# the teetotaller

**Carolyn van Langenberg**

**By the same author**

fish lips (Indra Publishing, 2001)
Sibyl's stories (Pascoe Publishing, 1986)

# the teetotaller's wake

## Carolyn van Langenberg

## Indra Publishing

Indra Publishing
PO Box 7, Briar Hill, Victoria, 3088, Australia.

© Carolyn van Langenberg, 2003
Typeset in Palatino by Fire Ink Press.
Made and Printed in Australia by McPherson's Printing Group.

All rights reserved.
No part of this publication may be reproduced, stored in a retrieval system, or transmitted in any form, or by any means, electronic, mechanical, photocopying, recording or otherwise, without prior written permission of the publisher.

National Library of Australia Cataloguing-in-Publication data:

Van Langenberg, Carolyn
The teetotaller's wake

ISBN 0 9578735 8 1 (pbk)

1. Single women – Fiction. 2. Mothers – New South Wales – Death – Fiction. 3. Lesbians – Fiction. 4. Dreamtime (Australian aboriginal mythology) – Fiction. I. Title.

A823.3

## Contents

| | | |
|---|---|---|
| Part I | cold beer | 9 |
| Part II | the teetotaller's wake | 31 |
| Part III | Christmas pudding | 135 |
| Part IV | under the tankstand | 199 |
| Part V | crushed roses | 226 |
| Acknowledgements | | 228 |

For my grandmothers, Edith Lane and Annie Kirkland.

*Fry me a sardine*
*the wind is blowing*
*and I'll be off*
*— Deborah Levy*
**An Amorous Discourse in the Suburbs of Hell**

# PART I

## cold beer

It was late of an evening when Fiona Hindmarsh heard the news. At the time, the television was off and she sat comfortably in a wide-armed chair, her eyes raised and her mouth ecstatic as she listened to a CD of Mozart's *Requiem*. A young woman glided where books were shelved, spreading her fingers across and down spines and titles, a glass held at about shoulder height. Her fingernails were painted True Red. Her shirt reached where shadows began.

Is this affluence?

The women were drinking whisky, a twelve year old single Islay malt, Bowmore. Fi rested her glass. She closed her eyes. A diamond of light winked.

This is complacence.

So when the phone rang and that winking light spattered, whirled up then crashed under the news that someone's mother had died — Fi's mother had given up the ghost, Muriel Hindmarsh had passed away — Fi was surprised how much the news shook her up. She had to spread her hand on the wall above the phone table to keep her balance.

The young woman curled her slender arms around Fi's

shoulders. Her lovely face shone full of care. With the fiery whisky in her belly, a flame shot through her body — there's a new love in Fi's life, there's a gorgeous girl — and lipsticked lips smacked, tongues rolled hungrily and hands slid over and buried into silky softness.

In love, Fi's heart burst.

After passion consumed grief and strong coffees were shared, a suit of clothes was selected for the funeral and packed with jeans and shirts for a few days in the country. It was just on midnight when Fi fumbled behind the wheel of her brand new bright yellow bubble car and winked at her new young lover and blew her a kiss. Then she swung the car down the inner-city side-street where she lived to follow green overhead signboards to the Pacific Highway.

Toll gates arched where thousand watt beams made holes in the sky. She dropped money in the basket and blinked sleep from her eyes. Spindly trees flashed past. When shadowy blue merged into grey bush, a gaudy billboard advertising a sandy bay for sale advanced and yawned. Guilt drove her hard over the several hundred kilometres from Sydney to the home farm at Newrybar. She sped. She had it in her to flatten the accelerator.

Fi half-expected Muriel's ghastly face to rise above the ad to accuse her of not seeing her for years, not once in ten years. Under no god's divine instruction would Muriel's ghost play at being the weeping, teeth gnashing supplicant in limbo. Haunting Fi, Fi believed, would be to Muriel her supernatural pleasure — she had great faith in her mother. And she pictured her standing in a blast of sunshine, proudly showing off her mayflower bush. That odd figure, long to a stretching neck and dumpy below the waist, was gone.

No more.

Dead.

She sped to be with her sister, Gillian. Together they were

going to cremate their mother, the dumpy and long waisted Muriel Hindmarsh who was born Muriel Dark.

Fi almost never went home to see her mother.

Gillian was the one who phoned with the news. "Mum's gone? This afternoon, you know, after tea? Died in character," Fi heard Gillian say through a shout in her head that this news couldn't be true. Muriel was how old, seventy-five? Fit as a horse! Why hadn't she gone back up there more often to see the old thing? "Mum died in character?" Gillian's voice strained. "Up to her neck in the shrubbery, pruning, culling, God knows what!"

Listening to her, Fi pictured her sister standing at the phone table under a mirror etched with swans. It stood beside the comfortable chair put there for those long conversations Muriel loved to have with the women serving with her on several charity committees. Gillian, overcoming tears, her nose lengthening, her voice squeezing through her knotted larynx, both hands grasping the handset.

Muriel had always approved of Gillian. She was the daughter who pleased her mother by being born pretty, the girl who developed from a warm, brown adolescence into a responsible adult and mother, her blemish being the single fact that she never married. But Muriel's face was stamped on Fi's — the wide forehead, white like a headlamp, the aquiline nose and the thin lipped mouth. The girl twitched and strutted like a game hen on the defensive. How could she be beautiful when she pursed her lips as if she was sharpening her beak to take a chunk of flesh out of someone? A girl had but several duties to herself, all of which depended on beauty! Did Fi believe any man would respect her if she wasn't beautiful? Did she think anyone would want to dance with her and take her out and be romantic with her if she wasn't beautiful? Did she think anyone would want to know her if she stared with such overt criticism at them? If a girl was beautiful, a man would respect her because if a man went with a girl who was not a pretty face he had other things in mind and those things were not respectable! In any case how could a man respect such a dreadful girl as Fi?

She whinged about the daughter whose face mocked her.

And the girl put her head down to steady her brains so that she could get through and up and out.

And away.

When Fi was twelve and entering high school, she displayed the grittiness of someone who knew she would do something significant with her life. She knew she would have nothing to do with her mother's cosmos of *Women's Weekly* beauty hints and wordless men like her father who dragged rubber boots through the mud and slush of the dairy. There was undulating in her a world of vistas, the way the hills undulated away from the Hindmarsh farm pressed high against the sky at Newrybar.

In her head and above her textbooks, Fi saw cities take shape. Towers thrust above shadowed streets. Rows and rows of grand doorways swung open. She stepped into the gleam of expensive foyers and strode through wide double doors down corridors of silence lined with smaller but no less portentous doors opening onto rooms of astonishing dimensions and long sashed windows. She wanted to be seated behind a big embossed desk in one of these rooms. She wanted to look smart in a black suit and a white blouse with long streamers tied in a bow under her chin. She wanted her nose high and her hands smoothing papers and her fingers holding the fountain pen reserved for signing documents.

At university, Fi enrolled in economics and government administration. These subjects, she believed, paved the right path to her imagined end. Her conviction then, when she was eighteen, led her to anticipate she would succeed to achieve her ambition by using a mixture of her intelligence, her aptitude and her guile. That some of this came true didn't alter

Fi's discovery that she hated bureaucracies, especially their necessary habitat, those towers of glass and cement and steel chilling mind, body and, if not soul, certainly the soil under their weight. The featureless interiors, honeycombed with boxy offices, the central columns filled with cables for elevators and telecommunications, plumbing and electrical works, disoriented her. She simply couldn't stay in these unnatural interiors servicing either the government or private sector long enough to be promoted above graduate clerk. She stayed nowhere for long, the vistas never ceasing to unroll, beckoning her to step forever forwards and into them.

Fi became a consultant. Her independence was hers. So, too, the vistas. But she had to be vigilant in order to catch sight of them before taking off after them.

And then?

Fi Hindmarsh loved to lunge for whatever was new.

Fi's little Mazda rolled off the highway to pull in at a roadhouse. Crunching across gravel, the yellow bubble drew to a stop in the dark beyond the neon light pooling an eerie shadowlessness on the asphalt. The yellow duco glistened, the silenced motor cooled. Old ghosts stirred where the bumper bar brushed against a straggly hedge of westringia.

Fi's eyes bulged over the steering wheel. Slowly sitting back in the driver's seat, she stared at the dark beyond the car's bonnet. In the rear vision mirror, the lavender smudges under her eyes puffed up. Appalled at the sight of herself, she ran her hands over her latest stubble haircut and dug into the bottom of her shoulder bag, hesitated with a tube of lipstick, slashed her thin lips Woodland Rose and threw open the car door.

The ground felt solid under her feet, the gravelly crunch under leather soles so natural a sound it might have soothed her weary nerves had not a ghostly pallor risen into an ink black sky. A cold breeze grazed the back of her neck.

Did her body fear premonitions?

Sometimes when reason caved in under doubt she consulted a clairvoyant. No wonder she marched with trepidation out of the dark to the roadhouse, set her mouth straight and wrenched open the glass door.

Although the greaseless grind of the door's hinges alerted her to think steady, the smells of stale potato chips reheated many times and bad hamburger meat raised her anxiety levels. She sniffed for the aroma of coffee. Finding none, she sank onto the hard seat of an aluminium framed chair, pressed her elbows onto the laminex top of a greasy table, and cupped her hands round her cheeks.

A wink of light shimmied round a tabletop where a pair of Woodland Rose lips blew kisses for Laine. Laine Macready, the androgyne Macready whose full lips pouted across a room when the music played and Fi's limbs jellied. That gorgeous young woman had leaned against her kitchen bench, a look of wry resignation shadowing her perfect face. It was then Fi wanted her naked. To lap her bodily, scoop her mentally, swim to where she might find a gland called *soul*.

What was she doing in a roadhouse?

Did her clairvoyant say she would make this trip?

A waitress waved her notepad up and down and tapped her foot. Fi looked up to stare at a face bloated with sourness. She thrust her chin forwards and said to the mottled face, "Tea! Three tea bags, please! In the pot, I want three tea bags in the pot! And ..."

Fi ran a chipped Woodland Rose fingernail down the menu. She winced at the list of pies, hamburgers and bacon with eggs. She waved the menu up and down and ordered a toasted sandwich. "Cheese. On grainy bread."

She wanted her brains steady. If Fi believed in anything, she believed in keeping her brains steady. Raising one eyebrow, she polished a greasy knife clean with a paper napkin, and she saw how her lips, curled between crumbed streaks, smirked at their image on the blade. With a gasped hah! moistening the sure belief Laine would love to see her, she rubbed at them vigorously, exposing the vaporous Muriel to a weird opinion that hooked her nose and made it snort.

A gushing wind whirled in the roadhouse. The glass door whammed open and shut, open and shut, open and shut. Old women, part of a group of pensioners on a tour, stumbled on numb legs and aching feet. Their shapeless bodies pressed against the counter, swollen eyes unable to focus on the menu boards hanging over the microwaves and the toasters, grey faces crumbling in an agony of sleeplessness.

One old woman, dragging her bag and moaning softly, shuffled after the hamburger she held in mid-air. She bumped Fi's elbow. Fi started up, eyes savage, but the waitress thrust her stomach in Fi's face and thumped a teapot with the strings of three tea bags looped around the handle on the table. The toasted sandwich fell with a thud. It bounced off the plate onto Fi's lap.

A man lowered himself in the seat opposite Fi. He grinned, "She'd be a right one!"

Fi poured tea.

"Going far?"

She knew the coastal farmer's drawl when she heard it.

Her blunt stare damned him. He shifted awkwardly on his buttocks, then he said, "I guess you're going home, too."

Swallowing tea, wishing it were hotter and stronger, fussily wishing for a flask of hot tea to take with her in the Mazda, Fi caught a glimpse of a not-so-clean length of pale yellow and brown tie strangling the collar of a brown check shirt. Her bag was of good leather. Her Cartier bracelet fell over the top of her hand. With an abrupt swing, she snatched at the bag and dumped it on her lap, and he, shockingly, wriggled to look under the table.

Her face and shoulders heated up, her feet scraped together.

When the man sat up again, he grinned, and his grin wobbled and died against her sharp glare. Apologising as if her anger reminded him of some old advice about manners and propriety, he grinned again showing nicotine and tea stained teeth. Then, perhaps thinking better of it, he looked at the dismal orange cottage curtains pleated over the greasy wall of greasy windows facing the road, but not for long. Tilting his head sideways, he took to studying her, and boldly. He said, "I'm from further up north, too. Round the Bay. Byron Bay."

Leaning over the table, he said confidentially, "Priddle's the name."

Fi bit into her toasted sandwich. A lump of it stuck to the roof of her mouth. She worked her tongue around the gluey plug to prise it free.

"No place like home, eh? Not even for a lady like y'sel'?"

Fi shot him a boiled look. His thinning yellow hair striping his red brown scalp disgusted her.

"You're a Hindmarsh, aren't y'eh?"

She spluttered and coughed. The corner of one eye watered. Her steady brains wavered under the sudden fear that she should she be able to place him. Was his a face belonging to someone she once knew?

The man, oblivious to her discomfort, whined, "You're one o'them Hindmarsh girls from up Newrybar way."

Priddle grinned again. His teeth were awful.

Fi coughed no. "No, no!"

Priddle raised his chin. He frowned, and he sat well back, folding his arms across his chest. His eyes stayed on her features as if he traced the lines of a remembered map — the nose, the neck, the hands.

Fi held a triangle of toasted sandwich in front of her mouth, her hard eye following the gaze of this idiot man who peered at her ringless fingers and the chain bracelet dropping onto the top half of her hand. The clattering of cutlery and crockery, and the dry voiced chatter of the elderly travellers, slumped under his unbroken attention.

"You look like one o'them," he said stubbornly. "Those Hindmarsh girls from up Newrybar way."

Affronted by the man subjecting her to his lunatic

scrutiny, Fi dashed tea down her throat to wash away the bitterness filling her mouth with riled words. But nothing was said nor admitted to wash away his voice droning, "But y' might be about ..." and he leaned back to inspect her, remarkably suggesting, "If you're the one I think'y'aar, y'should be in y'FORties. Maybe y're a few years too young."

At this, Fi raised an imperious eyebrow. "Mr Priddle!" A speech attacking him for his sheer cheek raced around her head. To Priddle, she decided, there was no point discussing liberal individualism and the niceties of leaving people alone.

In the act of pushing herself up, she recognised a resentful shift above her stomach. It collided with her understanding that where she came from, from the *up there* that was the hinterland of Byron Bay, she was not Fi but a Hindmarsh, one of a large tribe of old settlers who established dairy farms where a rainforest once grew. At the edge of her psyche sepulchral shadows as silent as absence itself darkened and others lurched with questions that remained unanswered overwhelming the insistent voice informing with knowledge acquired in adulthood that her family's farm was where Arakwaal land had bordered with Wiyabul, both tribes of the Bundjalung nation.

She simpered a polite, "Happy going back home!" And she strode to the counter where the sour faced waitress jabbed at the cash register.

Laine filled her brain and Fi thought *Keep Calm!* She looked over her shoulder at Mr Priddle. He carved a wet meat pie with gusto.

Fi hurried to the toilet block where a lot of old women slept on their feet before bursting in and out of cubicles. When a thought asking whether her mother would have travelled in groups like this wandered through her head, Muriel's face swayed, its whispiness buckling then disappearing behind the green and black water stains marbling the mirror above the wash basin.

The clairvoyant had warned her. What had she said at that last session? Actually said.

Fi washed her hands and brushed her teeth and rinsed her mouth thoroughly. She puckered her lips, slicked on more Woodland Rose, sent a little thank you to Innoxa, and blinked at herself. She was, after all is said and done, expecting company, none other than Muriel to swim through the ether as it were, appearing to employ all hoodwinking methods to cause her wayward daughter to squeal away from shadows and smash up her new car.

Her Mazda.

It needed a name, her Mazda did. If Muriel should cause a smash-up, better to make the incident memorable with a name.

Her brain although steady, took in the remembered fact that the clairvoyant had said nothing about collisions on the Pacific Highway.

Fi strode across the bitumen to where she had parked. Maisie. Aah, yes! Maisie, the bright yellow Mazda. She walked closer to the little car, beaming at Maisie's yellowness.

Loving Maisie, Fi suddenly and achingly missed Laine. Missing her, the gorgeous young woman who loomed in her brain puckered her rose red lips to say, *Play it again, Sam* ... In another room, lovely lips smiling with the lights turned down and the music turned up, a movie trailed a nightworld through Fi.

*Play it again. Sam.*

Fi's steps sprang. She flung open the driver's door.

Priddle stood in front of the westringia hedge. A shadow fell across the upper part of his face, and his chin moved without a mouth. "You got to be a Hindmarsh ... Goin' home to y'r mum's funeral, I'll bet."

His hands sank in the pockets of his jacket.

Fi threw her bag onto the passenger's seat and turned round quickly. Her heart thudded, but not enough to obliterate his high drawling, "Yeah. One o'them girls'd never go home."

Resenting how alarmed she felt, Fi said very quietly, "I'm from Sydney."

Priddle turned away, his heel scraping bitumen, his disbelief a nasal whine striking the crisp night air.

Fi strained to see what this going home was all about.

There was a boy she might have shinnied up a tree with in the man who had sat opposite her in the roadhouse. Or was that man hamming up the role of a redneck, was he a drop-out bit-part actor from a prime-time soapie?

What *did* he say?

She's a Hindmarsh, he's a Priddle.

An old impatience flared. Wavering briefly, it subsided to gather strength for a better moment to burn her up so that her hands sweated, the steering wheel spun and a throb jabbed at her temples when the faces of Muriel and Priddle suddenly overlapped high in her brain. The absurdity of them leering together made her giggle.

A headlight swerved.

*Turn down the lights ...*

The back of her head glowed. She pressed a button. Maisie's cabin swelled through Coffs Harbour with the prologue of *Carmena Burana*, then over a stretch of highway said to be spooked coasting north of Safety Beach. Her rational and well if not elaborately educated mind insisted, when the soprano sang in solo, those hundreds of written-off cars and buses were driven by sufferers of sleep apnoea and drink drivers veering to avoid nothing other than optical illusions. But when a light flickered through the mistiness onto the papery bark of a sapling, she muttered, "M'God!"

Something swirled out of the tree trunk and struck the windowscreen with a thud. She waited for the glass to shatter above the steering wheel, cutting her hands. Leaning forwards, her head turning from one side to the other, she found herself staring at what might have been Muriel's howling teeth or a ghostly man's black chest striped with feathers.

Whatever it was, it looked like anger, vented anger, had struck the windshield, threatening to lacerate her hands, perhaps smash her skull.

She drove on, the music in Maisie's cabin her best defence against …

… Muriel looking for her.

She shifted in her seat and laughed to herself, satisfied her expensive chestnut brown stubble would prick Muriel's exploring fingers, her mother Muriel, the mothering demon loving chocolate box prettiness and despairing of her daughter who had her hair cut ridiculously short.

The choir reached its crescendo.

Fi, breathing carefully, strained to see the white line snaking down the middle of the road. Her eyes ached but her brains were steady and her hands on Maisie's steering wheel were in control and not injured. Nevertheless, beneath the lingering notes of the celebration of spring, an uneasiness about Muriel and Priddle simmered. Her wakeful body sighed, premonitions sharpening her nerves. Surely he was a dream with no clue suggesting who he was. She shook her head, shaking the idea of him out of the part of her brain damned by Muriel, a shadow night-hunting with the escapees of graves.

The music opened silences.

Night pulsated.

Limbless, and this is happiness, Fi slid into a cocoon of fish and nutmeg nightsmells where she was thoughtless, and she lost control, let her brains wander and slide dreamily with Laine. Swimming in and out of post-party excess, she landed in the delicious lap of the new girl on the block. *Turn down the lights, honeybun! Turn down the lights!* with that beautiful and slender young woman, her undomestic hand sliding round shoulders to vanish in Fi.

Aortas and ventricles fluttered. Sphincters winked. Let slip a sly slurp.

The car jerked.

Fi looked at the fingers curling around the steering wheel. Lifting the longest one up, she recognised they were her fingers, the nails painted a nice pink. Woodland Rose.

*Here's looking at you, kid!*

Near dead eyes stung.

Inside her yellow bubble car, enduring the insignificance of being human, she angled her head and squinted one eye when trees huddled for an instant on lime green swathes of grass.

The speed of the dawning was painful. Flashed creamy yellow moments quivered followed by a burrowing into the grey sky which shook itself out. The land bulked and widened and billowed with the sky to take the mad blast of an exhilarating sun.

When Fi turned Maisie inland to climb the hills to Newrybar, her neck ached.

Was Newrybar where she was headed? Newrybar's where she was headed.

Did Fi mean to drive so far, so far away from her brand new Laine?

Had she, in her yellow car, arrived *up there*?

Was *up there* home?

In the morning, singing in a perfumed shower, one long arm curved high above her head, a sponge pressed to her underarm, Laine was not real. She was a series of photo-shots, an instant pose of everything men give to women. She was the beautiful girl who liked to wear a pin-striped suit, a white business shirt and a Hardy Amies necktie. Fi had driven twelve hours in a northerly direction away from her, that gorgeous girl. Twelve hours away from Laine, who was (at least for the time being) the girl of her dreams, therefore (at least for the time being) where home was.

With the sun behind her, home, that place *up there*, was a twelve hours' drive north of Sydney.

Her stomach hungrily growled.

A few big trees blocked Gillian's view of Maisie coming up the Old Byron Bay Road. These were not meandering eucalypts. These were pine trees that had been violently ripped and charred by lightning during electric storms. When Fi's little car turned into the farm track, bouncing up and over the uneven surface of the grassed drive, one old man pine tree hummed, long mockingly cheerful whirrs rustling up its branches.

Gillian slipped the latch of the garden gate. Her throat was dry, her jaw stiff. Maisie bumped to a stop under the anxious yet unbending tree. Unable to sweep a saccharine tune round Gillian, it creaked its woods and moaned.

Gillian advanced suddenly to stand by the driver's door. Fi's spirit flattened.

Scratching round the back seat for crumpled tissues and anything out of place, she avoided Gillian; then, with a sharp jerk, she thrust her face out of the car window to look straight at Gillian who abruptly grasped both Fi's hands in hers.

There was an awkward breathing, a nervous moment of exposed trust in each other's resilience. Fi, alert to Gillian's pained introversion, said, her voice barely above a whisper, "I'm in need of a shower." The space between them ached, the silence awkward, when through the garden gate and grinning, "New car?", ran Gillian's nine-year-old son, Leigh. With an enthusiastic tug at the door on the driver's side, he slammed into the sisters' high tension. Her assurance lost to sharp edges and grumpy fatigue, Fi snapped, "Just wait a while! I'll show you all the snazzy whizz bang bits when I'm good and ready."

Immediately regretting her irritability, Fi expected the boy to retaliate with a well-placed punch at the bodywork, accompanied by the shout, "Sour old bag!" But Leigh surprised her by taking a step back. He stood in sunshine, his legs and arms long and brown, his dark chestnut hair a clipped frame around his apple-pink cheeks, and he bestowed on her his beautiful smile. It widened as he leaned forward to offer over the warmth of his being to help with her bags.

With her open mouth hanging empty, she made apologetic noises. *Home*. The word dropped into her mind, flagging up demands of warmth and reciprocity. Glowing bright red, embarrassment rising with her unexpected hot flush, she half-stifled a gulp. She tried to say, "Good to be home," but the words dropped like hard plums, sour and untested by teeth and lips.

A baleful groaning shuddered the pine tree's highest branches.

There were other things to understand — the crispness the sun snapped up. The quickstepping down the hallway to the kitchen. The breathless anxiety about which room she should sleep in. The long gazing through the wide window down the splendid hills and valleys to the far distant glittering of sea. The jug boiling, a knife bouncing, and the walls squeezing in to shrug off the violence of visitors.

Home! Was it really where the morning light was luminous? Or was home Laine, leaning against the kitchen bench when Fi said, "Goodbye!" as if she were driving away forever. She meant to say *See you later!*

*Auf weidersehn!*

*Au revoir!*

*Totziens!*

*Sampai bertemu lagi!*

Laine was home, and Fi would go back to Laine. She was visiting Gillian, she was visiting her sister, Gillian, in that place which used to be home because their mother died there.

Muriel had died.

*Adieu, maman.*

The visiting Fi, the errant, prodigal, self-centred, stubborn bitch, the acquisitive snob and couldn't-give-a-fuck lesbian daughter of the decent and respectable old settler family, the

Hindmarshes, hunted for the corners of the kitchen that Muriel had filled up. Overtaking the floor space lumbered a fridge partnered by a large freezer. A microwave oven was balanced on an old worktable that was nothing other than a warped, single slab of timber, a relic of the family's pioneering past. No one got around to discarding it in favour of formica units when fashion invaded the kitchen during the fifties. Gillian fluttered over breakfast things, describing how she and Leigh were coming up the drive "... after seeing friends at Byron. Thought we'd pop in on the way home, Sunday visit, you know? And there's Mum. Up a tree. Waved ... Then her whole body lurched towards the sky, sweeping up to heaven, you might say, before falling, crashing through branches."

"We ran!"

"Too late!"

Leigh splashed milk and crunched through a bowl full of Corn Flakes. His mother smeared butter on toast. She said over lumps of sleeplessness, "Heart attack," then she drew the newspaper closer to her plate, and directed a square of toast towards her mouth which, opening up, dropped the words "We'll sell all this," with a crunching bite.

The boy rocketed out the door.

Fi heard herself asking, "How's he going at school?" The words slid down a sun-bleached curtain to hook on the dusted weave. Her eyes goggled when Gillian's head jittered up from the newspaper to take a better look at her boy, the older sister's neck lengthening, nostrils narrowing as if to snort up pain, eyes threading blood red with congealed yellow, lips mumbling, "Pretty good." Something natural between them splintered. Nevertheless, they elbowed the kitchen table together, toasted crumbs pitting their flesh, and they drank pots and pots of tea.

All day, the boy Leigh whittled the shape of snakes from a piece of tree root he took with him into the Hindmarsh barn.

He ran his hands over the silken wood, wishing the oil of the grain would enter him somehow to soothe the hard spot that hurt at the bottom of his gullet and the top of his stomach. Unlikely. But he had to stay out of their way. The way of his mother and his aunty. That's when the pain hit him like a punch and the light went straight through his head.

In the afternoon, Muriel's sisters — Daphne Howie, Elsie Johnson and Lorna Scott, aunties, all — clattered up the drive with plates of scones and loaves of sandwiches and bowls of soup. They conveyed lots and lots of expressions of sympathy, and uttered surprise when Daphne made it clear she hoped their brother, Jack Dark, should come to the funeral. Jack? Come to Muriel's funeral? Why would he? After all, they hadn't spoken, those two, Jack and Muriel, not in years. Lorna, chin tilted as she gazed at something fluttering above the canopy of a small tree, vaguely conjectured "Has Jack? Called?" Gillian, over-anxious among flowering shrubs, flinched. Couldn't-give-a-fuck Fi frowned. Elsie widened a clumsy smile to cover an awkward "Dear Dear. Remember That Day!"

Gillian, with a lot of nodding and folding of arms and nervous fingers fluttering around her mouth, said she remembered a day when car brakes screeched and doors flew shut with a bang and Uncle Jack strode through the house to the kitchen where his quiet rebuke drilled holes in the ceiling boards. His fury shook Muriel. At the time, her small daughters felt her backbone writhe with silenced rage. Fi recalled lying under the sofa in the back room, listening to Muriel's barefeet pound the lino as her mother marched through the house to see Jack out, followed by the slam of the front door and the shudder of the verandah boards under his shod feet. Gillian, rigid with fear, tried to be good and do her homework properly at the kitchen table, her head jerking on her stiffening neck.

Fi, softening in the moment of remembering how miserable

was Gillian the night after Uncle Jack rebuked Muriel, held out her hands to steer Daphne, Elsie and Lorna — their aunties — away from their perplexed speculation about whether Jack would come to the funeral or not. She asked if any of them remembered an old photograph of Muriel, "The one of her disappearing in a splattering of sunshine by this?" And she dropped her arm down the length of a stunning mayflower bush.

Amiably over a cup of tea — "Just One!" — there was a lot of chat, part of the ritual warmth shared around teapots with the scones and jam. "One of Mum's," said Gillian. "She'd want you to have it, I'm sure." The aunties agreed — "Dear Dear!" — that Muriel made a good peach jam, that she was tough, most especially on herself, and that she was sometimes difficult. "So easy to offend." They knew she had not looked well the last few times they had seen her, and Elsie remarked the doctor had said … Oh, dear. What had the doctor said? Heart, was it? She looked aghast that she could not think what it was. Muriel had confided in her that she had … "It was a funny word, Very medical. Was it aneurism? It was *aneurism*." Lorna chorused, "Aneurism." Daphne nodded energetically, adding for everyone's benefit, "Family. It's in the family, aneurism."

Gillian, tired and pale, vaguely smiled.

"Quite nice, this tea," Lorna mused, arthritic fingers lowering the cup to its saucer with care. Elsie held a forgotten scone in her bent fingers and looked at the spot in front of her, fearing that her memory was as if wrapped up in a cloud. Looking firstly over all the assembled heads, Daphne stood to her feet, expecting everyone else to follow suit in one brisk movement. And they did, pushing at chairs and smiling mindlessly at each other.

Fi asked if Jack was still on his farm. But, no. His sisters, their heads rising to the question, layered their answers one over the other. "No, no." Gillian said, "Didn't you know, Fi?" "Sold up. Big sale." "Lots …" "Pots …" "… and pots."

"Of money." When Fi was on the brink of exploding with frustration, Elsie's voice quietly intoned, "Jack. He's at Tallow Beach these days. The house is beautiful. With ocean views."

Lorna said, "He spends his days watching the dolphins go by."

Fi didn't like to ask after Lydia, Jack's mad wife.

Following the clattering of cups and saucers in the kitchen sink, the women took another stroll around the garden they knew well, and they paused again to admire the mayflower bush that was Muriel's pride. Fi smiled at the aunties. They smiled, and loudly talked at their cars. "Must go." "Go." "On our way." Then Daphne, Elsie and Lorna farewelled their nieces. "Thank you, dears, For tea."

Fi and Gillian privately wished they were free of performance.

Fi wandered onto the verandah. It was a warm wintry day. She shivered in a stream of western sun, hugged herself and gazed at the trees.

Despite the beauty, inner calm evaded her. Bitterness ducked beneath a sudden memory, stark images looping back, locking in her grief. A late afternoon shadow billowed and the pine trees winnowed the fragments of lapsed time, perhaps a day when a little girl sat in warm wintry sunshine on a stool in the corner of the living room.

Tears froze at the back of her eyeballs. Arms crossed, her hands cupping her shoulders, her face skyward, her lips parted, Fi received the chilliness of something remembered on her tongue. Abruptly, she burst into the kitchen where an old brutality rattled the windowpane, a foot shot out to slam the door, a draught slid under chair legs. Gillian sniffled and peeled vegetables. Fi wanted to hammer in a border round a real picture of grief, but everything spilled and the picture hung slantwise. Fi blurted, "You know Gilgil, I hated her!"

Gillian swayed as if she'd been hit and she piped, "When we advertise, Fi, we describe this place as 'rustic charm'."

Fi caught a fast sob.

Leigh sauntered in.

Neither his mother nor his aunty remarked on the quantity of sawdust in his hair.

In Muriel's garden, russet and pink and old gold braided together. The passionfruit vine weighed down the old dunny, and pushed its door wide open. The front of the roof tilted upwards, away from the heady downward slope of the back.

Fi saw him again. Priddle. At the funeral.

Standing by the entrance to the chapel, a hand shoved down in one pocket and with a surprised grin on his face, he started up to greet her. "I wuzz right! ... Wunteye!??" (He was pleased with himself.) "At the roadhouse!" He cocked his head to one side. "S'pose you didn't want to know anyone back there!" He added, his voice dark with his simple understanding, "A woman. On a lowanely road!"

Fi shook his hand. She stood beside Gillian and together they committed themselves to the duty of accepting condolences from their mother's mourners.

Uncle Jack held the sisters' hands in his, each for a long moment, looking squarely at them, facing his inner bravery to come at all to his much loved and long estranged sister's cremation. Fi, her anxieties translating into her impatience with ceremonies, waited for him to hurry on.

A lot of people stood in a silent line, waiting to file past, and the sisters bowed their heads and pressed hands and they murmered well modulated and polite thanks many, many times over. Fi recognised her aunties and uncles but she had forgotten who most of the other people were, remembering only the slow footedness, a drawing back of the head, and a hooding of eyelids shielding pale eyes against bright sun. Perhaps that was a habit to protect the soul from fierce inquiry. Perhaps, too, they were shy people, defending themselves should any sort of person or thing crowd in too close.

Priddle watched her. He stayed in one spot, and he watched her.

Fi performed a surface act of great but fragile calm. She rose in an unctious state, and she saw herself, elegant in her neat black trousered suit with the pale grey silken blouse, her aerobic limbs firm and clean and her tummy flat, her bottom tight and high. Beside the soft armed women whose mounds of freckled flesh rolled against the seams of cheap cotton interlocks, the silly pinks and appliquéd blues diminishing the grandeur of these big women, she felt how insubstantial was her fashionable body. Fi wanted to be a girl again. She wanted to curl into their massive womanliness and scream like a bad girl that she knew she was guilty of neglecting her mother but, please! would they understand she didn't like, not not-love but not *like*, her mother? And she wished she could remember their names.

He watched her.

Priddle watched her.

With alarming cool, she glanced at this fellow who had become a nuisance, the reddish farmer under the deep brimmed hat he wore to protect his face scarred by the surgical removal of worrying freckles and moles and by the sun itself.

Priddle!

He was the kid at the back of the primary school classroom who threw wet spitballs at her when their teacher said she did well. The kid who walked through bracken water holes with her. The one who once gave her a small green frog. It was a prize.

Priddle shuffled to a bank of roses.

Priddle, the reddened farmer, the upper part of his face hidden under his hat, stood and stared at her. She squinted to see more of him, and the black of her suit brightened, the silk blouse, iridescent in the harsh light, hung limp.

The clairvoyant hadn't warned her about any of this.

All the events of her life swung around to compound the

differences years of experiences may have put between them. Fi moved comfortably between cities and lovers. She guessed Priddle lived as his father had, farming what had once been rainforest. Did this make him a noble character, natural like knotted wood and wisely simple, too? Or was he a coward never to leave, never to vanquish this verdant part of the planet?

From the corner of her eye, she saw how he watched her shake the last hand, nod with the last words of sympathy, pause to collect the last enduring sighs. The roses clawed at his feet on lumps of red earth. Fi turned away, knowing his light eyes stared at her back, burrowing into her, further and further in and a long way through the layers of all that life proffered to find where she was small and unchanged — further and further in to where Muriel terrorised her.

Fi pointed her chin at Maisie.

She wanted a cold beer.

# PART II

### the teetotaller's wake

When the stunning young woman let herself into her silent flat after a long morning at the library, the sound of her own breathing too much, the university teacher, her paper on *Habitual ceremonies: tea drinking and other portable cultures: a post-modern study of adaptations among women members of tripley migrated families* not advancing at all, she undressed to reach past the academic whose skin was perhaps drying in front of electronically transmitted negative ion heatwaves, whose nostrils were inflamed from scratching through the *aspergillus nigra* flaking off the pages of rare books, whose vanity desired the other part of herself which she steeped in a perfumed steam, and when she was lying in her foaming bath waiting for the telephone to ring, waiting to hear her latest lover's voice describing the rhythm of the day spent mourning the death of her mother in the company of a large number of relatives and friends she hadn't seen for years, Laine Macready squeezed a sponge and pointed her pebble pink toe towards the ceiling, and she saw Fi

Hindmarsh riding a helicopter over the magnificent Byron Bay, and Fi leaning out the passenger's door with her mother's ashes. She was shaking the vial, watching as if spellbound the grey dust sweep in an arc downwards into the deep blue, over the glittering crescents of sunshine skipping across restlessness until the sea lapped the sooty particles onto the lip of a wave that raced towards the beach where it scudded, and vigilant dawn healthwalkers accompanied by dogs, perhaps an energetic beach angler swinging in fish might remark a tracery of tiny black specks mysteriously staining one section of creamy beige froth at the northern end of the bay.

Fi's day was nothing like this.

Calling "Be My Guest!" to her nephew, Leigh, Fi legged into Maisie, occupying the driver's seat. Grinning, and sweating the terrible stink of a nine-year-old boy, he bounced into the passenger's seat. She looked sidelong at her nephew, turned the ignition key and sped out of the town. He stuck his head out the wound down window and screwed his face into the force of the wind sweeping over his scalp and down around his neck. He exuded something like good nature as well as a rich body odour.

They were headed for the Hindmarsh house where the relatives wordlessly understood they would meet.

Fi recognised the set-up before she got there, the teetotallers' wake, the time after the funeral of a relative when everyone got together to see people they 'haven't seen in years', 'to have a bite to eat and a good long chat'. An old aunty, her elbow gripped by her frail husband, groped for the front steps with her shod foot. A young cousin, waiting for the elderly pair to negotiate the climb up onto the wooden verandah, sighed and brushed his hair back from his forehead with the flat of his palm. His strident sister, gathering her brood of two curly-haired girls, instructed them at every one of their patent leather steps that they should keep their floral and lacy skirts clean. Another cousin's little girl sprinted round the house in a big T-shirt loose over floral pink tights.

She braked, and Fi's heart skipped into her throat.

Gillian waved.

Leigh chucked his mother a grin, and Fi pulled a sour mouth. Gillian turned away, chatting to someone neither of them could see. Aunt and nephew exchanged grins.

Quickly they shut Maisie's doors. Fi fussed with tissues and her handbag in the shade of the pine trees. She prepared to be social when her spirit demanded solitude. And she was blindly furious when Leigh sprinted to her father's barn, leaving her to shoulder on her own the business of being an adult, leaving her to wander into the house, through the chatting crowd, smiling, smiling, nodding, smiling. Fi made her way to her old bedroom. She wanted a moment up a tree or in the barn, somewhere away from the oppressive press of bodies and the big well-meaning faces. She wanted to be a kid again.

The clairvoyant mentioned loss.

Financial?

In rooms near one of Sydney's universities, Fi had studied the fairground pink and spangled woman. "No," she said. "It'll be an emotional loss. Difficult period ahead. But you'll ride it through."

In her bedroom where, on Muriel's instructions which remained in force, the blinds were drawn against a strong sun burning up the rosy pinkness of a chenille bedspread, Fi fumbled with her clothes, sniffed and snorted and wiped her nose. She hung her black suit jacket up. Her eyes, searching for something to fix on, avoided looking at the painted walls, the chintz curtains heavy with dust and the ballerina dancing upside down inside an imitation rosewood frame. The mushroom pink stool took up space in front of the dressing-table, its mirror filling one of the walls in the small room. Fi sat with a harumph! on the stool, sat with the thought that Alice had things to do with mushrooms, but it was the caterpillar who lost his shape on one. Unscrewing her lipstick, Elizabeth Arden's Garden Rose, she slicked it on, pulled a face at the pouches under her eyes, leaned forwards, put her head to one side. Fi liked the idea of growing very small, changing her grieving body to a flying shape, winging away from the clutch of relatives milling on the other side of the door. Fingers pinching the pearl studs she had chosen to wear, she checked how secure were the stirrups. And, my goodness, who should ghost the mirror, disgust on her mouth when she held her head sideways, but Muriel, lips sneering, eyes hooking an arrogant chill into a panicked heart. Fi very nearly screamed. A sound made it into her throat and stopped there. Fi's body shocked dead still. To bring herself back to life, she brushed her hand over her broad exposed forehead. The apparition winced, the face capsized. Fi began to tremble, even as she counselled herself that toughness rode her successfully through the soggy patches of life. She steadied herself on the crest of her anger, strode to the door, swung it wide open, and slammed it shut behind her.

"How do you do!" she boomed, quelling her anxiety by greeting a nameless uncle. Or cousin.

It was Fi's job to do the tea. She stood at the kitchen sink and filled pot after pot.

Uncle Jack Dark took a tray of scones out to the crowded lounge room and verandah. He didn't forget to go into the garden where several of the men found a bench to sit on, a good shade to stand in, a shed to lean against. Aunty Daphne Howie busied herself at the old kitchen table. She instructed her sisters, Elsie Johnson and Lorna Scott, to butter bread for asparagus sandwiches, thin white crustless squares furled over an anaemic tinned spear.

Somehow bum first, Uncle Harry Dark lumbered into the

kitchen carrying a baby bath brimming with fruit salad. He beamed and glowed for a rush of women's thankyouing voices. And he paused to admire the way Gillian's dress shivered down her back and over her bottom. Her body seemed to offer little resistance to life as she arranged sandwiches and vol-au-vents on plates and trays, farinaceous gifts received from the members of the various charities Muriel belonged to.

Lorna lowered her head and raised her corseted bottom to obliterate the fronts of the floor cupboards. She searched for sweets bowls, she wanted to 'apportion' the fruit salad. Fi looked for cupcakes with butterfly wings and thick sponge sandwiches oozing with cream. There weren't any. There weren't even any lamingtons, no white desiccated coconut speckling chocolate coated squares of stale cake that she could see to remember things by. She muttered to Gillian, "What d'you say, they're all on cholesterol-free diets or something?"

They only drank tea. For her aunties and uncles, tea was the only drink.

The canister was full first thing that morning. Testament to Muriel's increasing forgetfulness, an old person's anxiety that she might be found short, there were packets upon packets of Black & Gold stacked at the backs of the kitchen cupboards with unopened packets of Boh from Malaysia and some fine graded qualities from Kenya sent by Fi as gifts to Muriel. Those packets were labelled in a shakey hand, *From Fi*, followed by the name of the country Fi was working in at the time of postage. Irritated by this discovery, Fi complained to anyone who cared to listen, "F'r chrissakes! What did she THINK. They're fuckin' OIL paintings? Gemstones?"

Lorna looked shocked.

Her niece measured tea, making some sense of those routinely written letters she received from her mother, letters that were so alike they precipitated despair.

Home                                    4th Jan, 1973

Dear Fi,
I received your lovely letter from Nairobi yesterday. What a long way to go for tea! What do you eat in a place like that? Do they have bread? Where do you stay? You must love your job to put up with strange things — hardships and uncertainties. — I have just come in from hanging out the washing. I have peeled potatoes and skinned pumpkin and topped and tailed beans in readiness for cooking tea. — We had a windstorm yesterday. Houses were dumped off stumps, the wind stripped bark and leaves off trees. Fruit trees ruined. — Rosie is looking at me over the fence. She is in calf. Poor dear is getting on a bit for breeding but the new neighbours let their bull at her. Your Dad said it would be all right. — Must run — life is a fast track — pots are boiling —
Love,
Mum

PS I keep the fridge well stocked so if ever you want a holiday here you won't starve. XXX
PPS Your Dad says to say thanks for the tea. It looks too good to use. I will keep it for special occasions, stop him from having goes at it. Always after the fancy stuff, he is.

The little word 'thanks' dropped with a dull plop!, thudding with Fi's grouch that her mother understood her job so little she told everyone the family was peculiarly blessed with its own tea lady. And at Muriel's wake, that's what Fi was.

The warmly welcome image and improbable promise of Laine crossing long pinstriped trousered legs at a table set with the best from Sèvres on fine embroidered linen, imbibing tea, soothed Fi. That glamorous girl, smiling from the edge of Fi's line of vision, endorsed her courage to strike a pose that suggested edgy resistance. And busying her hands with the taps over the sink, Fi wished she could mingle with her laterally extended rural family free of wary discomfort.

In this company, teas were all one and the same, the same brew wherever the leaves came from, hot liquid swigged with sugar or milk, a combination of the two or blackly unadulterated, something to swill through the dentures clogged with breadstuffs and doughy pastries. None of Fi's rellos bothered with the experimental teas like MANGO selling at Caddies on Carrington Street around the corner from the nursery where they bought fertiliser and weed killer before Goulds sold out and Lismore changed.

Fi didn't expect any one of them knew enough to distinguish the Assam of Williamson & Magor from the same variety of leaf packaged by Twinings or by Jacksons of Piccadilly. Like Muriel, they thought the store brand from the local supermarkets was good enough.

Tea it was, tea it is.

Was that a problem?

Fi wished for indulgences with delicate smoky and richly earthbound aromas packaged attractively. Assam, Darjeeling, Earl Grey, Prince of Wales, Queen Mary, Russian Caravan, Lapsong Souchong, Formosa Oolong — Indian, Chinese, Javanese, Sri Lankan — Twinings or Belaroma. Laine, in extravagant moods, will giggle and touch her sleeve and gently accuse Fi of being, simply, a tea sipping snob, a conservative with a complex way of doing things. Fi identified herself as the discriminating palate (meaning the one and only) in a big agrarian family.

It should be said that at the first hint of a socialist revolution, Fi Hindmarsh would — more than likely would — change her name. She would do her best to avoid lining up to face the firing squad with her relatives, these land grabbers who, when she was studying school history, she thought of as *kulaks* or *boers*. Whatever the label, they were descendants of the world's most efficient demolishers of the rainforest the populous tribes of the Bundjalung nation once thrived on. Fi was a Hindmarsh, she was one of them, and she loathed the way they didn't seem to change. Except to fatten.

She wanted to be someone else. Painfully she wished she were in a bath with Laine. But, whether laterally extended, nuclear or dysfunctional, families are ceaselessly demanding.

In boardrooms, Fiona Hindmarsh saw another world. A cool elegance. Pale shirts. Expensive hair. Fine watches. There she was a thing among things, as well honed as a micro disc, nicely perfumed and stylishly clothed in discreet but high fashioned suits substantiating the quality of her products which were, in the main, economic reports and futures assessments. As component parts of a bigger machine, the besuited men circling boardroom tables expected only the conclusive end of the consultant hired to do a special study. And that's all she was to them.

Within this big untidy thing called a family, whatever was expected of her was always a beginning. She was always the person her aunties last saw, not the woman standing in front of her uncles or attempting small talk with cousins while desperately trying to remember their names.

But the elegance of her business life did not gloss over hollow moments. Sudden longings, rheumy and pre-dawn, when, cast up somewhere in Africa or overlooking a paradisiacal *sawah* in Central Java, Fi longed for an unequivocal belonging as the complicated simplicity she liked to think she was.

Laine may understand. The clairvoyant let it pass without comment. Gillian may, in a future moment, say that Fi was damned to see only the worst in her relatives. She will say to Fi, "They've kept me sane, believe it or not. And that's important for what I am now."

"Shit," Fi'll say, and then she'll fart.

Gillian will screw up her face to argue the point with her

sister, and then she'll laugh. Laugh and laugh. She'll drop her wrists on Fi's shoulders, and they'll press their foreheads together, and they'll laugh, knowing there's nothing they can do but accept who they are.

After the wake, they will talk about their relatives well into the night. Over a pot of tea.

Tea for the wake, tea after the wake.

Always tea.

Fi admired her sister's choice of quiet words of gratitude when yet another box filled with pritikin diet savouries was handed to her. She admired Gillian's attractive mannerisms, something about the hands having a long fingered expressiveness.

Was she mature? Had maturity meant she resigned herself to the exigencies of life? Perhaps having a nine-year-old child imposed a special discipline on her. But Fi preferred to resist conjecture and assess the evidence, and the evidence that she lined up for her better understanding of her sister's social elan conglomerated around sacrifice. Gillian had not completed her PhD thesis. Indeed she had drifted into becoming an exploited research assistant at Southern Cross University — judged by Fi as absurdly provincial — so that she may provide for her child. Fi wanted to know why forgoing ambition to become a providing sole-parent should encourage serenity. Then she overheard Gillian explaining the best way to make a good pavlova is to begin by checking the barometer. "So much," she was saying, "depends on the lightness of the meringue. And the humidity up here can be a Reeeeal Problem."

The woman Gillian bent over repeated, "What's that, dear?" Her face was a twist of coloured papier mache partly hidden under a wide frothy hat. Gillian peered under the brim to reiterate the details of preparing a pavlova. "Beat until stiff like mountain peaks six egg whites with six ounces of castor sugar, one ounce of cornflour, just under a dessertspoonful of vinegar, a few drops of vanilla and a good pinch of cream of tarter. Whip dairy cream with vanilla and castor sugar," she enunciated. "So much better than the shop pavs."

Her eye on Fi, Gillian's mouth kept on shaping words, advising, "Slice the fruits. Steep slices of kiwi fruit in lemon sweetened with a sprinkle of castor sugar." And she recommended Lorna's passionfruit, "For that final oomph."

Gillian patted the old woman on the shoulder. The old woman's hat dipped. Her nose protruded from under the brim and, looking up, she caressed Gillian with a soft-eyed gaze, then she began to waddle away, her feet at painful angles to each other, her body twisted at the hips.

Splashing water, her dutiful hands clutching the electric jug, Fi wished time would madly reel to drop her headfirst into Laine's lap. But an emptied sandwich tray slid with a wink under the flowing water and her shoulder brushed Gillian's who asked, "Remember Bessie?" Fi said, "No." Shaking her head, she lifted the jug out of the sink to plug its cord into the wall socket. She repeated her No at the wall.

Gillian, believing her sister resented being marooned at the sink, said, "Don't worry," in a motherly sort of way. But Fi was adrift with a beautiful woman's pout puckering through her brainy grey grooves. Laine Macready stirred hot waves that lipped over Fi's face. That girl smelt of nutmeg and the sea. When she slept, her arms curled around Laine on their first night, Fi dreamt of swelling waves breaking blue over blue. And in the morning when she looked with disbelief at the exquisite face of her blonde lover, she saw how her eyelids were lit the colour of sunshine.

At the sink, Fi's face was hot and shiny. She emptied a teapot and rinsed it clean.

"What? What's that you say, Gilgil?"

Gillian, taking in skin loosening over the muscles around her sister's mouth, assured her that they all knew, "Fi. They all know about you."

The teapot, its spout hesitant, stood in mid-air. The sink

deepened under it. Neither woman at the bench moved. And the red-faced Gillian dragged "What I mean is ..." over her appalled larynx.

When Fi said "That's okay, Gillian," smartly jibing "I'm not an unmarried mother," she didn't see or hear Uncle Harry lumbering through the kitchen door. She jumped, water splashing the front of her blouse, when he slipped his arm around her waist, and she swung the teapot into his face, but he pulled her into his embrace. "You were always a slender one," he said wetly against her earlobe. "How's the tea, eh?"

Gillian backed out of the kitchen. Her eyes bright with embarrassment, she called out, "You okay, Fi?" And fled.

Fi jabbed her hip at his crotch. Harry quickly released her. Not looking back, he walked straight into the crowded living room, the back of his head striped with long thin strands of chestnut brown disappearing behind an overlapping of hats and lips and fingers wiping crumbs off lips. An ancient child raised her head and snarled through Fi's anger that Harry was a fuck-up, an incompetent turd.

Life in segments, the linking of bits, linking him to her, a chain of associations — to establish what?

Kinship.

Now there's an old word. It has an old buzz. It has a meaning bigger than family. Nevertheless, whether family or kin, blood is thicker than water, and *they* say, in the BOOK OF *THEY* SAYINGS, there's nothing in this world quite like family love, it's so murderous.

Fi Hindmarsh, slopping at the sink, was blissfully submerged with fleeting images of Laine. The silken skin and shadowed hollows of the girl's long body spilled with tea leaves into the silver pot. Fi drew water and waited for it to boil. She wiped the sink. She fiddled with the kitchen curtains. She looked for things to do. She looked for things to look at. Her thoughts strayed with derivatives and a reckless client whose management practices she judged dilatory — the punctilious professional, the one with a reputation for being exact, was a returned girl slamming a cupboard shut, discovering boredom. Staring through a lattice of branches and twigs to the place where she knew the fence slumped, she considered that the only way she could endure the day was to believe she was a newcomer.

Whatho!

She swatted a fly.

Above the roar of people talking, Harry's laughter hooted. Fi watched him use his bulk to press a cousin against the doorjamb. That womanly cousin raised a puritanically sceptical eyebrow, humouring Harry's excess. Excess. Solidly built, a man wearing a brown suit and suede shoes, his face and his hands and his ears pock-marked by treatments for carcinomas, Harry was marked by excess. When he laughed, his belly and his third flabby chin bounced.

Marjory, his red-faced wife, grabbed at a large triangle of pavlova. Her wide mouth opened, her face became a mouth. She tipped the wedge between her big teeth to devour light meringue, fruit and cream, the wedge sliding down her neck in big muscular thrusts. Her tongue flickered. A handkerchief flapped open. Rings flashed. Marjory, dabbing at the folds creasing the corners of her mouth, wiped at the cream smudging her puce lips. Unseeing, she stared into the kitchen, and Fi caught the chilled glint of eyes that were the colour of coins.

Running water over her hands and looking out the window again at the dunny sighing under the passionfruit vine, Fi wondered if the tea ever warmed Marjory up a bit. That's when she caught sight of Jack Dark lifting a cup. Jack had a delicate way of pressing his lips to its rim. She stared at him, watching Jack ease the pressure off one foot, then the other. She sifted through the half-forgotten when as a child she had no thoughts about him. The Uncle Jack of long ago made no impression. He was the grey man married to the mad Lydia.

Was that a stupid thought?

She had got it from Muriel.

Muriel hated Lydia. The hurt pricking the centre of Lydia's glazed eyes was enough to condemn the woman.

Then there were her strange cousins, Jacqueline and Kelvin, where were they?

Jacqueline and Kel.

They smelled sad when they were kids, and Fi, on the old school bus, heard the boys throw vicious jokes at Jacqueline. Even though she kept her head down in her books, the girls targetted her with their shrill spite. Fi, amazed by her cousin's weirdly expressive eyes, learned how ugly it was to be so reviled, and she took what she believed to be the lesson of belonging to the crowd on board. And Muriel insisted her girls should keep their distance. "Let them drift under whatever dreadful star sign they were born under," she sniffed. Then she conjectured that Jacqueline and Kel must have done something bad in a previous life, "… to be landed up with a mother like … LYDia."

Distracting herself from Muriel's hold on how she saw people, Fi shook out a Wettex and spread it on the windowsill. Looking up, she saw him again, Jack Dark replacing his cup in its saucer, and she caught a glimpse of the way his soft glance somehow took in the mourners. She fitted a fist to her waist. She would like to speak to Jack. She will talk to him. But an airy silence breathed through her resolution translucent ripples that made her nervous.

Rolling her eyes back under her closing lids, she was almost relieved when, his arms big, Harry lunged in front of her with the flowered Doulton teapot. Then he hovered. His hands slid down his shirtfront, stopping above his belt buckle. He squared his knees and flexed his thighs, jockeying his pelvis forwards.

"Howy'goin' anyway, Fi?"

Her hands cradled the teapot. She had a go at being friendly, replying, "Not bad, Harry. Y'self?"

"Aw."

Not too sure what she was supposed to make of that response, she dumped wet tea leaves in the slops bucket and stood with her back to the window to face him.

Over the beak of his nose, he peered, beady eyes merry, "We're at the Beach now, y' know, Sold the Farm, 'n' got ourselves a Retirement Maisonette, y'know? A Beach House." He grinned, his hands fidgeting at the top of his fly zipper. "Should come'n' visit now y'up 'ere!?"

Fi, staring through red, snapped, "Thanks but no. Not likely."

"Why not?" he whined, fingering his belt buckle.

Turning away, Fi angrily rinsed the teapot and thumped it on the sink to wait for its next journey around the gathering. Harry didn't notice she was angry. He asked, "Have y'got a house?"

"Wha'd'y'mean?"

She jammed the plug for the electric jug into the wall socket.

"Well," Harry persisted, "do y'own y'r'own home? The one y'live in?"

"No."

"Got kids?"

Fi stared at the jug, willing it to hurry up and boil the water. For tea. More tea.

"Kids? No."

"…! Married?"

"No."

She wondered if another pot filled with tea would persuade her Uncle Harry to leave her alone. But he was not going to desist, he would have his say, pass judgement on this bad-tempered one who …

A free thought flung itself above Fi with the shuddering fear that Harry had his memories of her.

"No kids, Not married, Don't own y'r'own home," Harry sneered, itemising his assessment of the woman pouring boiling water into the Royal Doulton teapot at the kitchen sink. "What have y'got then? A car?"

Afraid she might lose her temper with the irritating man and throw scalding water at him, she dropped the lid of the fine old teapot in place. She made no attempt to defend her apparent failure to meet the standard for success Uncle Harry set. Unchecked, he whined on with, "What's an attractive woman like you doin' not married, eh Fi? Them City Guys. They blind or somethin'?"

Fi's eyebrows wiggled across her forehead and her lips pursed and unpursed and her mouth worked to suppress the words it wanted to release. The teapot stood near her hand, its curved spout elegant, its lid topped with a perfect knob. Her mother's. A wedding gift. Waiting for Harry to lift it into the mass filling the house, their cups ready to be refilled. It was an object suggestive of polite wealth or acquisitive desire, signalling one was too poor to own the complete teaset. Fi touched its fine handle as if searching for some kind of reassurance that the day would end soon.

Secure in his idea of himself as a good bloke, Harry was oblivious to any restraint she may be kicking against. Looking at the floor and stuffing his hands in his pockets, he rocked on his heels. He hoped to catch Fi's eye. For her part, when he succeeded to catch something of a glance from her, she half expected her uncle would blush at the resurfacing of an old embarrassment and then scurry away. But he had his surprising ways. With a quick smile, he said, "Y'know. Most wakes aren't tea soaked." Then he added with a knowing eye on her, "See y'in the Baarn."

He winked.

Harry and Jack: Brothers.

Quite a few heads crowded the living room. The roar of voices carried gossipy bits of information about weddings and the lack of them, babies and deaths. Fi snatched a snippet about a hip replacement. Big hipped and round rumped, blustery complexions shining under curly hair, these people looked more prosperous than some of the mourners who were at the chapel service, those friends and acquaintances who took it as understood they were not invited to drive out to the farm for the wake. One or two of the women identified as aunties wore floral frocks, but most of the older women wore navy blue dresses with little jackets. The uncles wore dark suits. Their sons and nephews, Fi's cousins, displayed a newer attitude about menswear. They paid careful attention to getting the colours of their light casual trousers and the tie knotting the pale striped or beige shirt exactly right. The younger women cousins dressed like city people, differing only in their clear preference for overbrightness.

Another teapot rounded its belly at Fi, her hand slid under its plumpness, she hoisted it to the sink, lifted its lid, hurled its slops into the bucket and held its body under the tap. Water streamed over its silver surface, beading thickly. Slowly wiping the outside of the pot with a thoroughly wet tea towel, Fi screwed her mind around her observation that there was not much anxiety rolling out from under all that related flesh. A quiet unpanicked grace governed all their movements, she acknowledged. They lacked pretence. She tipped leaves into the pot, knowing her relatives were cheerfully certain. Complacent. Stolid.

She plugged the jug into the wall socket yet again. And waited for the water to boil.

Stretching over the sink, her elbows finding an awkward place on the sill to peer into the garden, she craned her neck to see if she could see Uncle Harry heading off under the cassias to the barn.

How long did she have to make tea?

A sadness radiating through her stomach made her want to break loose when a sudden pressure sank into the soft skin near her elbow. Caught witless, blood drained from her face. She spun around, the hair spiking her neck tendons standing up and hurting. A twisting mouth slatted by clawed fingers, moaned, "I frightened you."

Aunty Lorna. A faded woman dressed in navy and purple. Fi stiffened, visually offended by the sight of her aunty's deeply lined dark rose mouth and sad eyes.

"I frightened you."

The nose. It lengthened, the face dismembering, dry skin finely creped with wrinkles, the mouth uttering, "I'm Very Sorry." Then Lorna giggled, briefly recovered, in a mood for taking over. "I'll do the tea, dear! You go! Shoo!"

"Go!"

She waved a heavily ringed and knobbled hand at the living room. "Talk! They haven't … Seen You in Years."

Fi didn't take her eyes off her aunty who, lapsing once again into attitudes of dejection, repeated, "I frightened you." When Lorna's lips trembled, Fi made no effort to reassure her, pointedly grunting in a rough voice, "Suit y'self."

A clear grey light shallowed through Fi's brain, exposing a lurid sensation of skin sliding off the bones of her face. She wasn't about to dissolve in tears, but what demon forced her to be so damned rude. Lorna insisted she should take a rest, "From making tea. It's wrong. You shouldn't be making tea today. Circulate, dear …" Through a room filled with people Fi scarcely knew. For a wild moment, she believed she should sit like a headless and naked doll on one of Muriel's dilapidated armchairs, wrists and ankles crossed and knees pointing at her well-fleshed relatives. Her corporate image, aerobically honed, would distinguish her.

What would Elsie's husband, Sid Johnson, have to say at that?

Daphne's ex, Uncle Philip Howie, would run hurriedly into the arms of his new bride, a crisp tart, Fi had been warned, who dressed like a meringue, Gillian'd said, but she was absent. Uncle Philip was somewhere in the house and nowhere to be seen. If disturbed by one of his nieces, he would know to look over the bulb of his nose to assess her body as if it never bothered to own a head. He would do that whether she was dressed or not. Would he notice if she lolled her tongue, let it roll as Maoris do when making a point. Perhaps he would, if she pinned a diamond in it.

And what about Uncle Bertie, Lorna's husband, the nervous one? The massing of related flesh and blood, kith and kin drawn together at ritual ceremonies like this wake, brought him out in eczemas. They all understood. No one asked why Bertram Scott avoided family gatherings.

Compulsively, Fi took Lorna's hands in hers. She ran her fingers over dry, loose skin. Then with her palm, she cupped Lorna's cheek and gently pressed her cheek against her aunty's. The elderly woman's skin, under Fi's hand, was cold. Her aunty smelled sickly sweet and powdery. Fi pulled away too quickly, uncertainty dragging doubt and anger and fear across her face and, in the depths of her bowels, everything hurt.

With a laugh, Lorna pushed her away. "Fiona! You go. Talk!" She said, "Talk to them!"

Fi's mouth dried up. Was her city veneer flaking off? The matte finish was cracking to reveal something once known by her. It was a something flickering under the chair her most elderly cousin Boyd Dark sat on, her wide old legs bleeding spontaneously. It was a something snaking around the legs of the old family table where a Hindmarsh aunty crouched alone to chat at the wood grain. It was a something sliding along the mantelpiece where cousin Elliot took his space, his arm pushing back the vases and a clock to make room for his conversation with Uncle Sid.

The enigma was in seeing again.

A widening, an enclosing. Uncle Harry, back from the barn, waved. He beckoned her to join him at the mantelpiece where he butted into Elliot's talk with Sid. Fi ignored him, splicing like cold steel through the big bodies and perfumes masking body odours, pushing passed pudgy fingers grasping for cakes and biscuits and large, ruddy mouths biting into saltless savouries. Harry's big smile hung on loose jowls. He stuffed his mouth with a whole slice of limp quiche. His cheeks fat, he munched and swallowed and pulled his handkerchief from his shirt pocket. Smacking his lips, he wiped his face with the dingy cloth, and then his fingers as if he had washed them. Beside him stood Sid, hand in one pocket, gaze fixed on the paint peeling away from the pressed tin ceiling. It was edging away from the roofing beams. Then a bright one bearing an empty teapot bore down on Fi, her shapeless chin wagging, "She'd've loved to see us, dear?" This one crushed close, she smelled of cheap lavender talc dashed on skin flaking under pubic hair. As if she was at elocution classes, she announced, eyes rolling under puffed lids, "And I'm sure she's watching. Making sure we are all having a Nice Time." Fi smiled into the fluffed perm. But the dear thing continued with her praises. "WONderful woman. Your Mother was a WONderful woman."

Fi drew in a long breath. She wanted a beer. She wanted a cold beer. It would fit in her hand ...

Her Cartier bracelet dropped over the upper part of her hand.

Dressed in black pants and a grey silk shirt, her hair — "A girl's hair, said Muriel, was her crowning glory!" — cropped to within a whisker of her scalp, Fi strove to imagine how wonderful her mother might have been. She fiddled with her pearl earrings, self-consciously worried that her aunties and uncles were looking at her, the one who rarely came home to see her mother. Were they whispering behind their hands? Were they damning her or singing Muriel's praises?

"Quite a woman ...

"Always on the road ...

"Never stayed at home ...

"Never knew her to hang about ...

"Always out ...

"On someone else's behalf ...
"A good woman ...
"Always busy ...
"Charity or garden ...
"Never an idle moment ...
"Poor dear ...
"Good legs but ...
"Head too ...
"Bad heart ...
"Up there in the tree, wasn't it?
"Pruning. She was pruning ...
"I Ask You."

Muriel, dispenser of charity, she who imposed what she believed was right.

At the top of her stomach, a lump of anger hardened, and something like bile soured Fi's mouth.

Like a tropical fish under water, the little girl dressed in a pink T-shirt loose over floral pink tights spliced a trail through the crowd. Two floral and lacy girls followed in her wake, their firmly girded and plump mother flapping after them, reminding them of "Manners! Manners!" and "Girls! You must not dirty your dresses."

Fi stretched her neck to get a better look.

The three girls grabbed plates of cakes and sandwiches. The mother snatched away the cakes, complaining her two girls must not eat too much. Those two fumed, their faces red with protestations and graceless rage. Their mother disappeared into the kitchen, announcing she would find them something suitable. She would find them a good sandwich and a proper thing to drink. Her voice was shrill. It whipped around heads that perked up and peered across and over every other head the mother in her panic ducked behind. She repeated several times, "Tee Vee? Where's the Tee Vee? You kids Stop running Stay inside Watch tee vee Where is it?"

Gillian called from the hallway, "Tee Vee's in the bedroom."

Bedroom?

"Muriel liked to watch it there."

Disregarding adult witlessness, the three girls quickly snatched a cream and chocolate cake, and they headed off to the great outdoors. The pink one leading the girlie file militantly concentrated on delivering her cousins from being shamed. The girls' mother emerged from the kitchen with two glasses of water in her hands. She caught sight of the chocolate cake, borne high like a trophy, jogging step by step down the stairs. She blustered forwards, alarmed her girls may stuff themselves sick on that cake, staining their dresses and getting a taste for rebellion, too, but her surge down the hallway was blocked. She bumped into a damp-haired middle-aged man who grinned, "G'day! Sandra! Howzit, eh?" The woman hesitated, her exasperation bubbling through her thickly smeared and powdered face. Her larynx squeezed a tortured, "Very good, Stan. But I can't stay and chat. I must catch up with my girls!"

Sandra's anxiety to reach her girls, to rescue them from the dangers of chocolate cake, the girl in pink and any other unforeseen evil, worked a laugh through Stan. He was a short round man wearing a white shirt and grey jeans. His dark tie was knotted too tightly round his thick neck. "Eh, Sandra!" Closing off her push through the crowd, he asked, "What are y' doing these days, Now you're a Mum? Still teaching?" He laughed. "Tell me," he said. "Tell me. What's life like up at Mullum?"

Struggling to free herself of Stan Hindmarsh who insisted on describing in infinite detail his latest holiday which seemed to have been spent in Bali, Sandra's body signalled distress. She wheezed through dangerously narrow nostrils, her pink skin blotched. There was something about her blonde hair, too. It gleamed brassily.

Fi, her brains steady, looked through her cousin Stanley Hindmarsh to gaze on her cousin, Sandra Weir, a pretty blonde with a prim mouth who married some bloke from the Department of School Education. Muriel had written a letter about the wedding, and she had sent Fi a photo of a lanky fellow staring too seriously at the camera. Sandra was at the fellow's elbow. His stare at the camera was aggressively defensive, and she was glowing at him as if she'd landed a treasure or a big fat fish. She was, Fi recalled of that photo, extraordinarily dolled up in wedding finery.

The sun thickened behind a curtain. A chair leg creaked. A mirage took too long to sink back in memory. The dolly bride Sandra Dark was the present day Sandra Weir. In Fi's sights, she was clad in a purple linen and viscose suit and a black and white 100% polyester flowered blouse. But Fi's steadied brain held the image of a girl. Such a pretty little thing who had, perhaps predictably, become this woman clinging to frothiness, a mother desperate her daughters should be 'pretty little things', 'fluffy heads' with nothing to think about but colour schemes for lips and hair and bedrooms.

Fi concentrated on the woman trying to get past Stan. But other things were added. A schoolgirl giggled behind the shelter shed. She did favours for persuasive boys. Her skirt rucked up, her lips livid, she swayed for gropes and lost control, her body leaping sweet agonies. Wasn't that the joke? Anything for the gimlet-eyed boys whose strong fingers brought her to her thrilling point, but she drew the line at cock sucking.

Strong swings with a softball bat won her official school accolades.

Below her purple hem, patent leather black stiletto heeled shoes severely pointed at Fi. Her toes, her poor toes, were rammed into the bulbed bit rising at the pointed front of those shoes.

Sandra was ten years younger than Fi who shared no highschool days with a bit of hot stuff spicing the gossip, the softball champion swinging in the prizes for the school principal to gloat over. Letters from Muriel must have filled in the days Fi was missing. She thought that was more than possible. Muriel's letters kept her up to date with the family news. But there was a Sandra who was hers, a memory ghosting the back of her brain with those many things not shared with Muriel. For the furthest back she went with Sandra was kneeling on a bed at Nanna Dark's, pressing her twelve-year-old head close to Sandra's two-year-old curls to direct her gaze through a wide window at a golden moon. A story book moon. It was huge and golden in a dark purple-blue sky.

She was, Sandra was, the prettiest little two-year-old.

One small, one tall, they knelt together, the palms of their feet crossed. Pillows and coverlets buckled around their legs. Silhouetted, the backs cut a woodblock print of a svelte girl tilting a protective arc over a little one whose blonde curls spun a halo, her doll's head at her thin shoulder. The prettiness of the picture, for all the world like something designed for a Christmas card, swiped Fi's eyes and she looked up with tears welling along the bottom lid at the terrible mess the little girl had become.

Sandra, flushed a desperate pink, stumbled on cramped toes.

Fi, slyly, smirked. Sandra would keep.

In this questionable state, she saw herself clearly — Fi Hindmarsh, a stranger in her mother's living room surrounded by well-fleshed and well-meaning relatives who yarned and yarned about real estate and other people's children and the terrible effects daylight saving was having on curtains, cows, carrots and everything else.

She studied her laced shoes. Hoped her mouth dared anyone to come close. Then a general growling agreed there were Good Old Days, and Times That Were Tough.

"It was, I'm tellin'y'z, a good life," Sid was saying. "This was a good place to be. Until th' hippies. Bluddy Nimbin."

The room filled with nodding sunburnt faces. "That's when a rottenness set in. I'm tellin'y'z, our children went orf the rails."

"Drugs'n that."

"An' the Scrub," said Elsie. Fi looked up surprised to hear, "Weir's old farm. Used to be corn all along the flats right to the banks of the creeks. They're plantin' trees all along there now. No corn."

Lorna put in a grumble. "All that trouble to get rid of the Scrub," she said. "Now they're putting Scrub back in."

"But the floods," Gillian protested. "The floods aren't as bad now the trees are growing again. National Parks have begun weeding the willow out of the creeks. That's good. That means …"

She was cut short by an elderly voice ignoring all that had been said about the derailing of children and the reforestation of river flats with a reminder of the time when the EEC got up. "The poms, remember? Mid to late sixties? When the pommy bastards stopped buying our butter?"

Fi tried to point out that the problem had moved on from the EEC which was now the EC. "It's 1992. You've got GATT now." But she was drowned out by the general growl rumbling around the room. The assembled relatives lowered their heads heavy with dark memories of those days in the sixties when farms lost value overnight. Elliot said, "Yeah. Poor old Uncle Jim. He had it rough."

A bodily silence rolled through the room like a dense coastal fog.

Why does the grieving for one spill into the perhaps unfinished grieving for the other?

Fi's face fell in, the poorly remembered letters by Muriel flagging guilt through her brain. The words jumbled together, the contents and the dates lost to repetition.

Muriel might have written *Home*, the letters much the same, only the date changing. *1975, 1979, 198 …*, endlessly …

Dear Fi,

I received your letter, lovely to hear from you, when will we see you? — I have just brought the milk in from the dairy and I have peeled the potatoes and skinned the pumpkin and I have topped and tailed the beans, in readiness for cooking tea. — Your Dad is unwell with coronial occlusions. — Gillian rang, expects to be back from Penang soon.

And she always sought to distract Fi with items about
... *your old school friend Lyn* ...
... *your old school friend Judy* ...
... *your old school friend Kay* ...
... *married with babies* ...
with the qualifying declaration:
*They do not want to live anywhere else.*

Did Muriel believe the ever-repeated *I must rush, life up here is in the fast lane* softened whatever it was she should have been saying clearly? Unambiguously? Did she want to write *please, Fi, come home?*

The letters, in all their banality, were abstruse, Fi reading the *PS Your Dad said to say Hello with XXX* as code for Muriel's message that she should come home. Perversely, she refused to read between the lines that Jim was sick. Muriel never actually wrote *Your father is very sick, Fi. He does not have long to live.*

Therefore, it followed that no one knew where to find her when he died. So they said. He was cremated when she was 'on one of y'r rambles.' That's what they said.

"Where *were* you? Africa? Mozambique, was it? Some place like?"

She was told the phones were bad, and Muriel nodded, gripping close to her mouth a handkerchief around which she had crocheted a dainty edge. Slowly, with the nodding, the story came out that no one had tried to phone, it was too difficult '... understanding all those foreigners, Fi. They say they speak English, but I don't know, you can't work out what they're saying, all gabble to me. I kept giving them the name of your hotel, and the town you said you were in, but ...' The look of crumpled helplessness drove home to Fi where she was from, and she didn't like it. Back then, Fi choked on dismayed anger and roared at her grieving mother's frustrating ineptitude.

Poor Jim, dear Jim, her Dad.

Living room. Collapsing lounge suite, and big faces turned away from her. Her mother's funeral, a tissue pressed against her cheek. Sodden, it was, and Fi grappled at the edges inside herself where she interrogated what she is and what was her life. In a sense, she was torn apart. The one resentful of home and possessive of it, too, was eager to rip shreds off the complacent and much-travelled city slicker who flicked at crumbs pocking her grey silk shirt with greased stains.

Muriel's wake was no sweet dream.

Fi scratched for another tissue, lifted the flowered Royal Albert teacup, and watched the teapots — the silver wedding present and the beaten aluminium pot and a brown enamel one someone found under the sink — swing around the room. Raising an eyebrow to maintain a respectable degree of cynicism, she tried to keep her spirits up and her brains steady. But grief bowled fast and bruised the thick muscle behind her eyes. Her tears stung, her tears too salty. She shoved the tissue at her eyes, and Gillian drifted to her side. "Fi," her sister softly cautioned. "Bear up now, Fi! Bear up! I'm talking to you, Fi! I'm talking to you."

"Okay okay!"

Gillian waited for a certain redness around Fi's eyes to fade, for the sting at their centre to go away. She waited for her sister to take a mouthful of tea. She waited for her to dust herself down, to pull herself together and compose herself. Gillian took a plate of something from a passing hand, calling, eye on Fi, "I'll look after this lot."

Fi hated Gillian's composure. She took a slice of wet quiche from a fussy plate. "Whyn't you having some yourself?" She swallowed bile, gulped the tea and pulled a terrible face, complaining "I need something stronger than this puke." She dabbed her nose and eyes, then scratched around for more tissues.

Stan touched Gillian's arm, Sandra brandished a box of tissues.

The elderly Boyd, seated on a chrome and vinyl kitchen chair, stared blankly, her legs seeping blood whenever a child's hand or a swishing skirt brushed against them. Gillian glanced over the assembled heads. Imbedded in her quiet question, "Has anyone seen Leigh?" was a suggestive fear for him. Fi said glumly, "In the barn. Last I saw him, he was heading in that direction."

The barn. That was where Jim tinkered, his tools hung in formation on a panel he had made himself, quietly by himself. Alone. Away from the fussing. The women. And that's where Leigh retreated, away from ...

Gillian moved fast, taking the tissues from Sandra. Sandra, finding herself relieved of both the tissues and Stan, raced for the front door with Gillian. She will rescue her girls, no matter what.

Fi, catching her breath and feeling sorry for herself, studied the slice of quiche Gillian pushed on her. Its sunken pale cream and milky green filling looked as glum as she felt. Against her better judgement, she sank her teeth into it. Her bite stayed, she controlled a gag.

A girl in pink stood at her feet. Her rodent nose twitched. Her shoulders, squared and bony, hunched forwards. She held Fi in the quizzical depth of her huge grey eyes.

Fi masticated slowly, her eyes fixed on this young pink thing. She wished a crack in the skein of real time would open so that she could fall out of the room. But she was no Alice. She was no pretty kid dropping through wonder, stepping into looking glasses and running into rabbits. Nor was Fi one to like it when her brains slipped dangerously close to the edge separating the rational from the irrational.

(The clairvoyant knew her client well. She was wise, that clairvoyant, a small, plump woman who had worked for years behind the bar at a Mancunian pub, good training ground for learning to understand human foibles, you might say. She knew people fairly well. Even though the bright eyed and petulant Fi was well groomed, nicely scented, beautifully jewelled, she had about herself an air of abrupt masculinity. And Fi was flattered to accept without argument her brains were tough like those of the army general or the court politician she had been in her previous lives. She was led to believe hers was an intelligence relying, not on intuition, but strategy. She was focussed — one-eyed, like a bloke. The wise woman from Manchester got it right to tell that to Fi.)

Back on the farm, Fi, swallowing quiche, pulled a face. "Awful, is it?" the girl asked. She wrinkled her nose and screwed up her mouth in sympathy. Caught out, Fi blushed. Dabbing at crumbs around her mouth to cover her awkwardness, she said, "Suffice it to say ..." splayed her hand and mimed a terrible moan.

The girl cocked her head at an angle. She waited for Fi to say some more. Fi complied. "Quiche." She wiped her fingers, smacked her lips. "A quiche is usually a splendid thing. A quiche is meant to be an appetising entrée. True to say, you can invent your own combinations but *this* ..." Fi paused, the girl's eyes fixed on hers. "The pastry bleeds the flavours from the cream and egg mixture. No nutmeg, no herbs, no garlic, no salt, no pepper. No cream. Shape or skim milk is in that custard base. Tinned asparagus has been stirred through a custard recommended by the Heart Foundation to keep us alive and in misery for the rest of our days — flavourless, shrunken prunes that we'll be — the concoction little different from Polyfilla."

She took a long draught of tea for the practical purpose of washing the flavourless glug from her mouth. And she bent down to say close to the girl's ear, "It tastes like shit."

The girl opened her mouth wide in real surprise. Adults, where she came from, scrupulously avoided using swear words in the presence of children.

Unphased and revived, Fi asked, "What *is* your name?"

"Belinda!"

"Who do you belong to? Who's your Mum?"

Belinda, announcing names Fi dimly recalled, pointed at a woman wearing apricot lipgloss slicked on her full and appetising mouth. Mackinnon. Julie. Married who? Elliot? Stan? Gordon? Maybe she married someone from the football team. Wasn't there a Warren Mackinnon who was something of a star?

She had no mind to put flesh on boys' names — there were some she fiercely forgot. Distance helped the forgetting, the habit of relying on Muriel to keep her up to date on who had been added to the Hindmarsh and Dark clans creating a fold to cover up the bitter things that blighted her early life.

Fi, looking at Belinda, asked, "Are you eating?" At which utterance, the girl twisted her wrists round each other, threw Fi a coy look, then whispered wetly, "Why do you wear men's shoes?"

Fi, glancing at the girl, put her plate of rejected quiche on the mantelpiece. She looked at the toes of both her shoes then she propped the right one up on its heel. They were stylish black brogues that accommodated her orthotics, their leather soft and, being Italian, the toes drew to a rounded point. Fi loved the design, the elegance of the shape and the sheen of good leather. She looked at Belinda who was looking at her, her mouth open and her eyes cannily watchful and ever so slightly pink with embarrassment. Belinda, Fi saw, knew she had breached a rule of etiquette.

Attempting to take the child into her confidence, she

explained, "These are women's shoes. I hate those high heeled things, the ones that make a woman's foot look like a colt's hoof."

She blushed. She wasn't used to children, wasn't sure how to talk to this girl who seemed as if she was ten going on middle-age.

Having taken in Belinda's pink Reeboks (Expensive for the parents, Fi thought), she was about to ask what shoes Belinda liked, if only to make ungainly conversation, when she spied the soles of two little shoes appearing from beneath the curtain draped over the window. Fi peeked behind the drop to spy a little boy with the look of a page torn from a book by A. A. Milne, a Christopher Robin clone. He looked up at her, his pretty face soft with wonder. He wore a pink T-shirt emblazoned with a very yellow canary, and he balanced a plate of pikelets on his lap.

Fi sank to her heels, Belinda's face close to hers. The little boy, the heel of one hand against his jawbone, his fingers curled near his cheekbone, whispered with no breath behind his words. He was telling them something, but they couldn't hear him. Fi was surprised to hear Belinda's firm and quiet voice gently coax the little boy to speak up. She called him Joey. Joey managed to wriggle on his bottom and lean close to them, clutching his precious pikelets with his move.

Again, his fingers curled over his cheek as if he meant his palm to fill with his words so he might physically lift them across to Belinda and Fi. They heard a high pitched rasping whisper: "I frighten'." His eyes rolled high in their sockets, his head formed a peak.

Fi looked for Belinda, expectantly, deferring to the wise one, the one skilled with children. When nothing was said, Fi began to ask, "Do I frighten you, Joey?" But Belinda cut her short. Speaking slowly, the girl asked, "Are there frightening things in this room, Joey?"

Fi looked at the pink girl in astonishment, and she looked at Joey. He nodded, "Yeth." Belinda's hands pushed hard on her kneecaps. One hand slipped, bumping her words, "What are the things, Joey?"

Joey wriggled again. He leaned close to them, and he whispered, "Painted flowerpot ladies."

Fi rocked back on her heels, a laugh hitting the back of her teeth, but Belinda looked serious. She nodded with understanding. "Are you safe behind the curtain?" When he nodded vigorously, she stood upright.

Fi stood up too, fighting her laughter.

The shoes pointing up from under the curtain wiggled. She was sure they looked like happy shoes. "Belinda! Who …?"

But Belinda had dashed off, a pink slip streaking into the kitchen.

The hump of a little bottom poked the drape out and the hem heavily dragged over buttered pikelets. Fi pushed at her teacup, accepting that Muriel's golden drapes were greased.

Fi lapsed into a grey space where the memory of Muriel's fierce temper pounded holes in her brain, Muriel forever defending herself against her daughter's tart comments, Fi sinking her heels through floorboards against her mother's obsessive preoccupation with domesticity. Whether it be her curtains, her cushions, her crocheted toilet roll and tissue box covers, those efforts to make the rude farmhouse comfortable, cosy even, they were Muriel's only conversation. Perhaps the table weighed down by plenty straightened up a thing or two when things got bad. Excess revealed the quality of the woman, her waist thickening at the stove.

Caught in a time warp, Muriel was God's child — God, the misogynist who dropped women like Muriel in black holes in the universe to give'em something worth screaming about. And the son, Christ, lent no hand to help Muriel.

With a criss-cross in the middle of her eyes, her nasal voice calling the chooks, her harsh sighs vibrating around her flower garden, she was trapped on a hill with abundance, with the quantities of cakes and puddings she always had at the ready, the flowers constantly blooming in her garden, the ingenious little housekeeping devices 'to make the place look a bit better'. Nothing she made was made to last. Fi pointed that out to her. 'All those crocheted edges around face washers ... What for? Cakes, garden, the crafts you do. Nothing is for forever. And none of it makes money.'

What would the asparagus, ejected from tins to be squashed on sandwiches, cooked into quiches, speared as fingerfoods, make of a life so spent? Would the mushroom vol-au-vents and those pritikin things that were soggy and grey have a better way to explain away the blandness of it all? Fi was sure the lamingtons would understand. And she had no doubt a sponge leaning over its fat filling would too. But there were none, not any, of those sponge sandwiches topped with strawberries and cream. Not at this occasion. It was as if God's spite snuffed them out. There. Where Fi dragged her finger over the surface of a French-polished sideboard where Muriel had of late forgotten to dust.

Above Fi's head, a green and ox-blood vase jutted opposite two oval portraits, photographs of old people dressed in dark clothes gripped at the neck by a tie in the case of Grandpa Hindmarsh and by a cameo pinned into soft pleats and lace in the case of Grandma Hindmarsh. Smaller photographs, framed and hung on the walls, of brides whose headdresses failed to flatter and of grooms who looked worryingly shortchanged, celebrated the size of the family. Babies balanced on proud laps disappeared regally in finely smocked layette sets and layers of crochet and lace knit wrappings. Their necks were too feeble to support their heads. In one, girls dressed in lace socks and buttoned shoes and long hemmed and lavish dresses, their hair fastened by ribbons, beamed beside a birthday cake. They were Muriel's sisters, Daphne and Elsie. They had beautiful wavy hair.

Hair. A girl's crowning glory.

Fi swung a foot, kicking out at memories of Muriel's

bullying, her anguish and Jim's passivity. And for the first time in her life she saw that in this room, there were no photos of Muriel. None on the walls, none in silver frames on the occasional table. There were no memories of Muriel's hair in the living room.

Fi shifted her feet, held her teacup aloft, wished for a glass of whisky. Her nose twitched, her lips rolled inwards. In this room, an unremembered dream fingered her.

She stopped fidgeting.

Fi remembered bullying alright. And anguish. And Jim's passivity. The way he sat and stared for hours at nothing in particular, hands idle. Even in company, Jim locked himself off from his wife and daughters, she believed, isolating himself in a world so private he shared it with no one. How much she had wanted ... How hard she worked at school so that he might, for a rare moment, see her. When she was a little girl, how much she had ached for her father to accept her as the next best thing to a boy.

Did he moon for a son?

With wry approval, Fi caught the sheen of polished leather — her men's shoes. Turned her foot to study one more carefully. Pins and needles took her by surprise. Wincing, she languished with the thought that she would see through the rest of the day, see through the hours until she turned the yellow Maisie, her car, around to face home, that other home where Laine Macready waited, that lovely girl opening the taps to heat up her cooling bathwater ...

*Here's looking at you, kid!*

*Oh, my!*

Fi very nearly rushed for the door. That girl, that dreamboat, stirred Fi's sinuous body to gasp and ...

She was sure her eyes were stark with lusty love.

But a Dear Thing, witchy finger pointing at the shoes propping up the edge of the golden drape, shaky voice exclaiming "Shame! That's Harry's grandchild!" insisted on having her ear. Vaguely following the Doulton teapot dipping round the thirsty relatives, Fi did her best to withstand images of the slender Laine, as she listened to the condemnation of a modern mother. She was distracted, she radiated adoration. The gorgeous girlie was a dream, an inspiration, long arms raised when, eyes steady, Fi slunk across a party room to smack a kiss on a deep red pout. What use had she for children and their ridiculous mothers fussing and bullying their children to suit whatever they placed most value on. Shoes. Food. Hair.

The old woman's mouth shuddered to a raggy full stop. Her sad eye was moist and defiant, her lips slid to form a haphazard clench of disapproval. And when Muriel's Chinese vase rocked on a high planter, catching on its minutely patterned surface for a second or two a glint of golden sunlight, Fi believed the sheen caught a dream called Laine Macready. In that same moment, that same Laine Macready ran a sponge over her wax white legs.

Fi loved the fine bristled hair downing Laine's elegant neck. She loved the feel of not having hair.

Laine was herself from an agrarian community but from a country town, her family not anything like the Hindmarshes. Those Hindmarshes were designated 'cow cockies', dairy farmers of small ninety acre holdings, the men said to be 'red necked', the women said to be 'generous at table', their large round arms expert at whipping cream for filling sponge sandwiches and knocking up a batch of scones at a moment's notice. Soaking in bubbles, she imagined Fi chatting with an uncle. It occurred to her that her lover would find talking to her old aunts difficult, remembering her grumbling before she left Sydney that family occasions were 'bluddy hell!'. It was an outburst she had smiled at when Fi's will collapsed for the longly gazing of her large grey eyes.

She assumed that after the funeral service and the burial

or cremation, a few hushed friends gathered with the bereaved to share memories before leaving the relatives with the lawyer and the division of property — and the discovery of how one had been valued by the deceased. For her, the occasion was one of grief and loss muddled with material gain or rage, and the lack of alcohol at the wake would be incomprehensible.

Steam billowed up to the ceiling. Her short hair plastered against her cheeks. She wished Fi would phone.

Faint for air in her perfumed and foaming bath, and well known for her loveliness, she resolved to wait for Fi, and her researches ran a story through her about teetotalling customs where women, lodged at a kitchen sink between the stove and the fridge, performed duties with the said tea, the tea drinkers descendants of Irish potato farmers or, quite possibly, Scottish shepherds. That is to say, ignorant and uneducated people. Fi Hindmarsh, Laine Macready believed, was not from that kind of background.

But she was.

Fi was the descendant of Yorkshire farm labourers.

Boyd Dark, the fine blood vessels of her legs seeping, balanced precariously on the small seat of a kitchen chair. Her hands slowly rose across her breasts and to her throat. Fi found her line of vision filled with her, a stout and reliable woman not succeeding to protect herself from the infirmities of old age.

When she was a child, a stringy girl with a pouting mouth and glaring eyes, Fi liked Boyd. She was a woman with steady brains. Her clarity of thought was a relief from Muriel's illogical muddling based on the fear that someone somewhere just might disapprove. Boyd's aura of calm — that's how Fi felt it — appealed to the little girl wanting to trust intelligence in adults.

Unlike Muriel who could spend an entire afternoon on the phone discussing the length of hems, or the place of a pocket on a skirt, Boyd did things. She had authority, got things done or not done, as the case may be. There was that letter Muriel wrote, back in the eighties.

Home,                                      ? ? 1981

Dear Fi,
A chook is in the oven with potatoes and pumpkin and onions and I have peeled peaches and put them on to stew in their own syrup. A jelly is setting in the fridge and I have whipped up some cream with sugar and vanilla. — Gillian is home. Hope you will come too. Dear old Rosie, remember Rosie? Such a pretty cow. She's looking at Gillian through the fence, chewing her cud. Taking in the day, and a story or two. Anyway there is always a bed for you and Gillian, just let me know when you are coming, give me twenty four hours to run into town for some extra things to put in the fridge. — On Saturday, I dropped in on Boyd, she is my oldest cousin and she still sews her own frocks. She is eighty-two. Everyone knows Boyd is the sole reason why Clunes cannot be planned and developed. Your old cousin Boyd is refusing to sell. She will not sell off several estate blocks at the back of her house. She says to sell would upset her chooks!!!! But her stubbornness means the new subdivisions run parallel to the main road. Mr Townley said the town planners cannot crown the hill with blocks, and put in sensible town sewage and water utilities. The town is being held back. All because of your Cousin Boyd. — Must run. I can hear the washing machine jumping. I am running in the fast lane. Don't know how to keep up with myself.
Love, Mum.
PS Try to come home soon. Your Dad's not real well.
Mum XXX

Boyd. My cousin, your cousin. What was that message Muriel wanted to deliver in the sub-text of her letters — don't ever forget, your cousin's my cousin, my cousin's your cousin? Fi's heart frosted up, knowing that this was Muriel's way of insisting Fi belonged, even with her irritating short hair and despite her refusal to have boyfriends. She was more Boyd's cousin than Muriel's daughter because Fi, like Boyd, was recalcitrant.

Boyd smiled in a tired sort of way. Fi lifted her chin and her teacup. She toasted her. Wished her, inanely, a good year.

Later that day of Muriel's funeral, Gillian will say, "When Cousin Boyd dies, the family will subdivide like crazy so they can sit on their tails for the rest of their lives." Fi, dazed from the day, will say, "What?" She will try a tentative smile, but Gillian will look over her shoulder and not at her. Gillian has already said, "It is a shame this land has been wasted the way it has. Remember Nanna Dark telling us how long the grass used to be? Now it's a stubble. One of Boyd's grandsons, was he called John? Anyway. He'd once been a maths teacher, and he gave up classrooms to grow avocadoes and bush nuts. Sorry. Macadamias. The rest? They'll sell sell sell." Fi will remind her, "And so will we, Gillian." That smile, small and sour, will slide down her mouth.

Muriel had sold a block. The concrete slab went down, red bricks piled up and a monster shone. Red tiles reached a thin edge of guttering. Aluminium frames squared, slatted blinds blocked out brightness. With no garden to soften its edges, the house stood, rudely abrupt against the big blue sky.

Muriel, hating it, hid it from offending her view of the green and blue world by growing clematis across a strategically placed lattice.

Gillian said, "She got scared. Mum, that is. No doubt about that." She got scared of visible poverty. And the loneliness of old age, "… which is not a lack of people in your life," opined Gillian. "The horrible fact is all your friends are dead."

That's what Gillian told Fi.

Fi, glaring at another quiche breezing by, curled her lips against having regrets. She nurtured no pity to gild her strained relationship with her late mother, Muriel. She thought, "Good," and ground her teeth. Then, her hand shaking, her brain darkened.

Damn the lot of'em!

Why?

No one listened. No one listened to the land. The valleys drained of swamp and the hills razed of forest growth heaved to smother an agonised cry when, with God's blessing, the remaining clumps of trees and bushes and ferns were hacked out of the earth for brick and aluminium houses. The sun was too hot, the sky was forever gleeful, a tough combination for a century long swing between godly irascibility and benign grace. Anyway, God seemed to lose interest, not giving Muriel even a fly-by look-in. Perhaps he got all hooked up with an answering machine, or lost his way, surfing on the Internet, wrapped, not in shepherd's robes, but in the virtually real. If God should give up on them, as he seemed to have done some time ago, why shouldn't she?

Fi went with boys from school who squinted at birds circling vainly for trees to perch in. Old rookeries had vanished. And with slingshots, the boys aimed and brought the homeless birds down. Some of them had pretty feathers, they said. Those were the boys who grew up when there wasn't much rainforest or wetland left. Their grandfathers worked hard to burn the roots of tall tree ferns and savaged the trunks of forest trees — for a kitchen table, a dining table and the dunny seat, the two seater, small hole for little kiddies and the larger one for big bottomed women.

The men turned tree trunks into struts and rafters for the barn and the dairy. The narrower boards were used for the ceilings and the walls of farmhouses. Like the simple house Gillian and Fi grew up in. It was no architectural wonder, and everyone's house was the same. A hall ran down the middle with three bedrooms flanked on either side and a living room squared off at the far end of the hall. In this elementary design, the back of the kitchen stove was braced against the fireplace the living room boasted, the chimney bulging up the kitchen wall squaring in the living room on the other side. During summer storms, the roof leaked. On wintry nights, draughts eddied in cold bedrooms, and the hall creaked.

But the child Fi liked the farmhouse. The morning sun shafted rays across the breakfast table, and the westerly sun warmed the front verandah. On hot days, the interior was cool and sunless. The garden had sunny and shady spots, the whole of it, garden and house, seemingly spacious — fun to run through and around. On the day of her mother's wake, she knew it was small and so poorly built, it was falling to bits.

"Poverty," insisted Gillian. "It's scary."

Laine, naked but for perfumed suds, stood on the edge of Fi's brain and blew her a kiss with a bubble.

When the phone rang, the pink Belinda blinked at Fi, and the crowd lowered its communal voice for the one who, lifting the receiver, answered the call.

"H'lo?"
"... Yes?"
"... That's right."
"... What Did You Say?"
"... With Muriel?"
"... With Muriel?"
"... Yes, Dear, I'm sure ..."
"... Mrs Digby, Do you want to speak with ..."
"... Dollies?"
"... toilet roll ...?"
"... Muriel's toilet roll ...?"
"... Oh, I see ... Did you, Dear?"
"... Yes, I' ..."
"... I haven' ..."

"... Mrs Digby, Dear, I haven't looked."
"... The Girls ..."
"... Yes Yes ... The girls are ..."
"... Gillian, yes, and Fiona is, too,"
"... Yes, Fiona's here too,"
"... They're sure to be here. Somewhere."
"... Yes, I Know ... You and ..."
"... You wa'"
"... You want the Purple one."
"... You want ... You and Muriel crochet' ..."
"... Mrs Digby, Dear, the girls're sure to ..."
"... purple ..."
"... with the dollie in the middle."
"... Spare toilet roll."
"... Cover."
"..."
"Bye, now ... ByeBye, Dear."

Aunty Elsie quietly replaced the handset with hands still wet from doing duty in the kitchen. Her lips compressed, she wiped the back of her knuckles down her apron front. Motionless for a pico-second, she faced some dark ache in herself with wordless anxiety.

That's what it was with them at this Fi's mother's funeral and wake. Behaviour, and all outward manifestations of feelings, emotions, were obliged to be constrained. Blood relatives crowded her mother's house to share grief. They were good at understanding the soundless dreams haphazard with tortured images that followed death. But for them words fell down dry throats, unspoken. They couldn't speak the words of condolence. The pain was too great. They looked. From embarrassed eyes, they looked, and with a terrible understanding.

Aunty Elsie looked straight at Fi. "That," she said with an appalled air, "was Mrs Digby. She worked with your mother for St Vincent's, you know, crocheting all sorts of things for raffles. Raffles." Then she picked up the skirt of the apron and wiped both hands thoroughly on it. "Without raffles, we'd have no renal unit at the hospital." A low murmur slowly ran through the gathering. Bodies faced Elsie, chins lifted and mutterings agreeing with her sentiment rose. When the sound of voices began to swell, the bodies, as if choreographed, turned away from Elsie into the folds of conversations about the bluddy government and its failure to honour its responsibilities. Held closer to raised chins, their undisputed opinions avoided the reminder that Muriel was dead, overcoming the ache that they were grieving for someone who had died.

Most of the gathering missed Elsie quickly informing Fi that a Mrs Digby would be calling to collect a purple toilet roll holder — "… one of those dolls with a skirt that circles in gathered tiers, and she wants the toilet roll in it …" — one of many that she and Muriel made together. Fi nodded, frowned, nodded. She bumped her hip against the table laden with god-alone-knows-what, hoping when she winced that Gillian would know what to do when a woman stood at the front door, anxiously loud, insisting that Muriel would want her to have a full-skirted crocheted purple toilet roll holder, one they had made together. God might strike me lucky, she thought. I might just miss her and her small but vital concerns about Muriel's contribution to the hospital's renal unit. Stifling giggles, her face dropped, the lachrymose clown stumbling away from her spectral mother beaming above a mound made of toilet rolls.

Fi longed for a strong drink.

The Hindmarsh living room was no place for feeling damaged and distressed. Her face bent at the centre, she twisted a mocking laugh behind her eyes where she beat it flat, extracting from herself the strength to be composed, to steady her brains.

Fi stretched her ropy body. *Be careful*, an inner voice whispered, as if care itself would care for her when she thrust her body past the thought, pushing herself into an act that might pass muster, something that might make her enough like them, for Muriel's sake, for as long as she stood among them.

The girl Belinda stared at her. From smoky eyes set wide apart in a frank and open country face, what did that girl see? A game fowl? A scrawny chook? A bit of town flesh, painted carefully and dressed in a disguise of sorts?

Belinda's eyes absorbed Fi.

Fi, tired of her performance, fidgeted. A hot flush rose up her neck and spread across her cheeks. She sweated. She hoped she wasn't bright red from blushing. Muriel would find a hot red face distasteful.

Fi rallied. She pointed her knee at the front door. Pulled her head up high.

If she was somewhere else, she would tell the kid to piss off. But, surrounded by people loosely associated by where-they-come-from, and closely linked by blood which, hard as one may try, won't wash away, Fi was embarrassed. Sinews washed in blood were too strong to snap.

Belinda's face was deadpan. She said, "Mum says you're rich." She was straightforward. No prissy miss, this one.

"Really?" Said Fi. Bile spilled through her guts. Spying Julie Mackinnon's full apricot lips flicker and whisp — no temperate mouth, this one — she ached to be evil and smiled beautifully at the child, inviting complicity. She enjoyed brushing her hands lightly on Belinda's shoulders and the long slink purring through her.

Legging through the crowd with Belinda under her elbow, Fi wanted to chat with the woman whose fingers fluttered in front of her face. Her fear of showing too much irritated tiredness with the social demands a wake might put upon her evaporated in the prospective thought of flirtation. Conquest.

"Oh!" Julie swallowed a bad taste. Looking at Fi, she loosened her lips and she said pleasantly, "How d'y'do? I'm Julie Mackinnon. You may not remember ..."

"No. I don't. And I'm not rich."

Fi watched for a sensuous movement of the apricot lips. The pretty blue eyes darted. Her skin was a trifle too pink, but she leaned forwards to smell the sweet breath exaled from the mouth. Muriel hissed through her brain, "You are Not Nice! Bitchery is Not Nice!" How she ground her teeth between the not and the nice. Fi bypassed distorting censure to ask, "Where do you fit in, Are you a cousin, darling?"

Julie blushed.

Fi made her eyelids fleshy.

Belinda's face glowed, a creamy lotus.

Was the girl blooming with love and admiration, or was she simply young and beautiful?

Julie stroked her daughter's hair, draped her arms around Belinda's neck, and the child rested her shoulders on her mother's stomach and she rocked with her mother's body. Mother and daughter. They formed a two-tiered, double-headed creature. Smiling slightly, happily together, they watched Fi, at the way her grey silk shirt bloused untidily out of the waist of her black trousers.

Outside the comfortable body they made together, Fi tried not to see them. She stood straighter than anyone in the room.

Adjusting her face to radiate the casual joy of motherhood, Julie strutted a leg forwards, lifting Belinda's leg with hers. Mother and daughter took a few clown steps, and laughed, showing off their unity. But Belinda broke free and shot her mother a red look as if she questioned the motive behind the display of Julie's affection. Her hair swung. She ducked and ran.

One hand on her pointed hip, Julie watched the girl disappear out of the room. She stayed like that for a long moment, a slim sportive figure among the abundant flesh, but she was not brutal enough to forget Fi altogether. She swung back to look at the cousin who others in the family said loved women and had no time for men. With a slight huffiness, she managed to confide "Great kid." Knowing the answer, she asked with more than a hint of malice slipped into her implied innocence, "Have you got any?"

Fi promptly said no.

After a short silence in which they stood awkwardly, wary of the distance time and place, experience and life-style put between them, Julie looked Fi up and down, mumbling something that she wanted to pass as sympathy. "I'm sorry," she said. "About y'mother."

Fi's eyelids dropped. She surprised herself so much her jaw lengthened. Tears would not fall, but her throat twisted around an awful desire to howl.

Julie, disarmed, fumbled. Her apricot lips protested a language of emotions not usually called upon. She took Fi into her warm arms, and Fi found her desire to act the bitch overtaken by Julie's performance of "There, there!" and "It's okay!" "You're allowed to cry." The rest of them lowered their gaze, horrified to be confronted by cuddles and tears and things. They were too repelled to take much notice of Julie saying in the way of a mother diverting an injured child from pain, "Well ... What do you do, anyway? I've heard so much. And I'm curious."

Fi, resisting the ribald, tried to grin. She pulled an awful face, and the voice in her head ticked her off and told her to stay calm. As if to assist the instructing voice, right in front of her wet eyes, apricot lips pouted and glistened. The devil in her couldn't resist turning a phrase out of an act. *Here's lookin* ... Indeed, Fi was looking. She was warming to the thought of tasting apricot lips.

"You travel a lot," the motherly Julie gushed. "You've a good job. *They* tell me you're rich." She waved her hand at the bowed backs and bent heads.

Fi turned sour, she wanted to say Fuck off!, but she managed to stay her tongue. She said nothing of her weekender in the Blue Mountains, the 99 year lease on a house near Ubud in Bali nor anything about a part ownership in the business premises she used as her office.

Julie grabbed a passing plate of sandwiches. They seemed to be tomatoes layered between thin white bread. Apricot lips, punishing a crust, worked through the glue. She reached for her cup of tea, teeth clicking the china of a perfect Arberg teacup.

"What do you do?"

"Sports. I'm sports head teacher for girls at the local high-school." Julie chatted on about softball and netball and, her eyes dancing, inter-school visits.

Something inside Fi collapsed.

*Oh*, what a *boring tart*!

Swimming up from the depths of Fi's anxiety came the ghostly sighing. Muriel's mothering advices insisted on passivity, a style that echoed back to the condemning word *ladylike*. Fi had learned, with difficulty, to smudge that one with the gentlemanly demeanour of not explaining, never excusing, always assuming one had the power. But the coy mother of the pink Belinda stood in front of her and chewed the crust of a bad sandwich. Her lips worked in the most adorable way, and Fi got defensive. She hunched up. She bothered very much that she should say something explanatory. Like: I don't own the house I live in. I have a lease on a place in Bali, and I own a weekender up at Leura. As for travelling a lot, that's part of my work.

She got it all out, and the apricot lips formed a perfect Oh!

Fi, hot all over, her eyes glazed, felt her desire was starkly exposed.

The pink point of Julie's tongue slicked across the surface of her lips and pouted. "… y'mean t'say … That's Graaaiiit! Wow! Y'kidding! Interesting! Indonesia? Funny place to go, isn't it? To own anything there, I mean. Leasehold? What a strange … Oh! I see! It's all for tea. Wow!"

Recognizing, and not for the first time in her life, how ubiquitous is incomprehension itself, Fi managed politeness. The hours were dismantling her equilibrium. Her head heavy and her shoulders slumping, she slid, pushed, forced herself through the press of bodies and out of the room.

"Fi ?"

She turned to see who might have called her name. And there she found it brightly glossed between lips abandoned to Arberg and tea.

Who's the bitch in flat shoes, then? Who stepped onto the verandah and swung around to lean against the rails? What's her name? That woman who pressed her elbows on the wood, tilted her nose up, chin high, neck twisting? Got fingers stuck up her nostrils, has she?

She squinted into the westerly sun, turned her head and ducked, amazed by its orange blast. When afternoon breezes rustled through the top branches of trees, paused, and murmured deeply under shadowed bushes, she waited to hear music rising to its crescendo. She looked like the well-travelled woman finding her feet in an atmospheric and rundown joint off the beaten track, the one in the tee vee ad who asked the beautiful hotel servant for the phone — to bring the whole world to her old Mum, she of the ear splitting grin that peered from under a battered hat softly panned through a smudged window.

Men stood at one end of the verandah. One moved a foot. Others looked across the southern ridges the road wound along, and they all paused in unison to sip tea, scratch balls, tug at an ear lobe and grab at a sandwich whisked by on a plate balanced on a woman's palm. These men scraped the collective heel, screwed the collective trouser leg, twisted the collective hand deep in trouser pockets. They stared collectively at nothing much. And somehow shook a leg without moving it.

They waited, not for music, but for serpentine shadows to glide across the crest of the hill and slither through trees and writhe around the house before swallowing it whole, for the energy in the house to get ready for plunging into moist dark night — for the women to wash up, pack up, put things away and get away. The scones had to be shoved into plastic containers, pikelets wrapped in Gladwrap, sandwiches sandwiches sandwiches pushed into the plastic tubes mass-produced bread came in.

Besides, the women had to finish their discreet rubber necking at How Muriel Lived. Cupboards, at first opened with shy resolve, were thrown open, the contents touched then lifted out then shaken shockingly and humphed at. One or two yawned at the lumpy armchairs, and two concerned older women stood beside the Chinese vase towering over old Cousin Boyd. There they whispered behind cupped hands "Poor Dear."

Who was the Poor Dear? Was it Muriel? To die and have her belongings poked at? Was it Boyd? To be alive, dozing, bleeding?

Boyd smiled. At the edge of her dream, she heard the wives and aunties and maybe the men's mothers beginning to chorus "Time t'go." She prayed to go, forever. Forever freed of the silliness and the routines and the pain of being alive in an old and tired body.

She heard no men's voices. Boyd was, it seemed, freed of men's voices.

If they spoke at all, the men hummed "Yeah," mumbled "rrr," giving no word to speech at all. They were content to wait for the women's voices to lower, for the quiet silence of night to consume the house. While they waited, they took in at the pointed tips of their big eyes the lone woman, the one who lounged and made no move to go inside and do what women do — help the others.

The men weren't sure into which branch of the family she fitted. She lifted her leg, hoisted herself to sit on top of the verandah rails, one hand spread, fingers long on the banisters. She ignored the men, her attention directed at her desktop hands, her manicured nails, at the chipped and nicely Cinnamon Pink. Or was it Woodland Rose? There was a flashy splash about her.

She knew herself to be a lover wanting her lover's sweet breath to cascade all over her.

At the movies, the woman the men had trouble identifying might have developed an eye for Marlene Dietrich, top hat and cane. Forget the tails. Perhaps she flirted with a womanly image of the forties in a crepe hip-hugging dress and a feathered beret. Possible, who was to know. Did she try a swagger like Mick Jagger's? Or did she go for the husky eccentricities of Mame?

The thing is — and those cousinly men will never get the gist of this — whatever she experimented with, whatever act she tried on, she always wanted to be Humphrey. Bogart. The hats and the suits and the twitchetty mouth. Swinging in a seat and lighting a cigarette and taking yet another drink.

*Here's lookin' at you, kid.*

This's a woman with a grin and a flash set of suits, flat shoes to match. As long as she remembered the gym and her advanced fitness and aerobic classes, she looked good. For this one wasn't quite Gertrude Stein, she wasn't literary nor graphic. She was cinematically informed. Listening for Sam. To play it again. She was listening, wanting to play at being Humphrey again.

Woman identifying Humphrey Bogart eyed the young slinky bit who walked through the door. *Turn up the music, turn down the lights,* and the young one blushed. The older one, looking on loveliness, was glassy-eyed.

Lengthening her neck and twisting her fingers, looking out across green hills, she was in a state called HOMEBOUND. At home among rellos, she wanted to be speeding down the coastal highway to that place in Sydney she believed to be her true home. No one in the city had any idea who her Mum and Dad were, what her name was, which tribe of fat people she called family. On her inner-city street of anonymity, no one bothered her with expectations like having a name, a house, a bunch of snotty-faced kids ...

... and she liked it that way.

Fi Hindmarsh. Balanced on the banisters, dressed in one of her compromises — a women's trouser and jacket set, the jacket off and the shirt slipping out at the waist — balanced in a crinkled bit of celluloid. At her mother's tea soaked wake where her suit was not quite right, she waited for the outside shadows to thicken, the bustling at the kitchen sink to peak and wind down, for the kids to stop squealing, for the cars to start moving off. Like the men, she waited for all this standing around trying to be ceremonious to be over and done with.

A cooling snap stiffened the late afternoon breeze.

When Gillian found Fi on her own, she made a straight line of her lips and her breasts rose up and she walked up the steps to stand guard beside her sister. Then, her body softening, she smiled and she leaned against the sill of the window of one of the front bedrooms. Fi glanced with a smile at Gillian. In the same movement, she looked at the garden again, the front beds of azaleas and the pine trees shading Maisie, her bubble car. Thin shadows mixed with a clear light.

Was this prelapsarian, this Eden of hills above the Pacific Ocean? Death surely had no place in its old trees, one energy exchanged for another that swam in an unimagined medium.

Fi asked aloud, "When did Gerard Manley Hopkins …?" She then rephrased her question for the observation she shared with Gillian. "When we did all that spackling and inscaping — Hopkins' poetry at school, you know, in English literature — I thought he was writing about this."

Gillian glanced quickly up and down the lean body of her sister, trying to catch at Fi's meaning. She was very often alarmed by whatever she thought Fi was saying.

"An odd thought, Fi!" she said, the light on her hair. "What an odd thing to be thinking! Just now!'

Did Gillian say that?

"These gardens and trees," she said. "When you take a good look at them all, they are rather imposed. Imposed on the land. Did you ever think the spackling was wrong to impose? When I look through the light foliage of a ti-tree, for example, something bigger than my heart shifts inside me."

Gillian said that.

Fi didn't reply. She looked at the abundance of trees with thick canopies cluttering the line against the sky, shrugged and turned to face Gillian, trying to work out what it was that they wanted to understand. They shared raised eyebrows. They regularly reminded each other travel taught them how to look with new eyes at old and familiar things — playing with new perspectives, rejecting some when, in the same breath, they sought to enhance others.

Both of them grew up with a beauty Gerard Manley Hopkins could never have imagined. They grew up with shadows that did daily battle against a capricious sun. They grew up with vivid colours, and they both had visited the place that formed his heart, that place of pallid skies and milky sunshine. For them — well, there's a matter of intensities intersected by …

Gillian's head titled heavenwards, and she confided, quietly, "It's all about trees, isn't it? Really?"

Fi's head jerked with the sharp question, "You mean, the way Muriel's soul, if she had one, took flight when she was up a tree?"

Despite her polite control over muddled grief, always more skilled at dissembling decorum than Fi, Gillian smiled. Shadows of trees bulked as if they, in their copses and groves, wanted to hear, to be part of this conversation. Branches stretched forwards after Gillian replied with "In the desert, aborigines put corpses in trees. Do you know if the Bundjalung did? Around here?"

Fi merely snorted, "Stink, wouldn't it. The flesh would fall off in nasty festering lumps. Too tropical maybe?"

"We don't know, Fi," Gillian said evenly as she turned her whole body away from Fi's strong gaze. "We don't know where their burial grounds were. We know nothing about what they did." The trees, thought pitching through them, stymied a gasp. Fi leaned forwards into their graveyeard hush, observing with a hint of malice, "We left our trees behind, don't you think? Sort of lost our way." Then she threw in "Have you been to England? Scotland? Do you think we should go back to those cold veldts of Yorkshire where trees like lone cranky parsons damned us to hellfire?" She answered herself briefly. "All I could think was how lucky for us the ancestors left."

Gillian pawed the floor, annoyed with Fi's cynicism and amused by it as she ruminated over her serious speculation. "We, as a people, emigrated from cold misery. And we dispatched Bundjalung to ... misery." Compressed in her mind was the knowledge she had acquired from historical documents that those Arakwaal and Wiyabul her people had displaced were sent to the reserve at Palm Island where they were forced to live in prison-like conditions with the people of other tribes they didn't like, among trees they didn't know, and ... She threw her hands up with an "Oh!" and "It's too hard!"

A quick breeze whistled through treetops, setting free a primal laughter bouncing from branch to rustling branch. The old man pine by the gate sighed, its cambrian layers creaking, fearing for the disjunctive lives it watched going past it every day of the one hundred years of its lifetime. Gillian will later say there's a lyricism, and Fi will insist there's a banality that barely concealed madness. But in the moment of looking across the movement of light at her mother's wake, she said, "Anyway. Patrick White said it better than Hopkins — about the beauty of place."

The old pine on stormy nights roared, the grief of evicted people tearing through its fibres.

Knees spread and face fierce, Muriel fell as if from on high into Fi's poor brain. Wickedly glinting, she sneered that hell was hot. Fi flushed bright red, and the haggard whisp gloated. That's it. Those hot flushes condemn the wicked.

Oblivious of the woman's battle with sudden heat — would it bother them if her conscience got at her? — the men contemplated the ground at their feet. Droned. Shifted the weight of their bodies. One glanced over his shoulder to see two women, the two who were sisters, his cousins who were mourning their recently deceased mother ... and then, quickly, he turned inwards, back to the blokish circle.

None of the men wore shined shoes. Not one.

Fi, to stay another embarrassing hot flush, diverted her attention to her shined toe, and she heard herself quietly reminding Gillian about feet. "Remember? Bare feet? Sinking into fresh, warm, sloppy cow pats?"

The whispy hag crouched in her conscience strained, her displeasure burning holes through Fi. But the errant daughter giggled.

Gillian smiled like the mother of the god who had long escaped the sun-and-dew-drenched hills.

"Slipping on the grass?"

"Swiping, wiping, uuurrrgh! clean?"

"Running to the tank?"

"Running to the tank? Turning on the tap?"

"Washing, washing, water everywhere."

"... and never getting rid of that *feeling* ..."

"... of warm, sloppy, fresh cow pat."

The women shared silent, wide mouthed laughter.

Gillian, a hand over the bottom half of her face, moved to lean against the sill. Her skirt ruffled round the calves of her legs, her hair fell in soft waves to frame her round face. Fi, rolling her eyes, swung her shod feet over the bareboards. She was about to say that perhaps creation began with a cow pat when a pink streak leggily leaped up the steps. Fi looked straight at Belinda's wide face, skin and eyes clear and glowing good health. The young eyes looked without baulking straight at Fi's gaze. But it was Gillian, not Fi who challenged the child.

"Belinda! Have you ever slid in a cow pie?"

The girl's mouth dropped into a horrified square caged with long slimy spittle.

"A wha' ...?"

"Cow pie."

The women moved as one, swinging from the crutch and turning on the girl, their leery smiles moist above restless long-fingered hands.

"Cow's Wet Fresh ..."

"Pooh."

"Poop."

"Aw, yuk!"

Belinda wanted to run, but womanly hips broadened across the verandah. Trapped behind their breadth, she pivoted on the balls of her feet, flexing to spring away.

"Have you?"

Should she humour them? After all, their Mum had died. "Heheheh!?"

But two moisturised adult faces bent to shine their lurid leers at her astonished grey eyes.

"Have you?"

(Why were they being so wicked?)

Belinda uttered a shrill "Naoh!" so unlike herself she said it again, "Naoh!" hoping the slightly lower register was truly her own. To be certain her voice had got her right, she added an emphatic "Not ever!" then moulded both hands, one over the other, on the knob at the top of the railing. Then she ducked her head under her armpit.

But Uncle Harry's vacuous presence intercepted the game, dissolving Belinda's expectations of sisterly quirkiness. Coming up behind her on the top step, he grinned wetly. The cow's poop, figuratively speaking, fell with an uncompromising splatt! when he paused to fill up the moment with his bulk. Fi's flinty eyes measured his pause, and she guessed he summed up the situation before he spluttered "Foundyez!" Belinda, desperate to escape the squeamish fear hardening at the bottom of her gullet, somersaulted through the wide open front door. Laine's body pitched through Fi, upsetting her dreamy balance on a crest of dazzled silkiness and below the bright sunshine the wispy Muriel screamed for the love of her daughter.

Two little girls, lacy socks tangled over patent leather court shoes, their floral and lacy skirts askew, pressed their heads together and giggled behind their hands. Then they snapped apart at the forehead as if they were Siamese twins, and they swung back to back to sprint around the house, running away from each other at a gallop, whooping, wild west style. And as abruptly they reined in, bums together, glanced over shoulders at each other and panted hard.

Their mother rushed towards them on spiked heels that sank where flower beds had never been delineated. The redfaced young woman, one hand upraised, one hand hunting for a balanced grip on events — the once blondely beautiful Sandra Weir nee Dark — sank and sank and sank. Her squared mouth gawped at Harry when he happened to mention that he'd been in the barn with all the kids, where, judging by the smudged faces, they'd had a fine time eating chocolate cake.

Chocolate cake with Uncle Harry.

Fi uneasily looked away from his wet grin. Sandra, her face bright red and greasy, very nearly burst into tears.

Even as she looked at Harry's loose lips gaining no sympathy in the garden where she sat, Fi appraised the lovely young woman who was losing her grip, her bottoms-up daughters running their show. They were intent on excluding their nice-enough Mum from protecting them. They wanted to share their joke but not with her, their Mum.

Two against one when there were three. Like Fi and Gillian versus Muriel.

When bees buzzed, girls giggled.

Fi, turning to Gillian and gesturing at the girls, asked, "Do you know them?"

Gillian mouthed, "Felicity." Then, "And Ashlyn." She knew Fi would find those names rather pretentious for a family of farmers who were becoming school teachers. Plus an engineer and an accountant. Or two. Fi was the only economist, she was the only (part-time) historian. Thoughtfully staring at the bareboards, Gillian quietly added that they were the Weir girls.

"Okay. Sandra's girls," said Fi, and she wanted to know, "Who's their Dad?"

Gillian frowned. Perhaps Fi would want to poke fun.

But one of Muriel's letters flagged into Fi's consciousness, giving shape and form to the woman she believed had once been beautiful. One of the ones who was 'beneath contempt' in Muriel's world, nevertheless Sandra made it into the letters, a news item to sit beside the formula that proscribed an exemplary if diminished life.

Home,                                   Sept 22, 1980

Dear Fi,

I am sitting at the kitchen table and I am looking at the old cow, Rosie. She has her head over the fence at the bottom of the garden and she is chewing her cud and she is looking at me with her big brown eyes. Such a pretty cow is Rosie, do you remember her? — a Jersey and quite a good milker. — Your Dad and I are going to Peter Avery's funeral today and I'm just throwing down a few lines to you before we hit the town and the post office. Peter taught history, do you remember?, he taught Gillian for a year, I think he taught her before you got to highschool. He had cancer of the pancreas. Poor man died a long and painful death. We are taking a large bunch of flowers from the garden. The may is out in thick clusters, I cut long canes and arranged them with fuschias and Erin lilies. Looks beautiful. Good thing he died when he did, the Dark's are all coming over to raid my garden next week for Sandra's wedding. No one came and asked me if I wanted my garden ransacked for that nasty motormouth and nosey parker Sandra. Your cousin. Do you remember the gossip about her? A bit too keen on the boys, she was. What a wicked girl! Well, she's marrying some dolt called Weir. — Must run — living in the fast lane. Your Dad's backed the car out.

Love, Mum.

Fi closed her eyes.

Was it a life, this thing that Muriel loved to live?

Names may recede under the cassia where old gossip rotted with the leaf litter, but there was no mistaking how Sandra's little girls' dresses frothed high up their pink buttocks. Chocolate smeared their thighs and fingercoated their knees, lollied up their pretty white skin. They were little girls that liked to run. They ran in all directions, calling out in clear sharp voices, "Catch me!" "Catch me!" "Catch me if you can!" They giggled hard, stirring a maniacal rush of air.

Under their running feet the earth quivered with a silent shout of victory.

Fi stood still, and watched Belinda join the Weir girls with a mighty jump. She missed all the steps in one big leap and giggled. Felicity laughed — she almost squealed — when Belinda landed on grass.

Ashlyn liked centre stage. She came forwards, put her hand on her hip and spun like a top, right on the tips of her toes. When she spied Gillian watching her, she extended her leg and pointed her toe and lowered her curved arms, and slowly bowed her head.

Gillian's attention was not arrested by the performance of a demure girl becoming Barbie doll. Something unseen, perhaps a rustling in a treetop, claimed her. Or the sun's old gold afternoon light hard on a bush.

Ashlyn, pouting and looking away from Gillian's neglect of her finesse, recovered herself with the pleasure of a scream when Belinda somersaulted. She rushed to make the most noise and she bounced her skirts high. Fi was astonished by the mass of lacy froth where the panty elastic clung to the top of her thigh. Then without pause, all three girls took off, running in all directions, their shrill screams splitting ears.

Clutching the rails, Fi's knuckles whitened. Muriel, squat in her head, gritted her teeth at disreputable little girls. It (whatever this *it* was) was all about sex, all about respectability, all about pirouetting on a fraction of life's endless possibilities and keeping that *it* sex under strict control.

Fi winced, and looked away when Ashlyn materialised, panting but sure-footed, and right in front of Fi. She lowered herself, one leg pointing long, one curled under her buttocks. A swan. She made herself become a dying swan. But she was not appreciated by one of the older women bearing a scone on a plate who stepped over the top of the girl as if she didn't exist. The swan, with a movement of minor irritation, folded her legs under her body to make a ball of herself and, notwithstanding scrunched skirts and petticoats, she rolled and hit the wall.

Thud.

Laine Macready, her sudsed toe pointed to the ceiling, her hands cupping her buttocks, had listened to Fi on the subject of her family several times over several evenings. She'd gulped down mad fragments of a family history about a people who settled on land overlooking the Pacific Ocean round about the turn of one century into another. By Fi's account, they were big people with many children, grown sons with big families who occupied several farms, filled pews in newly built churches and ran picnics to support the primary schools all the small settlements were building at that time.

Laine listened with fascination — or was it with the feigned entrancement of a lover? — to a strange story of passions dug into soil. Perhaps in time memory fudged over events, and other stories took off, parallel to the true ones and tangential to the narrative line of the original one. For how would Fi describe to Laine the oval framed photographs of Victorian era ancestors reverentially arranged around walls with studio photographs of weddings and baptisms, and not one of these less than sixty years old?

Laine may have been puzzled by the dour faces. She may have been inspired enough to observe it looked as if, in the 1920's or thereabouts, it was bad practice to show teeth to a camera's lens. Did the Hindmarsh graveyard expressions give them a sought after air of importance? Under the lift of a chin, the high arch of a nose, there was a sniff in the conviction they were worthy of observation and due recognition was not forthcoming.

Knowing something of the history of small settlements along the eastern coastline of Australia, Laine may have opined that they looked as if they were proud but ignored, most especially by politicians responsible for allocating funds to build roads and bridges and railway lines. But Fi probably would have countered with the pedestrian observation "There's nothing a certain Sigmund could not have explained," even though she herself didn't believe that Freudian theories explained ancestral seriousness. Fi believed they looked stern because they had to sit and wait a long time before the photographer under a black cloth got them all focussed and in the picture.

With a wry smile at the memory of sliding in the bath with Fi and her talk about ancestors, Laine sank her chin into bath foam. She should have been in front of cameras, advertising ... baths and bubbles,

bubbling under her chin and above a thought, straying to a cold glass of wine of Chardonnay she pictured in the fridge, Laine Macready gently believed Muriel and Fi, mother and daughter, never gave themselves a chance to reconcile their differences. When she rose, foam slipping down her back, her pink wet fingers reaching for a thick white and blue towel, she amazed herself with her belief that it's easier to mend strained mother-daughter relations when the daughter becomes a mother too. And the Fi Laine loved would never do that to herself.

In this same moment, Fi swung her legs off the banisters. One of her aunties, beaming from the doorway, rolled in a glycerine, "An' you're still a spinster? Eh, pet?" Fi's head jerked back. The fruitiness of her laughter cut through damp gold light.

Harry glanced at the men. The men. Whose backs were bleached by sunlight. He did not join them. He looked at the frowning aunty and the rudely laughing Fi. Striding down the steps, she brushed past him. He started forwards up the steps and into the house. When he hesitated at the front door to turn and look again at Fi, she'd gone.

Fi's skin lapped up the coolness of ocean breezes. Under a spell, she forgot her outline and merged with the garden.

God forbid! But then God, having abandoned them, could forbid them nothing. Left the lot of them, hadn't he, a bunch of murmuring and muttering and mumbling cow cockies among trees they didn't belong to, trees their grandfathers chopped out, trees young nephews and cousins carefully planted back in — in the faintly religious hope that some sort of redemption might be found. Would the men's mumbling muddle with the nasal whirring sometimes heard in deep gullies by rocky brooks?

As a child, she heard high in her head sticks clicking with the droning didgeridoo when she walked where the creek curved under an overhang of lillypilly branches and where a knoll jutted above a valley and rocks flattened under earth. But when she stood still, perfectly still, the imagined sound evaporated. Those people had gone. In her lifetime they'd never been there.

The land sighed under her feet, and sunny crescents stood up and shone. Did a face beam, smile on her? She wanted that. When she was a child, she wanted that smile from heaven.

Her mother sucked in her lips when she cut sandwiches at the breadboard, and her father allowed his hand to wander in front of his face. One of his daughters believed he tried to catch hold of his dreams. The other wanted to be one of her Dad's dreams. With a clicking stick and a didgeridoo and white smudges painted on her bare chest.

The adult Fi touched her face to remind herself she was standing in this moment on the garden path at the wake after her mother's funeral.

In the corner of her eye, a tear may have beaded, but none fell.

That's how it was, that's how it is.

Gillian, or was it Muriel?

Long-waisted and wide-hipped, her left foot too thin in navy pumps and hooked outwards at an angle, her full skirt swinging round her calves as an old song swung high in Fi's head, the middle-aged woman plied her course past the white flowers blossoming on the dark green branches of Muriel's prize, the mayflower bush. *Coming round the mountain, when she comes.* That old song, tinnily tuneless, ... *round the mountain, when she comes* ... in a dark navy dress sprigged with white flowers. It was a mayflower dress, the type Muriel would have chosen. But here in the garden, with the abominations served up as food, Fi witnessed Gillian transforming, transforming ...

It could be her. Indeed, it looked as though Gillian had dressed herself in this garment, something awful Fi was too distracted by her own inner-qualms to notice earlier in the day. Her sister's widening body, flowing in its soft sprigged dress, waded towards her, dark blue eyes concealed under fleshy lids. Should she splutter, blurt unambiguously, "Gillian! Where the hell did you get that dress?"

But even Fi drew the line in the shifting sands of decorum,

politely asking over the heel of her hand, "Gilgil, I didn't notice your dress earlier. Where …?" Criticism remained unsaid, except for the rebuke languishing under the inquiry, "Where did you find it?"

Was it the soft side of Muriel that widened?

There was the countrywide smile creasing up cheeks to make hoods of eyelids, those smiles never darting through eyes to flicker and kindle inner warmth. The woman whose body smelt warm and sunny, the woman who replied with a giggle embedded in a hiccup, "Fi! I have always loved op-shop shopping," smiled shyly and nodded, truly agreed, that the whole outfit had a frayed look about it, even the shoes that were surely the same as something Nanna Dark had worn forty years ago.

Fi believed she saw a desolate self — that Gillian's was a body vulnerable to the world in which it accommodated itself.

Fi crossed her arms. She rocked on her heels. She could be overbearing. But she desisted, allowing her "Oh m'god!" to drop straight into the dark depths of her stomach.

The harsh western sun forced Gillian to flank her cheek upward to protect her eyes. Warmth seeped through her pores into the roll of her neck. She held her head high. Nevertheless, she began to murmur in confidence, "… quite a few expenses. Lately …"

Fi frowned and looked away. The Cartier bracelet dropped over her hand.

Choosing with care the little information she wanted Fi to know, Gillian's face opened, her head turned. A segment of memory flagged up from her sun-warmed depths. Her old self parried and sparred, and so she bridled. "Fi, you do, on occasion, as now, look for all the tea in China like something off a David Jones' REDUCED rack. Ever so discreet. Ever so nicely priced for the quality."

The city woman, invented out of the flesh of a country girl steeped in precise frugality, is shocked that she should be so obvious. The city woman, assiduously created, will not be insulted. Her mind, bracing for a battle with words, hoped for a joust. The bad girl in the city woman grinned.

Gillian sniffed, nervous a conflict may become a battle.

Fi graced her world with milder manners than the clamorous girl could claim, the created woman a development away from the second child flexing her verbal skills to demand attention from the family she belonged to. With a tilt to her head that some may describe as shy, others ingratiating, Fi said, "Camouflage is a good way to go."

"You're being elliptical."

"Perhaps.'

"Who are you hiding from? In your camouflage?"

"Hiding?"

"That's what camouflage is for. Isn't it?"

Fi pondered the light glancing the teacup she held, twirled the object to catch more of the sun as it slid behind the big branches shading the gatepost, and spoke to the glint, "Not hiding so much as ... Masquerading."

"As?"

"Ordinary, Gillian. I masquerade as ordinary."

Gillian's eyebrow rode her forehead. Her lips looked at Fi's lips, her eyes questioned her eyes.

"You mean ..."

"Normal, Gillian. Normal."

Gillian moved her shoulders inside the soft cloth of her dress. She stood on the crazy path made of stones warmed by the sun. Held by warmth, Muriel's stories about heroic young men dragging river stone from creeks at the bottom of the valleys to hilltop farms for paths and dairies and pigpens stirred old feelings of complacency through her being. Nevertheless, the knowledge that her sister's black trouser suit worn with a grey shirt were not mourning clothes, rather a careful selection concealing a lifestyle, speared a chilling thought through her.

Her sister. Fi. Neutered in a suit.

Gillian, fingering the synthetic fibres of her imitation twenties' dress, weighed up a word or two.

Normal, was it? Or did Fi mean *acceptable*?

As if despairing, she winced when she muttered as if to herself the word *acceptable*.

# A suit.

Trousers and jacket worn with a soft shirt. Perfect for the woman seated in boardrooms who was once a girl running barefooted to school, running yelling along beaches, running noisily in brackish brooks, hunting frogs with despicable boys, and finding in clumps of forest growth stone tools, spear heads and axes belonging to a vanished people.

Gillian came up hard against the brittle edge of Fi's gaze that warily advised, and from the bottom of her heart — there, at the heart of the matter where sex is truth and truth is sex — Fi always believed she was born to be in love with loving women. She was a woman who loved busty girls. She wanted to shout into the branches of the old pine that guarded the road gate that she was Sapphic. That she was lesbian. And that being so very often left her lonesome.

Would Gillian understand any better than the bluddy tree that, on her overseas' business stints, she ...

... and striding across polished floors, she greeted pinstriped bankers crowding an executive suite. She extended her manicured hand, the men raised cut glass tumblers ... She extended her manicured hand, the men inclined bald heads ... She extended her manicured hand, the men shook it in their plump grip. They shook her hand and, overtly, studied her face. They knew her. She, like them, was a professional, an economist, and their consultant. Perhaps chic black, a single leather camellia clasping her jacket, folded into her being yards of well-tailored confidence. The men, smelling of good serge and the best malt whisky, hovered and smirked, their fleshy fingers anticipating a promised dalliance plunging into youthful flesh. Be it a boy or a girl.

All part of celebrating the successful closing of a deal. And she swung a leg. Their partner in consultancy swung her trousered legs, and drew to one instep an elegant leather shoe. Her heels were her firm support — she did not wear shoes that made her teeter and wiggle suggestively with the look that she may be vulnerable, therefore available. She looked good and neat. One of them. Their business partner. Although … After sharing a drink with them to celebrate the well-negotiated deal securing good business, when they began to look excited about the promised jaunt downtown, the woman in the neat suit would fade away. She was never around when their matey camaraderie got them anticipating a visit to the most expensive brothel for exotic girls and boys. Nor did she slide into place at the dining table with her partner at those dinners when business and industrial leaders squired their beaded and perfumed wives. Her eyes may glaze when the pretty waitress bent over the oval table to retrieve an empty plate. Her breath may shorten when a doe-eyed girl pouted over the cloudy fumes rising from an opened bottle of champagne. But, her feet firmly on the ground in her choice of sturdy shoe, Fi remained alone, and she kept her brains steady to sell her expert and expensive advice.

Did the men ever consider …

Some men might have felt moisture oiling their palms, others might have hoped she wanted to take a bedded tumble with them. She was good to look at, damned attractive. But … might be a dyke. And that's okay, they tolerated all sorts. Meaning: She'd be a bit of a challenge. And she was not, for everyday and all events, acceptable.

Fi rocked on the balls of her feet.

Could she confide in her sister that she dreamt of being cuddled by a huggable girl and her name was Laine Macready? But she got derisive when Gillian opined, "We are a cousinly people."

What a load of sentimental garbage Gillian came up with

when an afternoon breeze lifted and ballooned her dress and she pushed her hair off her tired face.

Fi's shoulders twitched when she snarled "Cousinly, my arse," but she controlled further outbursts. She had a strong sense of reserve that increased in her feelings of exclusion from country-headed cousinliness. She was the city woman, a sardonic individual who professed a love of good whisky.

Basking in careless winter sunshine, her grey shirt rucking at the waistband of her pants, she stood, weary bored, unseeing eyes gazing across flats to the sea and across hilltop farms to the inland horizon. She agreed with an inner voice complaining there had been enough of the bucolic. She wanted grit under her heel. City grit. She missed the heady brew of toxins mixed with stale perfumes and spirits and the uneasy silence of dawn in the inner-city suburbs of Sydney.

Fi missed holding the fragile stem of a wine glass.

And Laine.

Gillian's skirt billowed as if slowly lifting her into the embrace of clouds.

The standing around in the garden on the crazy path had become tricky, losing amiability to the edgy watchfulness that made blood thicker than water in some families. Gillian's pain tightened over her teeth. She looked up and down, eyes right then left, avoiding Fi who looked for a wall to lean against, something to take in her sigh and support her back as she tried to resist being where she was.

Old uncles, sun-pocked bald pates visible at the living room window, were talking energetically, hands holding down air, gnarled fingers rounding out the size of a point that had to be made. On the other side of the window, Fi knew their conversation by the cadences of their voices and the meaning in their gestures. The sad state of the dairying industry preoccupied them. Bluddy poms, bluddy Europeans and, most recently, those bluddy Yanks forced them to give up all hope for the pretty Jersey cows of their youth. She didn't need to hear: "And of course y'carn't trust the bluddy government to do anything. Hands in pockets of all them big business types intent on destroying everything we stand for." The thrust of the jaw and the pounding of the air by one large and work-worn hand was enough to know that that was what was being declared to a room filled with agreeing nods and defensive shufflings.

Time fell out of sequence, someone hurtling backwards from the nineties to the sixties when good blokes with good farms had to work as road gangers 'to make ends meet'. The heads moved with a certain shyness, making sure she and Gillian were out of earshot, and she knew the old uncles were discussing Jim Hindmarsh, and his inability to accommodate himself to change. By the fat rolling of lips over bottom dentures she knew that they agreed Jim had had it all destroyed in him, his small allowance of flexibility, during the War.

A pot of tea may have passed under her nose, perhaps, too, a plate bearing a pyramid of sandwiches.

She touched her eye to wipe away a salty tear.

Men. At the front gate, the men who were the fathers of small children had not moved. Those wordless young men, in their thirties, trapped in that awkward masculinity the national credo labelled as 'easy-going', were waiting for the time when they were bidden to take the women and children home.

Salt of the earth, those blokes. Pillars of salt. Immutable.

She held a tissue to her nose and turned away from these men, blokes, pillars of earthy salt, for a new focus on the wake.

In the shade of an ancient peach tree, Clarrie Dark, Boyd's son, sat on a collapsing wicker chair. Flickering light and shade spooled across his bare head. His fat neck, strung with a wide tie ending high on his massive chest, bulged over the top of his shirt collar, like a Christmas ham trussed for the occasion. Looking over the top of the crumpled tissue at him, she smiled vaguely but, as in a dream, her father's disembodied face drifted through her, through and through, his large, cracked fingers bothering the shadows in front of his eyes.

Gillian's back was between her and the remnants of the orchard where Clarrie sat, the magpies' afternoon calls long and sad in her ears.

Something tickled Fi's palm. Absent-mindedly as she squinted, she flicked her fingers, but the thing tickled her palm again. She was disturbed by grief, a huge wave of it swelling from within to rush upward and overtake her. But this thing tickled. In a sudden and violent gesture, she flicked hard and uttered a sharp, "Hey!" Then she looked down onto Joey's small face. White like moonshine, he gazed at her.

She sank to her haunches. Fi wasn't sure what to do with her hands, but she put one in the small of his back as much to steady herself as to give him comfort. "Have I hurt you?" she asked stiffly, as if he were a miniature adult who might take it into his head to sue for assault.

The little boy leaned against her knees. She tilted sideways, righting herself when she replaced her hand in the small of his back. He leaned hard against her knees, testing her strength. They both fell sideways, Fi's hand splaying across twigs and grass and hard earth, the little boy twisting across her, painfully digging his elbows into her stomach and biceps. "Joey!" she scolded. "Get off!"

When Gillian swooped on the tangled bodies, he looked as though a crying sound had stuck in his throat where it hurt. He hooked a free finger over his front teeth. His bony knees wobbled, and his calf muscles stretched under mottled blue skin when he stood upright.

Fi pushed him off, and dusted down her trousers. Something sticky made a gluey track across one knee. Not being used to children, she felt uncomfortable, not knowing how annoyed she should sound. The kid was slimy and weird. He slipped clumsily, and he stank. She wished Gillian would take charge. After all, she ought to — she'd had the experience, she'd been a professional martyr and, heaven forbid, she acted the forever heroine, otherwise known as 'mother'.

Joey snuffled. He was a rheumy sort of kid who might be asthmatic.

Fi rubbed at the sticky trace messing her trousers and asked, "Where's Mum?" But, sucking his finger over wet lips, Joey spun in a slow circle. His eyes rolled crazily. Fi, bewildered by his behaviour, stopped rubbing the sticky mark on her trousers and looked at him straight when she asked again, "Is she around here? Your Mum." He stepped backwards, and fell off the edge of the crazy path, this time landing alone on the stubbled lawn. She offered no helping hand for the feeble whelp to smudge with his slime. His ineptitude irritated her, and then he gagged on his finger. Disgusted, she looked around for help and found Gillian at her elbow asking in a fussy sort of voice, "Shall I get Mummy?" To be exact, Gillian addressed the side of the house and, not waiting for a reply, she walked off to find his Mummy.

Joey stayed where he fell, lying on his back with his shirt hitched high up his thin blue chest. He raised his finger high above his head to watch the spittle drop long threads onto his face, one bony knee pointing to the sky.

Examining the dirt on him from her high point, Fi questioned the value of neglect in that thing called love. As far as she was concerned, he was in need of his mother, one of those creatures who should come running to gather up her dirty little boy and march him off to the bathroom. Peremptorily she called out, "Gillian?" But Gillian had disappeared.

A single leaf flagged slowly to the ground beside him. He stretched out his hand to clasp then crush it in his grubby fist.

Belinda bounded down the pathway. Felicity and Ashlyn, their petticoats bedraggled, their hair in knots, their feet bare leaped behind her and turned cartwheels, showing off their frothy knickers. Belinda hoisted a plate of sandwiches to adult eye level and called out, "Last offering!"

Joey, his dash swift, darted up and tackled Belinda, head-butting her in the groin. The plate swept up to the sky, and sandwiches rose and rose and rose in a high long loop that slowly curved over to float to the ground. The plate abruptly dropped and smashed into a thousand chips on the stone path.

Clarrie, the leg of ham, stirred in his chair with a grunt. He called out "Joey!" The little boy's screwed up his reddening face, ducking and wailing and running away from the perceived rebuke delivered by his Grandpop.

Crying quietly, Belinda gathered up the sandwiches. Fi, helping her, was conciliatory. She uttered a mantra, singing in monotone "Not-to-worry Just-a-load-of-old-tomato-bad-white-sliced-bread-sandwiches-sparsely-buttered-and-the-tomato-Oh-m'god!-the-tomato-Honestly-Belinda-You-only-get-them-round-about-here-'n'-up-north-they-love'em-in-Queensland-White-bread-sandwiches-with-the-thinnest-slice'o'tomato-in-the-soggy-middle-Jeez!-the-secret-is-y'see-the-tomato-is-sort-of-milked-if-you-can-imagine-it-Carefully deseeded and unjuiced Then-it's-fit-to-lie-between-two-bits-of-sliced-white-bread. So! It's no loss, kid. No loss at all."

The plate?

"… may've been one of Muriel's finest, but you can't take everything from one generation to the next can you? I mean if a bomb dropped, if there was a war on, it'd most likely get all smashed up. Wouldn't it?"

In shock and in love with her adult cousin's line of appeasement, Belinda sat in a huddle, wiping tears, and giggling fit to split her sides. She heaved, her sticky red mouth madly retching. Felicity, surprised the unflappable Belinda was moved to make such an ass of herself, knelt up to make a mountain of the sandwiches. Ashlyn looked straight at Fi. Pouting through her abundant hair, she lowered herself, one leg pointing long, one curled under her buttocks …

Fi flinched. Her fingers reached the pink sodden mountain.

Ashlyn leaned against the trunk of the peach tree, her leg cocked, her exposed knee in the midst of filthied lace petticoats and frothy knickers. Fi stood at the centre of a sidelong glance cast by a coquettish child who pouted her lips and calculated to make her eyes sultry. Ashlyn held her smouldering pose, up against the peach tree trunk, leaning, tilting her chin high. She ran her hand through cascades of curly hair, then pressed them on the tree trunk behind her back. Her bare toes curled over a twig, her sinewy body bold, and she dropped her chin to her shoulder.

Frightened by the girl's precocity, Fi, her brain shocked, dipped under the shimmering second. Keeping her eye on Ashlyn, she spoke to Belinda, her whisper hoarse. "Tomato sandwiches," she said as if their presence mesmerised her. "Mum made them for my school lunch, day in, day out, for years."

Then out of the blue, Joey bullocked straight past Clarrie to thrust his pale face into Fi's stomach. He reeled round to rest the back of his head on her concave belly. He gasped for breath, his skin clammy. But, leaning against Fi, tugging at her hands to force them to fold over his chest, he sought to nuzzle safely in the warmth of her body.

Ashlyn, seeing Fi's arms round Joey, wrenched herself away from the tree trunk. With Felicity in tow, she took off, leaving Belinda alone in front of the odd muddling of human flesh Joey and Fi made together. Fi, trying to prise the boy's fists off her wrists and hands, offered him a soggy whitebread tomato sandwich and kicked her legs out to make his attachment uncomfortable. Swinging from side to side, he dragged heavily on her wrists. "Get off!" she hissed, and she forced his fingers out of their grip on her. He stumbled. She rubbed her wrists. Irritable and sticky from his clammy fist, she asked, "Belinda? Where's his mother?" She nodded at Clarrie, detached from the scene in the wicker chair. "There's his Grandpop," she said. The enormous man, whistling snores, raised one eyelid.

Joey sat cross-legged and whined.

The conciliatory Belinda bent over the little boy to help him to his feet. He rubbed at his palm. The stubbled grass had scratched his blue flesh. His cry, a low moan, drifted mournfully under the branches of the peach tree. Clarrie quickly shut his eyes.

A waif of a woman walked towards Belinda, Joey and Fi. Sandra suddenly appeared at the corner of the house, her ruddy face shining with the fear that her thinly pointed and spike-heeled shoes would snap under the weight of her dumpy body combined with her disapproval of the woman who stooped to pick up her little boy.

The thin woman pressed him against her bony chest. Joey's soft moan rose to an ear splitting scream, his feet kicked nothing. She gripped him in her motherly embrace, staggering with her burdensome child past the sturdy, tea-drinking relatives whose profiles and backs and silence firmly rejected her. Those in the garden wished they could melt into the woody shadows of the house and those in the house refused to interfere with mother-and-child. They stared, pouting and gawping at the young woman who walked the gauntlet of their judgemental silence to the old pine tree. Everyone could hear her sing-song murmuring "It's okay, s'okay," to divert his attention from his imagined woes.

Belinda muttered, "She's Lucy, she's a druggy!"

Amazed and shocked, Fi recoiled at the thought that the family should harbour such a creature, and when she placed a hand on Belinda's shoulder, she caught sight of Julie, her arms crossed, her thunderous look following the thin Lucy carrying little Joey whose yells sliced the air. Screwing up her face, she spun around and stared with undiluted rage at Fi who chose that moment to lean against Belinda to steady her shaken balance.

"That's Cousin Clarrie's grandson," she said loudly. "Boyd's one and only great grandson." Fi heard Julie blast someone called Neil Paisley in her condemnation of Boyd's daughter who had married a no-hoper called Paisley, had had several children including Neil. "Neil!" she snorted. "The sort that became a hippy because it suited just how lazy ...!"

Clarrie, under the peach tree, drizzled and simpered strangely.

Fi wanted to know if this Neil was Joey's father. She wanted to know what he did, if anything, what sort of a person he might be. She wanted to have a look at a member of the Dark tribe, however remote the connection might be, who had taken up with a hippy woman called Lucy and had had a son by her. But Belinda, eyes on her mother's expression of unmitigated rage, remembered she should avoid the nasty things in life by investigating the nicer things — like the bottom end of the garden where the passionfruit vine grew up a lattice and across treetops. She more or less dragged Fi down the crazy path to ...

... a tankstand and a fence tangled under ferns and devil's cup. Where rich green grew all over black wet wood, the smell of humus tickled membranes, and sneezes had to be stifled. The boughs above, grey and gnarled peach and plum twigs bristled with lichen, striped the sky. Far beyond, the ocean met the sky in a hard line.

"I love the beach," mused Fi.

Surprised to hear something stray free from an adult heart, Belinda looked up. She agreed. She, too, loved the beach.

Other thoughts about feeling companionable were not said. Both of them watched the horizon in the stirring, afternoon light. What else, when a love is simply shared?

That's how she said it to Laine Macready. "I love the beach." A girl-like-you said, *Play it again, Sam! Turn up the music, drop a bit of e, turn down the lights and play it again!* ... and sex is pain, sex is political, sex with love and a nice bit of e keeps on keeps on ...

and Fi, spotting red red rosie lips pouting words for kisses, walked straight across a room. Her eyes luminous, she hung on whatever-is-said dropping from those perfect lips. She was deaf to meaning and content. Fi fell, painfully, repeatedly, dramatically, in sexy love with loveliness.

Loveliness was to Fi a matter of alchemy.

Like any fool, she is in love with expressive feminine beauty. Finding it irresistible, she found loveliness with a little encouragement made itself available for her to love. Experienced with the long-eyed look of desire, she tread softly, danced a step, looked to see how effective were her strategies and, almost salivating, she drank in softening lips, the honeyed gaze.

Fi was a love addict.

Thrilled to bits, the love addict could kill for the zing and the bite that gripped her crotch and fired her lips. But rarely if ever had Fi felt herself fall headlong into the face of loveliness. Thrillingly, she swooped then slid into her lover's body. Such slithery sensations she had never before experienced, she had no way out, she demanded to be possessed and in possession.

Ah!

*Here's lookin' at you, kid!*

A beautiful girl lifted a glass, a glass of wine rose to the lips of a lovely girl. She pressed her lipsticked lips to the rim of a long-stemmed flute where she left a stripy mark. When, on their first date, Fi leant across the table to hear her and smell her better — Laine's voice was light — she squeezed a weak grin onto her thin Woodland Rose lips.

*Beautiful girl!*

Her knees ached, wateriness weakened her legs.

*Play it again. Again and again.*

*Sam ...*

Flushed with love, Laine, alone in her flat, held her old fridge door open against her naked knee. She lifted a glass, held it against the light, then poured a long stream of golden liquid from an opened bottle of Chardonnay. With a shiver, she tugged her bathrobe round her middle and, like a circus juggler, struggled not to spill wine from her glass and lift a slice of pizza off the fridge shelf before sliding it into the microwave. She waited for the ping! Sipped cold wine. Kicked her heel against the leg of a high kitchen stool.

*Here's looking ...*

Laine wandered dreamily into her bedroom. Lifting her eyes to look at herself in a watermarked dressing-table mirror, she raised her glass to toast her image, the piece of warmed up pizza swaying beside her head. Laine Macready, who had lain in Fi's arms and listened to her talking and talking, posed for the mirror, her full mouthed image swelling warmly,

*Here's looking, kid. At you, gorgeous. You.*

Fi promised to meet her at the house in Leura when she had finished with burying her mother.

Laine planted her long stemmed glass among the dried petals of pot pourri and the wild knot of scarves and belts muddled with framed photos and ornamental boxes that littered her dressing-table.

Fi's was spotless, she remembered that. Things were arranged in rows and by size. Fi's mind was ordered, Laine agreed with a nod at her image in the mirror, and she mentally listed her lover's possessions, monopoly pieces lined up in her head.

There was the house in Leura, the ninety-nine year lease on a house in Bali and her part ownership in the business premises she used for her office. Fi, wanting to make an impression, played at being nonchalant, pouting over a coffee spoon whose handle flicked around and chimed against the fine porcelain saucer of her coffee cup, perhaps making herself appear acquisitive rather than an independent woman of means. For Laine lazily smiled at the self-made woman whose chestnut stubble, growing up the long tendons at the back of her neck, bristled to be touched. Eyes the colour of horn gentled, glowed at her.

Laine loved to be adored.

Alone in her pale blue and shockingly untidy bedroom, she swung away from the dressing-table mirror to lift her pizza off the unmade bed.

Fi Hindmarsh, her lover, accounted for any number of selves. She was a chain of selves revolving in and out of each other, linking and inter-linking. For her girlie girl, she had pasted together an image of a city woman who was once a barefoot country girl running to school some forty years ago. She had gone rabbit hunting and skylarking around swamps and creeks with grimy boys. "Rabbits live in burrows," said Fi. "We dug them up, a kid called Barry and me. Very often, rather too often, a black snake'd whip out before the bunny hopped free. Of snake and us."

Running her hands lightly over the delicious Laine, Fi scooped shadows where light eddied between shoulder and shoulder blade. Resting her cheek on Laine's cool silken skin, she related the story about how her first understanding of *Alice In Wonderland* was sabotaged by the thought that the White Rabbit would've been killed by a red-bellied black snake well before meeting the Queen of Hearts. Fi was a scab-kneed girl in a floral print dress and an old Sunday school sun hat squashed down on her head.

Laine had trouble picturing the hat. She had never heard of, let alone seen, white straw Miss Muffet hats with narrow brims and lots of small fruits and flowers decorating the band. Not in shops, or on people's heads. "A bit Tom Sawyerish, my childhood," said Fi. "Sounds backwoodsy," murmered Laine, her glance drowsily tracing Fi's sinewy contours. She tried to imagine the tomboy striding through reeds to the soft edges of creeks. Perhaps Fi went hunting for platypus burrows. Water rat nests. "Did you go fishing?" Was fishing a possibility? Lifting the book she was studying and wriggling under the bedclothes she believed Fi had had a strange life shared with snakes and rabbits and rats and dogs and ...

Fi climbed trees, stole birds' eggs, collected star-shaped seed pods and ...

Laine turned the page, but the print swam out of focus into the dream she was dreaming of sinking on a soft mattress under a thick doona, daydreaming Fi Hindmarsh. She was seeing her lover standing in a troubled silence on a garden path.

Fi had not quite told Laine how far into forty she was.

Laine, at twenty-eight, was a dream in anybody's language.

Gillian burst in on Fi's daydream of her gorgeous girl blushing *(Here's lookin' at you, kid!)* with "Where's Leigh? I can't find him." And before Fi could ask the question "Not in the barn?" Julie Mackinnon hissed in her ear. "There she is, that's Clarrie's son's floozy. Common Law Wife. Lucy."

Grappling to understand why she was at the centre of an anxious turmoil, Fi recoiled from and stared at highly glossed apricot lips reiterate, "Lucy Osborne. Joey's mother. She's on a methadone program."

"I've looked!" bleated Gillian. "I looked in the barn."

"And as is often the case," finished Julie, her cold eye looking straight at Fi, "she is slothful. Filthy. Lazy. Neglects Joey. He is filled with fear."

Fi peered through the sharpening light for Gillian, hoping to extricate herself from Julie's spite, flicking, as it did, from her wondrous lips. Julie, the sports head teacher, believed the failure to take care of your own health and fitness was beneath contempt.

"Takes all sorts," said Fi.

Julie stepped back, her head firmly centred on her shoulders. "What I'd expect of you," she snapped at Fi. Her jaw stuck out and she clenched her fists by her side.

Fi thought it was such a shame her rage distorted her lips. She tried to look away from them, the lips, as she sought out Gillian to cover for her feelings of uneasiness. But Julie started forwards, as if she would swing her fist at Fi's face. Horrified, Gillian looked at the two of them and rushed without pausing to hear explanations, demanding that they should help her find Leigh. Fi was surprised by the fear sparking at the centre of her sister's eyes.

The mad thought crossed her mind that her clairvoyant said nothing about imminent tragedy or sexual perversion. Or, for that matter, gross acts of indecency. But she admitted to herself with an inner grin that she couldn't remember the woman predicting an event saturated in tea, either.

And just then Elliot Dark, stepping out of the shadows, said, "Got teevee?" Fi's temples stung. Old memories of her disgust for that one cousin stunned her brain blank. She turned her back on Elliot. Through her own distress, she tried to come to grips with Gillian's distress, to see it clearly. With polite rectitude, she asked anyone who might listen if Leigh was watching tee vee.

"Gillian?"

They looked at each other, and measured each other's discomfort.

"Where's Harry?"

"With the kids," Julie began to say irritably. "They're all in the barn, Gillian. Leigh's got to be somewhere in the barn."

Dashing off, Gillian called out "LEE ... igh! Lee ... IGH! LEEEIGH!" through the dread in her throat.

The boy didn't answer. When he heard her calling from the coastal side of the house, he was happily high in the black-bean tree behind the barn, keeping an eye on the cars parked under the pine tree, admiring or having a laugh at the execution of three point turns and the rhythmic bump down the grass track to the Old Byron Bay Road.

"LEE ... igh! Lee ... IGH! LEIGH!"

When he saw his mother flap around the corner of the

house, her full figure billowing near the front steps, her call thin, lost where aunties and uncles advanced to say their goodbyes, he didn't allay her fears for his safety.

"LEIGH! ... LEE ... igh! Lee ... IGH!"

The boy counted the few remaining cars. Uncle Harry's was parked near a loosely hung and rusted barbed wire fence. He thought he could make out the shadow of someone's head ghosting the passenger's seat, a silhouette of fluffy curls blanking out a shape. Aunty Marjory. Old Aunty Marjory. One of the painted ones who smelt of cheap talc. And a younger man — it looked like cousin Elliot — opened the driver's door, stuck his head in the car, then withdrew it, slamming the door shut and throwing his face up for Leigh to see how red it was with anger. Even as the nightdark fell, Leigh knew cousin Elliot was furious — pissed off — with something.

The fluffy head bobbed as if it floated on placid water.

Leigh's sharp eyes laughed, and the dark deepened, brightening the lights, framing small moments. He shifted his haunches on the branch, making the words 'pissed off' ugly with his rubbery lips just as he was reminding himself to ask his mother again for a video-cam at Christmas. Again. And again, until he got one.

He had left the barn when Uncle Harry tried to dance with Ashlyn, acting the fool male lead in a mock ballet. His hands grasped the frothy bottom to lift the girl above his head. Ashlyn obliged. She wanted to be on top of the world. She widened her legs and pointed her toes. Harry shone. But something got the better of him. He wanted a drink. The boy heard his old uncle gasp, "Jus'a ... Little drink."

Something to do with alarm stung between the tendons at the back of Leigh's neck.

Whenever Great Uncle Harry, smile moist, connived to sit beside Leigh at family occasions — what else brought them together? — a spot at the nape of his neck would sting. Or, to a lesser degree, tingle. He trusted the sensation, as he trusted Belinda who had warned him that Uncle Harry had trouble keeping his hands to himself.

It was in the stinging moment that Leigh leaned forwards, his body alert, tensed, ready to spring into action. But, equally as powerful in him was a reserve that pulled him back. He found himself staring at Uncle Harry's big face as it rushed forwards, the mouth shouting as if in song, fat hands open wide. He was an adult having a whale of a time with frothed up dancing girls.

To Leigh's relief, Belinda took charge and ran her troupe of girls down the grassy path to the house. The next thing he saw, and he laughed, was Sandra Weir stumbling in her high heels behind the barefooted, grumpy and grubby Ashlyn and Felicity. Their petticoats swished, it was clear they were most upset that their fun had been stopped by their big hipped mother who marched them down the front verandah steps and up the garden path to the parked cars. That was where he lost sight of mother and daughters, there, among the Mazdas and the Toyotas, the Mitsubishis and Hyundais.

If the old pine tree sighed, Leigh was unaware of its sentience, rather more distracted by his mother, backlit on the verandah. She seemed to be wringing her hands.

"Leigh!"

A few grey heads bowed over "Bye now! Bye! Byeee!" Barked and simpered, belly-laughed and muttered. Followed by the smacking sound of car doors. Slow big bodies heaved behind the steering wheels, meaty hands hitched trousers and sighs hissed under the thought of the homebound road looped over hills and arrowed straight across flats. Any pursuing silence died fast. Engines fired and rubber crunched dirt, the farewell at last achieved. But Lorna and Elsie and Daphne hummed in the kitchen, their heads nodding and shaking and jiggering, their mimed laughter winding from one to the other. Aunty Daphne's head bobbed and her hair, sometimes like fairy floss, took on the lifelessness of spun steel. Lorna, beside her, fussed with a tea towel, their pantomime of head movements rotating across the glassy screen behind the closed window, their usual timidity and fastidiousness lost in the colours of their clothing. Blues and lavenders and purples. Those colours that coordinated with the bluey grey rinses they put through their hair were said to complement the fierce red and merciless pink lipsticks they chose to smudged on the pritikin cakes and savouries they lived on.

It was quiet outside, under the living room window, as if the wall on the side of the house cocooned sound and held it in the small wooden farmhouse.

The city woman who was once a scab-kneed schoolgirl, her grey silk shirt ballooning out of the back of her tailored black trousers, tried to reassert herself. She wanted elemental beauties when she had forgotten to divert her mind from her feelings of discomfort. In Indonesia and Malaysia night dropped down fast. In Europe and in the UK twilight lingered. But on the farm at Newrybar, overlooking the Pacific Ocean, the western light behind Fi's head darkened. It became old gold striated with flamingo pink, and held its colours for a fast moment.

The city woman who had become the principal side of Fi was a reasoning and educated person. She understood why she had a preference for the dramatic ending of the day. She knew this was relational, an association of memories threading with perception and consciousness to take her back to her beginnings. And yet she stood in awe as the shadows drew back. Playing with the hounding away of daylight, the shadows, seemingly slowly, tongued the hillslopes. Perhaps she had lost touch with Wiyabul and Arakwaal, Bundjalung spirits that roamed where a valley seemed to hover strangely before dusk obliterated it. Perhaps they only had a hard laugh for her.

Falling dew dampened Fi's shirt sleeves.

No wonder she jumped, nearly out of her skin, when wide

shoes scraped over stones and twigs near her and a man's voice asked, "What y'doing?" Elliot Dark, her cousin, the ruddy faced plantation owner, grinned loosely, some would say salivated. She said she was communing with spirits, and she had no idea why she confided that she often wondered where the Arakwaal went. To hear his "Who?" was to know how rude was his rejection of her confidence. Irritably, she repeated the name of the aboriginal tribe. "Arakwaal."

Elliott ripped a leaf off the crepe myrtle and crushed it between his fingers. Ignoring the sneer curling his upper lip, she further explained. "The people who ... It's the name of one of the tribes who lived here before us. Us whites. Wiyabul's the other."

His predictable response "Aw! Never heard of 'em," preceded several questions about what she and Gillian might do with the farm.

Fi's mind bloodied, and she loudly interrupted him. "I'm talking about the aboriginals, Elliott. You know. Blacks." Guessing he had an edge over her, he raised an eyebrow at the same time as he tugged at a fern frond. "There weren't any," he drawled. "Not here."

Her heel scraped moss on the path and Elliott raised his head above the silhouette of ferns. An old memory of shocked discovery stirred in her the sheer glee of school days. Under the stilts at Richmond River High School, a collection of wooden buildings thrust up on a floodplain in Lismore, Fi fooled around with leggy girls, a noisy gang who were good at French and Maths and whacking a softball to the outfield. On a day bright with anticipation, her gang ignored their teachers' demand for quiet as they giggled and gossiped and dawdled onto one of two coaches requisitioned to take sporting teams from her high school to Tweed Heads for a big inter-school carnival.

The clear din of crazed youth rocked the coach. Boys showed off their ear-splitting whistles for girls who talked over the top of each other in high young voices as they sped north through timbered hills and country towns sleepily glistening under the sun. The trip took over four hours. And all of them excitedly hoped to be billeted for the three day and two night event with a fun family. What if they got stuck with Bible bashers? Or with a daggy girl? Fi and her gang curled over their stomachs and giggled and squealed, confident they would have a good time with girls like themselves, mad for Troy Donahue in *Hawaii Five-O*. Fi was loudest. She was not sure why boys were meant to be adored and she had no idea what *Hawaii Five-O* and Troy Donahue were because the Hindmarshes, in 1962, had not yet bought or hired a television set. With a hoarse throat and a sinuous determination to be like the rest, she leaped off the coach when it pulled to a stop at Tweed Heads High School.

Thirty years later, standing among the ferns dwarfed by Elliott's big head, her adolescent confusion about her sexuality had become an accepted part of her story. The other confusion that she recalled, the dark alarm that swept through her, lingered. Black and unsmiling faces stared at her, her gang and their coaches. Half the population of the host school were black, a mix of aborigines and Islanders. She was aware of only four or five aboriginal children at her high school in Lismore.

Recognising their absence at Richmond River High, recognising herself in their presence at Tweed High, accepting the geographic closeness of the two schools, merely a day's hard drive on a coach, Fi no longer resisted understanding that the clearance, the removal, the annihilation of aborigines to make way for white farmers was meant to be irreversible.

Staring at the black hole that Elliott's head made against the darkening sky, she asked, "Elliott? How long does it take you to get up to Tweed Heads these days?"

He replied that you could do it in about an hour and a half, "... if you got a good run and the speeding cops weren't out fining everybody."

Fi slowly made to move, her body heavy with the terrible realisation that she recognised way back then that, when the black faces stared at her, there was no guilt but a fear of history.

"Don't be greedy, Fi," Aunty Elsie instructed her when she was very small. "Only take one sandwich and one piece of cake." She heard her aunty say, "You must not guzzle."

Why did she hear her aunty's voice from the past when she stood in the dusk at her mother's wake with Elliot?

High in her head an imperious voice reminded her a *girl-like-you would never marry* ... And another voice answered, dark with glee, sneering *How lucky!*

Elliot filled the large space under the kitchen window.

*The past is never dead. It is not even past* ... may be true for those whose life is one continuous reel of predictable events. But Fi had been a girl knee deep in brackish water, bare feet skidding through cow shit, head hidden in high branches, mouth scoffing lamingtons ... and she, a downtown suit in her adult life, was a black-trousered oddity at her mother's wowserish wake.

Elliot's voice rode the distance she put between them, that Muriel unwittingly exaggerated when she wrote in a letter — when was that? Perhaps it was not quite ten years ago. Muriel wrote all about Elliot, and what Muriel believed to be his achievements, mixed up with warnings about her Dad's health that Fi didn't heed.

Home                                          May 2, 1981

Dear Fi,

Lovely to get your beautiful card from Singapore. — I have just brought the milk in from the dairy and I have peeled the potatoes and skinned the pumpkin and I have topped and tailed the beans, in readiness for cooking tea. I am doing a chicken fricassee tonight. Mrs D gave me the recipe, sounds rather nice. — Went to town, your Dad saw the doctor. He coughs all night. Something from the war is catching up with him, and Dr Charmichael said his lungs are full of gunk. We came home with a bag full of pharmaceauticals. And we ran into Elliot Dark, he's got out of dairy and into plantations. He bought us a cappuchino, at Caddy's. — Rosie's still with us. Remember Rosie? Such a pretty cow. — I ironed all morning, to catch up on yesterday, and the plum trees need a prune. — Must away. I'm running in the fast lane, don't know how you young ones do it.

Love Mum,

PS Are you going up to Penang? Gillian sounds happy there. She said your cousin Jacqueline turned up. What a fright. That's an odd one. XXX

PPS Elliot's doing well. Been to England, saw the Queen, He does not want to live anywhere else, says we've got the best.

XXX

He talked and talked about his trip to London, "... the bluddy Poms, the bluddy food. Chips with every fucking thing! The warm bluddy piss they call beer!" The heels of his shoes crunched twigs and stone and cement. But she was distracted by something calling. Was something calling for her? Something like a bird?

In the garden, a frog croaked. Gnats sang in the grass on the other side of the lopsiding fence. The dunny's roof forked up, a crazy triangle strangled and weighed down by the passionfruit vine. And then she heard it again, but not as a call. Fi heard the rustling of a reptile, a legged one, in the ferns growing through the cemented floor of the old dunny. That's where a sound was coming from. That's where she thought a slight and sinuous rustling came from. Perhaps a small muscular body darted to snap up a tasty morsel.

Fi, the businesswoman alert to several cultures and a thousand ways to smile hatred, felt her skin prickle.

Elliot, oblivious to any unusual rustlings, followed her under the passionfruit vine. He was reciting his distaste of Europeans, the smells of ancient streets, the Nordic blondes and their heavy-headed sense of purpose. He paused, and then he said he loved Brussels. "They," he opined, loudly. "Those parliamentarians. They're cleaning the whole of that stinking old Europe up."

He was not a surprise. His slack jaw motored on with "I bin to Bali f'four days, saw it all'n one, an' I don'know why I went there. Shoulda saved m'money."

What a fart he was.

Reaching above his head to tug at a twist of vine, Elliot loosened a showering of mouldering leaves. She sank away from the drifting mulch, cutting off her desire to shout "F'FUCK'S SAKE!" She looked straight at the featureless black hole he made in the garden.

With an angry frown, Fi headed off round the edge of the dunny. Her cousin's voice blew around her ears, until, scrambling out of the dark, she stumbled over an abundance of sand daisies and forget-me-nots strangling each other to claim the pathway. She reminded herself that Uncle Harry, Elliot's Dad, had been a farmer with a dairy herd, and Elliot gave up dairy for plantations. Someone had told her that he also managed a sporting goods' store. He may even manage his own sporting goods' store.

Was she trying to calm herself down with a vaguely applied rationalisation for his boorishness? Her mother loomed, nodding that Fi was right to let the boy talk, the unsmiling Muriel offering her tepid praise and folding her hands as a good girl would. And he went on with a eulogy to the best beaches in the world — "The ones we grew up on, Fi. Ballina! Byron! Brunswick! Lennox!" — rapidly followed with the information that he was diversifying. "I'm growing guavas," he confided. "Got good sales for the little cherry guavas. Y'know they're so sweet you'd die to taste one. Paw paws and avocados, too."

So Elliot was in sporting goods and plantations.

She sank into the dark, aware how close was the bullying power of his body.

She wanted to stand like a man, front on. Sometimes she did this in boardrooms, adopting an elegance that Laine described as equine. "You're elegant," her lover reassured her. "Like a beautiful filly." Fi might have loved hearing that, but in this instance, away from her professional self and merely a cousin of someone whose history she shared, she compromised her direct gaze by letting her head casually tilt towards her shoulder, and by looking at him from under eyelids. Fi kidded herself that the I'm-helpless-look was in her translated to be the look of cool assessment. She asked after Priddle. "Remember Priddle?" A memory slid under her elbows. "I met him in a roadhouse on the way up here. I didn't recognise him, but he did me." She broke out in a sweat.

"I nearly died."

Did she say that? She heard Elliot say, "Aw yeah." Was there a menacing sneer in his voice?

She folded her arms across her chest, her fingers, in the crook of her elbow, playing a tune, measuring time, hugging her old memory of distress with awful fascination. "Vietnam vet," said Elliot. "Came back fucked up." He qualified his opinion. "A good man, Priddle." She learned that Priddle worked on his family's old farm, that he never got away from his old man's clutches. "Never married."

Fi raised an eyebrow. She moved her hands with graceful calm to control the demon that suddenly blazed in her head to fire the shape the man took up in the dark. She stood there shuddering in front of Elliot, her cousin, who expanded what he said with a sly grin that he believed his old mate, Priddle, her classmate, "Should've pissed off t' th' Philippines." And in case she didn't catch his meaning, he further elaborated his thought with his firm opinion that Priddle should have — what did he say? — "... bought himself a wife."

She said nothing.

He opined "Better married to a decent bloke like Priddle than living in those filthy shacks they call houses!" as if it were an adage.

He wasn't prepared for her undisguised sarcasm. She pressed her lips into a firm line and instructed her cousin with a finality he had only heard from schoolteachers. She said, "Where's the luck in ending up wedded to a social cripple in a country you don't know?"

His head jerked back, then forwards. Like a striking snake, she thought when he spat his question, "Social *what*?"

Fi turned to walk away from him, up the darkened path to the front of the house. He followed. His tread was heavy. She sank into herself, measuring the breadth of the soles of his shoes. But when she heard him say "Remember the old times, eh? Under the tankstand? You, me? And Priddle," her head emptied of blood. She stopped walking. She couldn't think. Her brains unsteady, she found her mouth dry and wordless, her temples stinging, her legs uncertain.

Disbelief overwhelmed her. About herself. After all these years, after accomplishing so much, he could still …

She hadn't grown up. She hadn't changed. He could still make speech, her speech, stick in her throat.

Speech stuck in the throat of a woman in her late forties …

Tears threatened to well. She lowered her head, her body stiffening from the toes up. But another shape, slight, perhaps a light framed man, breathed on the path. With awful relief, she tripped quickly towards it.

"Uncle Jack?" Fi's voice was breathy. It came from her, a woman from a boardroom …

In the ordering of things, men were queuing. Elliot sucked in his breath, and folded his hands over his crotch. He had nothing to say. Did his chest deflate? His arms, floundering for an unnamed object to grapple and punch, were large.

Uncle Jack stood aside to allow Elliot a way out.

If this was a plot, she was no one's victim. Why then couldn't she roar?

As the old man quietly enumerated all that was unique in the distant black space filled with rolling ocean — from restless lights signalling streets and housing near the shore to the horizon itself — Fi tried to shake a leg into her Humphrey elan. She wanted to be Bogey in the slim suit, with the slickest grin, but after struggling with her ancient antipathy towards her cousin, she knew herself to be a slight if tall woman wishing she was bigger. With a rude red face. She wished her mouth bazookaed Elliot with a litany of abuses.

Uncle Jack lightly touched her elbow. "Shall we?" His palm opened, and he bowed his head at an angle. His tentative gentleness exasperated her, and it pushed against the heart of the matter, the truth about herself where shame mixed with anger and guilt and helplessness.

"Shall we wander up to the barn?"

The quiet voice of her Uncle Jack brought her back to the present. Her beautiful Italian shoes were matted with dewy grass and gravelly dust. She wiggled her foot from side to side. "Yes, she said, surprised she sounded so shaken. She had to steady her brains.

"Okay." The Cartier bracelet felt smooth.

Jack's face glowed with the gentle restraint of a priest.

Walking with her elderly uncle's hand in the small of her back where her silk shirt rucked above the waistband of her trousers, her Italian brogues slicing through wet grass, her legs moving easily, her hands rubbing her forearms against the dampening chill, her head tilting back to laugh carelessly, Fi absorbed something she had very nearly forgotten — a man's warmth. But Jack's maleness was not unfamiliar to her. He was like a gay boy, the gay boys she knew.

She guessed in an eyelid's rapid blink how his life might have been spent. Lydia had given in, eventually, to dementia. She had always been unstable, some said mad. Rumour had it that Jack endured violence. She knew her cousins, Jacqueline and Kel, were quite strange to the point of being unapproachable. With memories of their heads bowed to watch their feet and their grins failing to stretch convincingly across their teeth, her skin softened. Fi found herself in empathy with this quiet man who had spent his life locked in a marriage of dysfunctional celibacy. Impulsively she gripped his narrow wrist.

With a light movement, Jack held her waist more firmly.

According to Muriel, his children were creeps. "Creeps! Jack's kids're CREEPS." Muriel really screeched when she spoke about them.

They hadn't come to her funeral.

Were they mindful of their aunty's ill-considered opinion of them? Was that why they weren't sipping tea with the rells, bonded momentarily by grief for the death of one of them? Would Muriel have noticed their absence?

Gillian once wrote from Penang that Jacqueline turned up at her lover's house in a state of drug-induced distraction. Neither Muriel nor Gillian talked about Kel, a fat slob, and Fi hadn't given them a thought

... until now, walking up the slope from the garden to the barn with their father, Uncle Jack, a neat man in a dark suit, his white shirt collaring a gnarled neck. White hair curled back from a high, sun-spotted forehead.

Uncle Jack was like all the others, a farmer, and they were like the limbs of trees that snapped off during the fierce windstorms, left to weather under the harsh sun and driving rain. Some petrified, some gnarled, others beautiful. Most, hosting parasites and fungi, rotted. But Jack was not as big as his brother Harry. Or Sid and Jim and the others. And his shirt was discreetly striped. Fi knew about good shirts, and his looked, improbably, like a Liberty. Its fabric certainly was a good cotton. Expensive. Exclusive. His woollen tie, dark navy homespun woven with a lighter but too bright blue thread, had the look of a craft shop about it. An amateur's lurid achievement. A gift. That's what it looked like. Something chosen by a fond daughter.

Maybe the shirt came from her, too.

Fi didn't know what son's gave their fathers for birthdays and Christmases.

Jack roamed through the barn, listing the machinery Muriel may have sold.

Alert, her senses quick, Fi sniffed and recognised the smells of oils, chaff, sawdust and mites. This was Jim's barn, the place he chose to go to escape the mother-daughter plot. In the warm silence of his own company, he cleaned and oiled the tractor, the plough and the chain saw. There may have been tree logging contraptions, a chaff cutter and a corn shredder, and equipment to do with growing and harvesting pineapples and peanuts, a lot of it no longer serviceable, the kind of farm machinery benefactors donated to museums, the kind the uninspired threw down banks to join the rising currents of flooding rivers.

Ranged above a thick slab of timber, a bench with a lathe fixed to it, he kept his hammers and chisels and saws and pliers, bolt cutters and axes, tools he carefully hung on special hooks. Jim took special pride in his tools. The smooth wooden handles and the finely cast metal parts were well maintained. He liked the feel of them, good and solid in his hands.

Fi registered with sharp surprise no dust coated any of the tools, no dark triangles of leaves crumbled on the bench and no spider webs laced the hooks. She listened, too, for the unmistakable muscular slithering of long reptilian bodies.

The barn of old housed carpet snakes, why not the barn of today?

When she was a girl hiding from Muriel's obsession with the dictates of the *Women's Weekly*, perhaps a hairstyle that required curlers rolling across her daughter's skull, Fi wiled away hours, fingering tools, trying out some, sniffing in that mix of chaff and sump oil. Muriel's mood blackened when her attempts to make Fi beautiful were rejected, the girl flying out of the house, her mother riding on her fury behind her.

After hammering nails into discarded pieces of wood, transforming end pieces into toys such as drays and boats and guns, Fi's heart stopped thudding, her jaw relaxed, and she became a little girl at play with her fantasies. Sometimes, Jim was there. But if he wasn't, she explored its rafters, squirmed all around the machinery, and with proud reverence studied his tools. Jim had taught her that she must look after them. *Be careful, take care.* That's what he said to her when he taught her how to hold a monkey wrench.

The barn was cool, the barn was quiet.

One day she heard a rustling, a particular rustling — more like slithering through soundlessness. Her ears stung. They seemed to flatten with anxiety against her head. She spun around to look behind her, then some small vibration made her look up.

Two carpet snakes uncoiled at that moment her head dropped back, and Fi found herself staring in awe as they uncoiled their lengths from the rafters. In her first flush of fright, she thought they were going to fight for territory. But the snakes didn't attack each other. They didn't charge. Nothing about their movements suggested aggression. They danced. Transfixed, Fi watched the serpents dance. They slung themselves by their tails down from the rafters, curling round each other, soundlessly, sinuously, kind of kissing the air as if they were kissing their reflections in a mirror and, rising high without appearing to move, they plunged in one downward swoop before separating and gliding away.

She had been entranced, even bewitched and astonished by their grace and magical dancing. That's what she had wanted to tell Muriel. She had wanted to babble to Muriel about the magical dancing of snakes.

Jim probably saved the day. At that moment he had come into the barn, his shadow falling over her body. She turned around to look up at him with a radiant smile, and she ran into his arms, demanding "Daddy! Cuddle!" He picked her up, complaining about her size and weight, and he stroked her cheek before he sat her down on his workbench.

It was the beauty of still movement. The snakes had still movement. Like crows leafing up a blue sky. Like fish sleeping under riverweeds.

Did she say that to Jim?

Back then, she would not have known how to describe the dance. Back then she may have been nine, her body alarming her with the sudden and rapid growth of black pubic hair concealing her slit. She hated it, sometimes combing it, sometimes holding the scissors above it, sometimes crying that her body should be so marked. She was convinced that Muriel told Jim things about her. Important, intimate things. Believing Muriel discussed her body with Jim, her shame deepened.

True to say that back then at the time of the snakes, she liked hanging around Jim, chatting about the unremarkable, her fantasies warbled to herself for her private amusement, his larger presence coming and going from the barn. She would have been as young as nine when she witnessed the serpentine dance, his eyes shining at hers when he picked her up, her eyes shining at his, but she didn't tell him about the snakes. They were her secret.

Nor did she say anything to Muriel, fearing her hysterical demand that Jim should hunt the snakes out of the barn into the sun where he could murder them.

Staring above her, she heard Jack lifting and sorting and turning metal bits over, inspecting his brother's tools. She heard his breathing falter. She peered into the dark of the barn.

"Jack?" She hoped her voice did not expose how fragile she was feeling.

"I've found a light switch," he said.

Fi fumbled against overwhelming strangeness that familiarity with Jack may embarrass him. After all, she may have misjudged how painful were his life's compromises. She may be altogether wrong about Jack. She had no idea, none, if he knew what it was he had, all those years ago, resigned himself to. He may not have rationalised his situation at all. Jack, coming out of the belly of a conservative family of farmers, may have expected that he should be loyal to Lydia, that he was duty-bound to be protective of her, truly living according to his marital oath that "til death us do part'.

For Fi, the whole relationship — of acknowledging Lydia, and understanding Jacqui and Kel — was coloured by the rift between him and Muriel.

"The rift," Gillian will agree. "That made us what they believed we were, a pair of snotty snobs. And made us regard them as a greater embarrassment than they deserved. Perhaps." She will, at this point, pour tea from the Royal Doulton, then she will ask, gazing at the pot's floral excesses, "This prettily ugly thing, Fi. Do you want it?"

But in this earlier moment in the barn, the future life of the Royal Doulton teapot did not divert Fi's attention. She stared straight at Jack who walked slowly and deliberately to the front of the barn where he sat on a wooden block. Fi, her eyes steadily looking at the back of his neck as it disappeared into the white collar that concealed wrinkles etched so deep the skin looked like old bark.

"What happened?" she heard herself ask. "Y'know. Oh! (Then in a rush) ... Between you and Mum, it was all so ... LOUD."

When he lifted his head, which he did after a long pause, tears streamed down his cheeks from closed eyes.

Like a puppet jerking off its strings, Fi jumped towards him, stammering her apologies, staggering to overcome resistances in herself. She baulked when warmth, some gentleness, even appeasement, required her to do the best she could, which was to take her uncle in her arms. To her astonishment, she managed to circle her arm across his shoulders without awkwardness, and to her greater astonishment, he wept noisily, sobbing freely into the cloth of her shirt.

Something irrepressibly repulsive swept through her, slapping nausea smack into her gut. An implosion powerfully forced her eyes to bulge in their sockets. Her fingers stung at their tips. And they hovered, the needling pain sharp. But she eventually cupped them over her uncle's head of thinning hair. She held that head against her chest, appalled at the mess his blubbering was making of her shirt. Like a mother with her child, she held him — her arms circled around him, his head cradled in her hands. She registered how small was his body.

Down the hills, the void that was sea stretched to join the inky nightsky. The world: A black hole, the air wet.

When Uncle Jack's tears were spent, he lay motionless as if asleep in Fi's arms. She sat quite still, her eyes widened to take in all she was physically able to look at. A shadow wavered and buckled, and dark shadows overlapped still darker shadows, some lurching, backlit momentarily by the quick, wide sweep of passing headlights. She peered, her eyes round like globes, absorbing shapes to make out the mayflower bush, Muriel's pride and joy. But a deep boughed camphor laurel was no longer where she remembered it should be.

She shifted on her buttocks, her lips twitching at the realisation she was pinned to the spot by her dozing or comatose uncle. Then Harry sidled into view. His tread, cushioned by the grass, crunched the gritty floor of the barn. He held a bottle of whisky. His fingers poked into three empty glasses.

"Like some?"

Jack lifted his groggy head and, looking at his brother's big frame, he reached out and said, "Yes".

Fi nodded. "Yes," she said. "Love some."

A voice sighing in her exhausted brain wished the day were over.

Harry held up the bottle. "Laphroig!"

Fi disengaged herself, dropping Jack's head as if it were a

lump of lead. The elderly man fell forward onto his hands and knees with a grunt, but his niece, leaping away from his grief and sorrow and remorse, brushed herself down and reached out to grab the bottle, "Laphroig!? You like Laphroig?"

Harry smirked.

With no pretence at dissembling sophistication or graciousness or quiet reserve — those qualities that might be construed as feminine — Fi took the bottle out of Harry's hand to read the label. She simply could not get her head around the idea that her uncle would know one whisky from the other any better than he would know Assam tea from Madura.

"Laphroig! My favourite," she yodelled to herself. She handed the bottle back to Harry, and he poured.

Whiskies splashed in bell shaped glasses. With the old malt aroma a warm camaraderie exuded, and Fi felt jokey, raising her glass, calling, "Dancing girls. Hey Harry. Where're the dancing girls? Harry?"

His bright red lips, grinning at shoe leather, shook from a spasm of defensive fear that she was making fun of him. Was she?

Uncle Jack pushed himself off the barn floor. He stood up and grasped the glass his brother offered him. A stickler for protocol, his old body offended by his niece's lack of respect for himself and her recently deceased mother, he brushed his trousered knees with his free hand, looked at that woman who would call for dancing girls and snorted.

(Jack's a Pisces, his watery currents strong and deep, and he or they never let up. Or is he a horse? Jack's a horse. The clairvoyant said she saw a trusting horse stand by Fi. She warned Fi not to cross the horse. An equine dignity must not be underestimated, she advised, for that equine dignity is intense and most especially faithful.)

Jack stalked off with his whisky glass, swaying across the dark space between the barn and the house.

Realising she was abandoned to the barn, whisky and

Uncle Harry, Fi cried out "Hoy!" after Jack. She wanted to be with him. He had stories to tell her. About Muriel and the argument they had about a cake recipe. She needed to know why they refused to speak to each other because of a cake recipe. Her glass of Laphroig held high, her eyes trying to see through the dark how well her flat feet felt their way through the slippery glass to the slightly lit front garden, she swayed, calling out, "Hey! Wait for me, Jack!". Not answering his crass niece, he picked his dainty way, his shoulders shifting inside his suit coat, his head at an engaging angle. Like a proud horse. Down the slope to the house.

Harry drained his glass and slunk to the car parked under a large tree where he found Marjory patiently waiting for him.

Jack, hearing her slipping on the grass and trilling ooohs! behind him, stopped and turned. Her skin gleamed and her eyes sparkled. Her arms waved above her head as if she wanted to support her balance by hanging on to an airy rung. He gave up rejecting her rudeness, responding to what he believed was her rakishness. Putting on something of a jaunty façade, he crooked his elbow, patted her hand, and guided her through the gate, down the garden path and up the wooden steps to the verandah.

Smells of soggy sandwiches wafted out of the house. Gillian bleated from the kitchen door, "Fi!" And she said nothing else. She deleted and censored, her shoulders barely grazing Fi's, her hands never brushing her sister's skin, especially when she wanted to know "Where *were* you? You should've been here. They wanted to pay their respects. Say goodbye. And you should've *thanked* them. Daphne and Lorna worked so hard ..."

Gillian resigned herself to huffiness.

Fi loudly covered her tracks. "Where'd you find Leigh?" she asked. Pushing plates, Gillian explained, without concealing her anxiety for his well-being, that he appeared, "Simply appeared."

Fi prattled on, and sat with a thump, laughing about the kids all running in and out of the barn, a crocodile chain of frothed up petticoats and fancy knickers smeared with chocolate. "Didn't you see? With young Belinda, a hundred and forty centimetres of pink with flowers, marching them to safety. Those Weir girls. Ashlyn and Felicity. Trouble, that pair …"

"What!? What happened?"

But Fi didn't seem to hear. She offered Jack a chair, and gestured for him to sit beside her at the kitchen table.

Gillian, her face flushed and her yellowed eyes boiling, interrupted with her imperative demand to understand what Fi meant when she said safety. "You said 'marching them to safety.' Safety from what? What was in the barn that was not safe?"

With a throwaway laugh, Fi told her that Harry had been up there. "Behind the barn. When the kids were there."

Gillian, her imagination reeling lurid, went white. She squeaked, and her hand lunged at a doorknob. Jack and Fi heard her gallop up the hallway, throw open the bedroom door, whirl in and bang the door behind her. Then they heard the hard laughter of a television presenter mixed with sharp fast questions and a boy groaning, "Oh m'god. Mum! Rack off!"

The kitchen gleamed. It smelled lemony.

Fi pinched an embroidered throw-over. A plate of wet sandwiches and half a dozen vol-au-vents oozed together on a painted plate, an old one from Muriel's trousseau.

Fi dropped the cloth and stamped around the kitchen, demanding of Jack, "Tea? More tea?" He sat and she filled the beaten aluminium teapot, Muriel's favourite, an anodised cheap thing she declared made the best tea outside China. Fi shoved the vol-au-vents and the sandwiches in front of Jack, and she flopped into a kitchen chair. Sighed dramatically, her eye on her uncle. Tipped the teapot. Poured the tea. And fell apart.

Fi burst into tears.

Jack peered upwards into her face.

Gillian rushed into the kitchen, fussing at the sink and running her hand through her hair. She didn't seem to notice that Fi was sobbing when she reported that Leigh was okay. She muttered "He's been in the black bean tree behind the barn, watching, counting cars, and ...," as if it was a mantra composed to calm her down.

Leigh slammed into the kitchen, threatened the fridge door with a high kung-fu kick, wrenched the door open and bent over, headfirst into the cold interior of the fridge. His hindquarters jiggered and shifted as he rummaged through the contents, eventually backing out, his upper body emerging with a booty of cheese and salami and a loaf of plastic wrapped bread. He whacked the bread on the breadboard, slapped on fillings and stuffed the sandwiches he made into the sandwichmaker, messing the greasy Black & Decker with thick tendrils of baked-on cheese.

Straining to stop sobbing, Fi gasped for air. Her face was bright red, her eyes swollen.

Gillian didn't acknowledge her sister's distress. Complaining in a low whinge, she turned on her son with "Leigh, Leigh. Don't be reckless with the cheese, will you, love? The sandwiches you make are too fat for the ..."

Fi gawped at the two of them, Leigh with his eyes averted, not caring to look at his mother, and Gillian, her voice rising into a whine, at the sink, overcome with ineptitude, caught dithering rather than rescuing the sandwichmaker with a deft hand.

Fi heaved, one of Jack's hands cupping her shoulder, the other holding the hand that clutched a tissue and lay curled in her lap. It was Jack who pushed the sandwiches mouldering on the painted plate with the vol-au-vents away, the smell, perhaps, offending him. Gillian flopped on a chair, reassuring herself by telling anyone who might listen that

Leigh was fine. "He's watching *The Simpsons*. Yes. He's watching *The Simpsons*. And he's eating. Eating."

Fi looked up through swollen eyes, her body crumpling. She cried out, "Jack!"

Jack!

At the sound of the name Jack! cried out like that, Gillian shuddered, visibly pulling herself together to stammer through grey lips that it was alright to cry "... Fi, as much as you like. As much as you like," her back against the sink as stiff as a ramrod.

Jack looked from the swollen face of one sister to the worn face of the other.

Like Jacqui, he thought. No men in their lives. Like his daughter Jacqui.

But what did Jack know?

Fi bent her head to touch her knees, and rocked as she sat, holding her belly.

For a while, nothing was said.

The women looked at their hands or at the floor, examining nothing beyond their own numbness. Their tiredness. Those familiar strangers who came to mourn their mother may have reduced the size of their grief in the present, but they could not stem the continuing pain. The women's relatives may have wanted to redeem their mother to them. They may, too, have performed a duty without knowing why, or what its significance might be.

But where guts spilled to bake hard under a mad sun, the sisters tried to shut the door on their mother's dull rage. One of them wanted to rid herself of her mother's giant demands. She lived her life, she didn't live Muriel's life for her. That one, Fi, ground her teeth. The other, Gillian, in her navy print dress, an op-shop rag evoking Edwardian vapours, showed nothing other than control and reliability.

When the doctor had said, "Your mother, my dear, has passed away", Gillian blinked, the news like a fist flying through her heart. Sitting with Jack and Fi, fatigue seeping through her bones, she made herself penitent. She both resisted and understood the fist flying through her flesh, the hand knocking her head sideways.

There will come a time when Gillian will double over, giving painful birth to grief. In seven years' time and late at night, her head will fill with voiding blackness. She will hear a painful screaming. Minutes will pass, and then Gillian will realise she is the one making the terrible noise. But in the evening after her mother's wake, after the teapots had been put away and untouched sandwiches had been stacked in the fridge for future use, Gillian reminded herself she sat with Jack and Fi in her dead mother's kitchen. She folded her hands in her lap. Uncle Jack had that story to tell, the one about his argument with Muriel, the argument she and Fi heard when they were little girls erupt in the small farmhouse, making its walls and windows rattle and doors bang, followed by the awful silence before they heard his car door open and slap shut.

Under her straight gaze and with her body rigid, she wanted the story to be told. Every pore opened to listen to it.

Off-handedly, Jack said Muriel wrote out a recipe for a sandcake she wanted Daphne to have. And, as Jack said, Muriel being Muriel, she wrote across the top, *Don't show this to that bluddy idiot, Lydia!*

Muriel being Muriel.

At those words, Fi sparkled with something of her old self-defending brightness, and Gillian's mouth made a thin, straight line. That's when Jack's voice changed its register from off-hand to defeated. Wistfully, he said, "Lydia cooked good cakes. When she was well, she'd cook a good sponge. With strawberries and whipped cream. Loved a new recipe to try out. Muriel used to pass a few on."

For Jack, on top of everything, there was the question of Lydia's health. What was he doing wrong that made her ..., what was so wrong with her ..., questions that were too difficult for him to formulate. He could only manage to ask of himself was she mad? And was he at fault? Jack avoided asking himself, or the doctors he took her to, why was Lydia so violent. When he said "I took offence. With Muriel. Lydia, that morning ... She was more than usually ... beyond my reach," his lips trembled, and a tear wet the corner of his eyelid, and he dragged over his dried out larynx, "I needed help, advice, not a kick in the teeth from my dear sister," and he sounded very nearly bitter.

Fi and Gillian quickly exchanged glances that shone with embarrassment and "Was that all?"

He looked at the ceiling, his knees wide, his shod feet splayed on the floor. His hands agitating, his breath rasping, Jack's face shook. When his shoulders heaved, his two nieces stared at him through their mourning gaze.

Down the hallway came the muffled sound of Leigh laughing at *The Simpsons*.

Jack pushed the tea away. "I'd like a strong drink." Gillian's lips shaped up to say, "Mum never kept strong drink in the house." Pushing her chair back roughly, the chipped legs scraping the patternless lino tiles, Fi scored a tuneless bar across her blunt invitation. "I've got some whisky." She ran out of the oppressive atmosphere in the kitchen.

Jack, looking at the state the floor was in, inferred, with a fluttery sound at the back of his throat, "Money? Did she ...? Was Muriel ...?" Making a fan of her fingers, Gillian replied, "Mum was subsisting. She was cashless."

Fi, slamming back into the kitchen and brandishing a bottle, immediately took to hunting for glasses, obstructing the dutiful Gillian from making audible her answer that Muriel maintained a depression mentality. "Saved string. Rubber bands. I'd buy her knickers. Tights. Even her bras." Fi, who had never inquired after the personal effects of Muriel's financial state, thumped the bottle on the table with three glasses. "Good thing, too. Or we'd've had an ambulance man dead from shock. DREADful. The way she'd neglect her knickers and things."

Jack blushed for his sister.

Fi poured Islay. Gillian swung around to grasp the freezer door. Shaking the ice tray, Gillian flipped out ice cubes, twisting as she did so to ask Jack, "Want some?"

Fi, her face suddenly taut with fury, screamed, "ICE? You don't ruin good malt twelve year old whisky with ICE!".

Jack, one hand firmly around his glass, shyly admonished, "Girls!" but these were women, one indignant her malt whisky was being vandalised with ice cubes, the other recalcitrant, wilfully breaking epicurean rules.

The urine yellow liquid, Islay by Bowmore, a single malt, lapped the sides of the glass before Fi lifted the rim to her lips to take a good sip. Holding the liquor in her mouth, she allowed it to course all over her tongue, kindling a fire along its length, eventually to slide a heat up the inside of her gums and round her inner cheeks. Her chest glowed. Her brains steadied.

Gillian elbowed the table. Swaying the glass to hear the cubes collide, she nervously anticipated Fi blowing up and bursting. But Fi held Jack in her sights even though he looked as if he wanted to leave, and she kept an eye on her sister, taking in the image of Gillian's responses for careful examination. Then she said, her tone calm and dispassionate and professional, "The assets are considerable. Muriel's cash flow *was* negligible. But she's left an asset. The farm, I mean. We might hang on to it."

Hurriedly trying to work out how to protest "Fi! I have a child to think of," Gillian dug around her head for a reply. But Fi swerved. Sinuous and unpredictable, she swung the focus away from property to invite Jack to dinner.

"Sandwiches!"

She slapped the tabletop. "Toasted sandwiches. And you can always have another bucketful of tea." Seeing him hesitate in front of her aggressive invitation, she assured him, "Jack.

The variety of toasted sannies on offer is unrepeatable. Not be found anywhere else in the universe, not anywhere else on this earth. Now that's something you surely can't resist."

Ever polite, the small-bodied Jack, their mother's brother, a gentleman, smiled at the liquid colouring the glass on the table near his fingers. He lifted it to his lips, sipped the fiery liquor and, with shining lips, bowed over, "Thank you, but no. I'll be leaving you. You've got a lot to discuss." Words about Muriel formed in his mouth, words about his sister's wilfulness, their childhood together, school and hopes for another kind of future — words about her marriage to Jim who became sullen and withdrawn after he returned from the war. All those things confused his way of seeing his nieces after the wake.

Fi waved her hands to whisk up a nothing. She raised her eyebrows, making a comical oh! of her mouth. "Not staying, Jack? Sure you wouldn't like to stay?"

Gillian, emerging from something of a trance, took his arm in hers. The strength and warmth of her body surprised him when she led him to the door opening onto the hallway. She said over her shoulder, "I'll see Jack to his car."

Fi grunted. She pressed the rim of her glass to her lips and sipped the whisky, unwilling to hear Gillian's and Jack's simpering when faced with the truth. Muriel died with very little cash and a great big asset. Why did they feel embarrassed? Were they embarrassed? Was there something else afoot that she missed?

She played with the glass of amber liquid, muttering to herself about how Muriel set things up so she, Fi, neglected her. Fi. She accepted she was guilty of neglecting the old whatsit. A residual ball of nausea rose from the bottom of her stomach to lodge at the back of her throat. She stopped playing with the glass. Her hand touched her clammy forehead when a pout formed with welling tears she refused to shed. After all, she had wanted to be the neglectful daughter, the black one who made Gillian's white gleam.

She had wanted to be blacker. Nastier. More awful. But she came to the funeral. By adhering to the simple tradition of attending the funeral, she recognised that Muriel was her mother, making of herself a rebel in her eyes only. She hated to think that her relatives would see her simply as errant, a bit wayward, maybe eccentric. She wanted to be dreadful.

JEEzus!

The dammed up emotions ebbed and subsided, allowing a glimmer of how Gillian might be feeling to shine through her bewilderment. Gillian who, Fi believed, at least kept an eye on Muriel. The goody-goody deserved a thought or two.

Steadying her brains, she emptied her mind of all thought. Made it blank even of Laine. She was capable only of watching her hands shove soggy sandwiches into the sandwichmaker. The Cartier bracelet slid back and forth over her wrist and across the top of her hand. She gave it a flick at the same time as she tossed her head back. Then she had another go at squashing the sandwichmaker lid shut on the wet, bready mess.

The worst thing would be to underestimate what Gillian wanted, what Gillian needed, what Gillian needed for herself and Leigh. Surely, surely. Oh, yes, most surely.

Only gradually did Laine settle down to read an article about tea drinking among nineteenth century Irish flax workers, migrants to cities and migrants in time, trading places at the spinning wheel and the loom set up in cottages for the more regular and organised work in linen factories. She passed a comb through her hair, patted a freshener over her skin, smoothed a light moisturiser over its pinkness, and sighed at her reflection for Fi who, she believed, was probably putting on a kettle in her deceased mother's house. She pictured her, splashing water, dumping the kettle on the stove, striking the match and standing back, a hand on her hip, noisily.

How could Laine know that, in reality, the farmhouse was all electric.

# PART III

## Christmas pudding

What's there to see in a garden?
Where the bees buzz, is there tranquillity?
They say there is, that's what they say.

Fi, numb from feeling too much, stood on the sunny path of a gold and green garden. The shock of her mother's sudden death made her body feel hollowed out and bruised. Her nerves quivered. Her stomach ached as if it had been scoured clean, as if she had been disembowelled. The back of her throat strained from resisting its involuntary need to retch, perhaps from mourning.
    She ached for Laine.
    Contradictory sensations of weightlessness and heaviness dismayed her in the moment when she understood death and sex, grief and love strung her out for exquisite

torture. She lacked the language to describe the sensation of swimming through the skin of her lovely lover's body. Into her organs. Into the fibres, the filaments ...

Lovesick and sick for love, Fi wanted to sup at Laine's body. She knew this for certain, and she knew the physical and mental sensation of extreme feelings for someone else was one of life's mysteries.

Fi fell to her knees — not out of religious devotion, but because her legs had gone to jelly and couldn't support her any longer. For good measure, she wrung her hands, looked to heaven and cried out. She was afraid that she was unprepared for the intensity of her love for Laine.

Amazed by the sight of Fi praying on the garden path, Gillian put her arm around Leigh and hugged him to her hip. He said, "It's probably not ..." His mother completed what he was about to say. "You're right, of course. It's probably not what it looks like at all."

When she looked down on his young face, he looked up at hers. She tightened her grip on his shoulder, pulled him closer to better share their joke at Fi's expense — the ropy aunt with the Cartier bracelet, the one with more cosmetics than his mother ever owned, the one who sat and stood like a man. He liked that chiacking unfemale woman. She knew about snakes and rabbits' burrows.

On the hot path, the ghostly Muriel raged above Fi's flesh as surely as any of Grimms' fairytale witches determined to make a guilty daughter howl.

Her clairvoyant said she saw the power of the medium in Fi. Fi, sceptically, listened. There'd been premonitions, accurate dreamings of exam results and the days when lovers posted her letters. Then there was the frightening one she'd had of Gillian swimming under a dirty sea with a lipless ghost who burst through blood and churning water into a dining room. Music — thirties dance band music she thought — wafted through the dream with the watery shadow of a young

Chinese man. He walked with his arms outstretched as if he was about to dance, but he tripped at the grey edge where the dream evaporated into Fi's waking moment, her hand on her forehead, her body wet with perspiration.

Was there sea? She was troubled by the remembered surging of sea.

That dream repeated itself until Gillian gave birth to Leigh.

The clairvoyant, a wise woman from Manchester, ran her fingers over cards. She invoked a power from an American Indian whose headdress hung above a closed fireplace. She advised a range of insecure women — senior public servants, dentists, engineers, distraught schoolteachers — above a real estate office in Kensington, one of Sydney's eastern suburbs.

The wise woman from Manchester spread cards across the desktop and listed the names of people who would be important in Fi's future life. Fi scribbled notes. She wrote the names down like an accountant writing down digits — in columns. The woman looked startled. She said she had never seen anyone do that to the things she said, and passed her hands in a feathery motion across the front of her watering eyes.

She described a big event. A clan gathering. "Like a tribal meeting," she said. "Somewhere where the sun laughs," she said in her strong Mancunian accent. "Somewhere where storms brew." Her hands worried the air above her temples. She couldn't see the name of the place. "But," she said, "it's near, it's behind, it's above Byron Bay." Then she drew back from the cards to look at them from a great distance. The mauvey-white Indian headdress shimmered in the corner of the room. The woman from Manchester then said, "You are angry with your mother."

The woman's busy hands spread wide and circled near her ears and behind her crown, drawing her strength as a medium together to say, "She is furious with you. You don't pay her enough attention."

Her client grumpily interjected. "My mother and I don't hit it off."

The woman shuffled and dealt the cards. Fi cut, and the cards were shuffled and dealt again. The woman glanced at her client, a woman with a tough look. "Your mother's a bright person." She squinted above the upturned cards and slapped them up into her palm. She said that Muriel was artistic. Swallowing a lump, Fi looked away, confiding "We have nothing in common."

The Indian headdress, luminous in the unlit room, grew large and distinct from the wall when Fi's brains grumbled that there should be some sort of redemption for Muriel, one of the living dead rotting under that laughing careless jackass of a sun.

Appalled at her client's ugly thoughts, the clairvoyant's hands sprang up to cup her eyes. Her client, she divined, based her being, the essence of her character, the spiritual beginnings of self, on deep pain. At the netherworld edging her consciousness, this woman who sat in front of her in a neat trouser suit snarled through lianna vines and poisonous red-bellied black snakes.

The Mancunian yelped, "Your mother! She'll die soon."

In a small voice, she repeated, "She'll die soon."

Fi closed her face against any expression of interest in her mother. She wanted information about her newest lover, an elegant young woman called Laine Macready. When the clairvoyant screwed her face in an agony and said, "It's a pity you despise your mother," Fi's mind blackened. Her flushed face took on a belligerent grimace. She would have none of this.

Quickly rummaging in her bag, she took out her leather wallet clearly labelled Louis Vuitton, and paid the woman her fee of sixty dollars.

Her "Thanks!" a dull sound reverberating nowhere thwacked the woman's desk top. Fi strode from the room without looking back. When she'd gone, her perfume, a flowery one, thickened and swirled.

Shaking from within and without, the wise woman from

Manchester poured a neat Scotch. Her hand shook so much the whisky splashed down the front of her tracksuit pants. Mopping at the wet patch, her lips quivering and her brain in turmoil, she sat aghast in the window overlooking an intersection. She lit a cigarette. She blew a cloud of smoke upwards.

Through the whispy cloud, the expensively suited Fi strode into the sights of old Mancunian eyes. Her client walked to the street corner and looked right then left — looking for a safe pause in the traffic to cross the busy street. That's what the wise woman saw in the very same moment as she felt the ground under her shift. The uncertain space between the mundane and the spiritual world precipitously widened over and through the ground of shock — the shock of recognition. Fi had been her mother. Fi — the woman on the street corner. Fi — the client who had not a minute ago shut her out of her mind. Fi — the woman whose lingering perfume was daintily floral.

Staring down tunnelled time to another era, the clairvoyant watched herself, a mewling baby girl, slide from visceral heat into cold air. She lay gluily between her mother's legs, a girl born in 1744 to a woman who had not wanted her, that mother being in 1992 the client with the swinging stride and the dainty perfume and the bad attitude about her mother.

The wise woman from Manchester gripped the hand holding her cigarette in her other shaking hand. Agony and remorse and fear swung around her head dizzying and unbalancing her. She quivered and, with a sharp cry, she fell off her chair. She curled like a foetus, clutching her stomach and heaving with distress and gasping from the despair suffered in her previous brief life when her feckless mother dropped her, newborn, in a cold creek to let her drown.

Was Fi so awfully alive in her previous life? Was Muriel's anger viscerally part of her daughter's blood and organs and glands?

With a soft moan, the clairvoyant sat up at the same time as she flicked hair off her face, her body tensed and leaning forward to concentrate on what might have been possible in this life or that life for Fi. She stared ahead of herself at spaces empty of faces nevertheless labelled as belonging to the neglectful daughter, the possessive lover, the precise businesswoman. Fi was all those. At least in this life she was.

The clairvoyant was unaware that out in the street a cleft opened in Fi's head to fill up with Muriel. She believed she saw Muriel, clenching her jaw and glowering at her.

Fi's soles scraped greased grit, and she hailed a taxi. One stopped, a door opened. She sat back on vinyl Muriel maddening in her head. She shivered and complained of cold. The driver stopped the taxi and said if she was sick, could she please get out, he was not an ambulance service and he was not going to start cleaning up other people's vomit. Not now, not ever.

Perhaps the passenger was the mid-teen Fi, that abominable daughter who despised her mother. Or she may have been the Fi from a previous life, the young woman so careless of motherhood she dropped her baby daughter and let her drown without ceremony in a creek. One of those Fis looked at the mouth talking in the rear vision mirror and said, "Mate? I'm just a bit cold. Okay? Not sick. Got it?"

The driver raised his large hands in exaggerated despair then dropped them onto the steering wheel, which he grasped and massaged. "I dunno," he complained. "I got calls. All day. Sick kiddies. Sick mammas. Sick punks. Enough to make anyone sick! I wan' no more SICK!" But his passenger wasn't listening. At the side where the wavering edge of dream challenged daily life, Muriel bared her toothless gums. With skeletal fingers pointing at the bright sky, she let free a screech like unlined brakes squealing to an abrupt halt.

In the taxi, Fi believed she stared at a hag covered with ash and smoking chipboard.

Not a pretty sight.

Above the intersection where she liked to have a smoke and watch the day go by, the clairvoyant, the wise woman from Manchester, sobbed uncontrollably.

Muriel wanted everything to be out in the sun. When the morning sang, it was as if the world, spangled with dew, was threaded with glittering jewels. By mid-morning, droplets pearled in cupped leaves. By midday, above blue hydrangeas, condensation thickened and seeped through the cracked putty plugged around the windowpanes.

Moisture saturated the atmosphere where the sunshine bathed the wooden house. A small orchard on the northern side shaded the bedroom windows. But an old terror dissolved against the kitchen window. Slinking under doorways, it rolled like a sigh under cupboards.

Fi, troubled brat that she was, heard the hard rustle of snakes and lizards slithering under bushes. When she went hunting around the hills with boys like Barry Priddle, she looked straight into reptilian eyes, her teasing stories about their evil coldness causing Gillian to shriek and dense clouds to overshadow Muriel's sunny world. She wanted her girls to be pretty in their Sunday School frocks and new Miss Muffet hats. There was that time when, with much fussing, she bought them the latest fashion in handbags, plastic latticed buckets, one pink and one lemon. Fi put a pet frog in hers. "My, my!" Gillian said. "Won't it jump, Hindmarsh? It will jump." Muriel was too astonished to do anything other than retreat to the garden with the mattock.

The magpies' rich carol rippling through the warm wet air of Newrybar reassured her that 'everything'll be alright.'

Nevertheless …,
Hack hack, smash smash.
Hack hack, smash smash.
She destroyed the wistaria archway to let some sunshine into her life. She hacked at an old rose garden, tore at privet

canes and dug up a thorned bougainvillea. Muriel poisoned an old palm tree underplanted with waxies and begonias. She wanted banks of pink and white Marguerite daisies, pink and white dianthus and purple and white alyssum under pink and white crepe myrtle to grow around the Hindmarsh farmhouse. She created pathways leading through irises, ferns and salvia that tunnelled under raining yellow cassias to her 'pride and joy', her mayflower bush.

Christ might have looked askance, beseeching His Father's forgiveness for these female creatures who dug their fingers and their heels in the dirt of life without recourse to verses of spiritual enlightenment. Would the Son who yearned for His Father's forgiveness have understood that Muriel forgot the pain gripping her heart when she turned the red soil and lifted the bright green kikuyu to make way for her daisies? In the stone and wooden church that the Hindmarshes attended most Sundays to worship God the Father through Christ the Son, there was no special place for Mary the Mother.

There was no one for Muriel to talk to about being a mother snared by daughterly willfulness. Nowhere inside the formal structure of religion were precious girls allowed to see that the genesis of their battles with life were sparked by the demeanour of those standing around at their mother's birth. The research that showed the story of the daughter began in her mother at the time of conception was not known to Muriel. Nor to her daughters until the twentieth century crossed the imagined time-line into the twenty-first.

Laine, dozing lazily over the printed page in Sydney, pictured the high arch of Fi's mother's nose out of her knowledge of her own mother's when an unalterable opinion on dress sense, gardens and a girl's good looks was delivered. Wondering if all mothers demanded to intrude aggressively on their daughter's free will to think, Laine Macready moved her legs under the doona. Her dirty pizza plate rode the high seas of her bed. She watched it with the lugubrious thought that perhaps Fi was lucky enough to have a country mother, something like blandness bathed in sunshine.

She had heard so many country stories, but the dull thud of the mattock on hard earth was elided from them all. Fi tried to avoid listening to her blood when she talked to Laine about rabbit hunting and frog catching with boys. She didn't talk about the sound of Muriel in the garden. Hack hack, smash smash. Until the long shadows cooled and the chooks fluttered at the feed bin.

In one of her brainy grooves where pictures dropped between dream and memory, Fi loved the image of a mother in a candy-striped dress, a *Women's Weekly* mother who wore high heels and an apron which was an overall with frills all around the hems and the shoulder straps. At the back of the mother's waist the overall tied in a big bow. This mother was very slim. This mother smiled pleasantly. She stood over a saucepan and handled a wooden spoon. It disappeared in the saucepan. And her face dripped. Perspiration rolled down both cheeks. Then suddenly the kitchen vaporised and the mother's face melted all over the stovetop and snarled. She was Muriel in a fury.

Gargoyle to gargoyle, Muriel's temper frayed in the heat. Over a hot stove and during hot summers and always in a panic to do the right thing for the benefit of her little girls, Gillian and Fiona, Muriel whipped up a storm to spread on the table, in the absence of devotional calm, plenty. But she wasn't ill-at-ease with the mess of contradictions that added up to who she was. God forgot to watch what He was doing when He blessed her with daughters.

But Wiyabul and Arakwaal, ancients of the land, mesmerised by new disharmonic lyrics, droned when the light fast disappeared at the day's end. They set up their whirring and click-clacked their findings late at night when the single lights shone from the rooms of farmhouses dotted across hills that once keened their hymns that celebrated vitality.

None of them knew, no Darks or Hindmarshes cared to know, the spirits of the land they wrecked. Yet Wiyabul and Arakwaal planted flat barefeet on knobbly knees and hovered close by the little girls.

Gillian and Fi wandered down the pathways of wonderment to collect axe heads and sharpened stones that looked like the tools they saw pictured in the monthly editions of their *School Magazine*. Muriel ranted that they should not touch filth. Jim grunted and turned his back on lumps of rock.

Mr Piggons, their primary schoolteacher, raised a weary eyebrow at the stone implements. He encouraged a discussion about the shapeliness of the implements, how the owner may have chipped them from larger stones for hunting, carving flesh, chopping branches from trees. The children eagerly suggested bashing bush nuts, making fish traps and cutting bark for canoes. Suffering their enthusiasm, Mr Piggons had the senior classes make an inventory titled Ancient Tools. He arranged the inventory with the implements beside fossils of leaves and teeth and fish skeletons, the empty scarab of an insect and a snake skin Barry Priddle brought one day.

Curios, all, for speculative children to prize.

Arakwaal sank long toes into the rich earth and sighed. Looking for a resting place where three streams met under the deep boughs of a river gum, he found a sprawled weeping willow, its roots widening the creek bed, weakening the banks so that they collapsed.

Bereft, Wiyabul slid under a black rock and curled there with a red-bellied black snake — out of the hot sun and the driving rain and the early morning winter frosts.

"Where'd all the black people go?" The girls wanted to know.

Muriel told them bedtime stories about the thick jungle letting thin rays of sunshine strike the strong backs of her pioneering relatives. These big people hacked out the Scrub and put in the dairy farms. Sunshine and shadow striped the debris that went black and mouldy on the tracks where they walked. And they sat out of the sun, under deep shady trees, when they held picnics to raise money for the schools and the churches they built, those small wooden functional buildings that were freezing cold in winter or boiling hot in summer.

The lines in Muriel's face softened, her eyes brightened, when she described how they all dressed up in their Sunday best and climbed into sulkies when they went to picnics at a beachy part of Emigrant Creek. "Your Great Aunty Cissy wore a red hat," she said with admiration for her aunty's daring, a faraway smile playing on her lips. "When Aunty Cissy wore the red hat, I was ten," she said, dropping her eyes — to flick at unseen dust, they thought, realising their mistake when she curled her shoulders inwards and said with a blush, "That's when I first met your father."

Gillian and Fi, anticipating Muriel's stories about the picnics, pulled funny faces and giggled. Imagining their Mum at the age of ten meeting their Dad made them squirm. Such an event was hilarious. They clasped their hands over their mouths, their laughter mixing with shy pleasure in their Mum's and Dad's happiness. They thought Great Aunty Cissy was the photographed personage in a lace blouse that was gripped at the neck by a cameo brooch. Putting together a scene of adults murmuring their admiration for her large jaw protruding from under a red hat was beyond them.

But, then ...

Then came the moment for the tragic story.

Smoothing the sheets under their chins, Muriel lowered her voice, and they held their breaths. There was the picnic when the terrible accident happened. "After the picnic," she said. "It was for the school." Folding her hands in her lap, she sighed sadly and her words flowed under the silence their anticipation opened. "Lydia was a little girl, about three or four maybe, and she must have climbed up into the sulky. No one knows, no one knew, but she was on her own in the sulky when something happened. Something frightened the horse. Perhaps a snake. Anyway, it bolted. Lydia was tossed out of the sulky. One of her ribbons tangled round the wheel. Or hooked somehow on one of the straps. Anyway, she was dragged under the sulky over the unsealed road for about a quarter of a mile. We all had to search for her. Her mother, Aggie Kinross, a strange one, was beside herself. She was new to the district — English, very pretty, loved new clothes, had grown up somewhere ... Malaya, I think. Anyway, she was, well, a bit of a lady. Liked dancing. She wasn't one to offer to do anything useful. That day, that day — she wept a lot. Not much use, all that weeping. And it was getting dark and we still hadn't found Lydia. We called out Lydia! Lydia! No answer. Then a breeze ruffled one of her ribbons. She wore a pink sash that day. Aggie dressed her like a doll. Like a pretty little doll, she was. Anyway, the breeze picked up the pink sash, made it rise above the long grass that hid her from view. The ribbon ... Old Uncle Hugh and Aunty Edith saw it. Pink. Dancing. That's how they found her."

The girls were silent, sensing the depth of sadness and wondering who Old Uncle Hugh and Aunty Edith might have been. That Lydia had suffered was irrefutable. Gillian at this moment in the story-telling usually ran her hands across the sheet folded under her chin to find the right voice for the question, "What happened next?"

Muriel's lips predictably drew a straight line when she said that Lydia, dressed beautifully in white voile tied at the waist with a pink satin sash on the day of the fateful picnic, lay in hospital. She was in a coma for a long time. Her head wounds were slow to heal.

"Lydia." Muriel winced when she uttered the name. The girls anticipated Muriel would venomously add, "Never right in the head since."

After Muriel's story-telling, Fi very often slid into sleep disturbed by a dream filled with cacophonous birdcalls and a girl flying through the air to land in a crumpled heap at the edge of a gravelly road. In the dream, noise drove her mad.

She struggled to cover her ears. No matter how much she struggled, she couldn't escape the shrieking jungle. She was somehow in front of herself, her dreamself the girl bleeding on stones, her head and eyes an agony of white until a long black shadow blanketed her. It made the ribbon stand up and dance above where she lay with blood spurting out of a large hole in her head. Blood sprayed through the dream saturating Fi's sleep that was suddenly shattered by high ringing. Birds? Were there birds shrieking in her bedroom? With the gasp of one escaping direful Fate, she heard loud bells. The alarm. It rang loud.

Through its loud clanging, Muriel called out "Breakfast!"

A properly sun-drenched voice announced *Here is the news from the A B ...*

Fi blinked at dust motes dancing on bright sunbeams.

Warm from sleep, she sat at the table and smelled burnt toast soaking up butter. She stuck her spoon in her boiled egg and asked, "Mum. When you went on those picnics like the one that Lydia smashed her head up at, where were the black people?"

Muriel, her hand jerking and her jaw stiffening, said, "There weren't any." She insisted on toast with vegemite. Weet-Bix and bananas. Tea. Lots of tea. Breakfast, in other words. None of it stopped Fi's commonsense.

"I betcha there were lotsa birds. And lotsa blacks, too," said a grumpy girl.

The candy-striped and aproned mother fell off the pages of the *Women's Weekly*. Her stiff jaw lengthening, she was Muriel, boiling angrily.

On the day after the wake over an eggy breakfast, Gillian asked Fi if she remembered Muriel as anything other than angry. Hugging a mug of hot brew close to her, Fi felt the ghastly whisp at the edge of her brain seethe. "Giligil," she said, ignoring the pall the whisp set up, "I once saw an exhibition of statuary that explained Mum to me. It was Khmer,

I think, Buddhist influences. The female deity was manifest with something like seventeen pairs of limbs for seventeen representations of Woman. When I saw it, I understood. That was Mum. You know. Seventeen moods, seventeen selves. All in one body. The problem for us was guessing which self, which mood, was dominant at any given time." She looked at Gillian in despair and asked, "Enough moods for Muriel, y'reckon?"

The shadow in Fi's brain faded, Muriel's ghost losing shape to the discomfort of her daughters sharing grief with each other.

Fi followed Gillian into Muriel's floral, shell and musk pink bedroom, asking "Do you know who Cissy was?" "Not at all." "And little Lydia. Is there a photo?" "Not a one." Then, on reflection, Gillian said, "No. That can't be right. The school photo. Lydia might be in an old school photo."

Fi sat on the shell pink eiderdown and ran her hands over the satin. It had lost its sheen. She touched the finely crocheted cotton and silk doilies Muriel had stitched over the thinned sections. She did all this with faint disbelief, as if mortified by visible signs of Muriel's frugality. Gillian had her back to her, but she could see her face vacant of expression in the dressing-table mirror. She looked at Gillian's mirrored hands. One picked up the hairbrush that had been Muriel's wedding gift and the other picked up the matching hand mirror. She weighed them, it seemed, her bowed head turning from the held brush to the mirrored mirror that filled with shell and musk pink. Her mouth opening, her lips softening, she replaced both on the crocheted doily at the centre of the dressing-table incongrously supporting on its left the television set.

The rustling of the sisters' movements altered the silence in the bedroom.

Fi, smoothing old satin that had lost its sheen, old satin that was daintily patched, heard her mother call out — for Fi to stop jumping off the lounge, for Gillian to check if the cake had risen in the oven, for Jim to quieten those girls down. At once! Muriel may have been absent, but she was present. It was her bedroom, cool, sunless, pink with floral curtains and decorated with crocheted antimacassers and doilies.

Jim had shared this feminine retreat with her. For many years, he was its nightly guest.

The room smelled. Fi's nose tickled from chilled dust. She sneezed from the smell of absence, that breathless absence that is Death. Her mouth trembling slightly, she whispered, "Gilgil? What do we do with her clothes?"

Gillian dragged open a drawer. Her feelings were knotted tight in the pit of her stomach. She touched folded panties, she lifted folded bras, she let pale petticoats fall free, and she folded them again. She dropped them into a green garbage bag. "Really, Fi. No use, these under things, no use at all."

Fi slid off the bed.

"They're no use to anyone."

The mirror of the dressing-table saw it all. Fi, it caught, bewildered in front of a tin of Johnson's Baby Powder, a large pump-pack of glycerol and sorbolene lined up where Muriel once kept perfume and dusting powder — where she once slowly opened a round cardboard box of face powder to the amazed eyes of her daughters. A pink powder puff sat on top. "She used to keep her lipsticks somewhere." Fi's voice was rusty. She lifted the lid of a cut glass jar and found it empty.

Fi turned to the wardrobe. She opened the doors. The racks were stuffed with cotton frocks, pink cardigans and two well-worn trouser suits, one tastefully grey and white and the other black with biscuit piping around the hems of the jacket and its pockets. She held them up. They surprised her. Gillian nodded, advising "She lived in those trouser suits all winter." So the frocks were for summer. But Gillian contradicted Fi's thought. The frocks were for the garden.

As she lifted out the frocks, slipped them off the hangers

and folded them for the bag intended for charity, Fi allowed feelings of remorse to dissipate. She chattered about the floral dresses, churchgoing outfits when they were new, shifts for the garden when they were old. "I remember her standing there, do you? In the garden with the bucket full of bulbs, barefeet flat on the ground, the sun on the back of her head, face totally obliterated, shaded by the hat. Her face. Totally blanked out. *Good grip,* she used to say. *Barefeet on the ground, good grip on earth. God's earth.* Do you think, Gillian, that that's when she felt closest to God? When her face was obliterated and her feet were flat to the ground?"

On the bottom of the wardrobe, a mess of shoe boxes with torn lids sat on shoe boxes with mismatched lids.

"She threw nothing away." "Depression mentality." A giggle, an admitted "I carry on the tradition," followed by "Really?" with shared self-parodying looks and laughs.

The room lightened with the day. Gillian knew what to do. She thought she knew what to do. She bent down to secure the top of the green plastic bag for St Vincent's. It was softly packed with dresses. "We'll put the cardigans and coats and the trouser suits, winter things, in a different bag. Mark the bags, will you, Fi? Put summer frocks on this one we've just filled."

"What did she read? There's nothing to read in this room."

Sighing over green garbage bags, Gillian muttered that Muriel read borrowed women's magazines. "Books, according to her. She called *New Idea* a book." She couldn't keep a tone of exasperation out of her voice. Fi then said, "I don't actually recall Mum opening a book let alone reading it to the finish. Never a book opened, never a book satisfyingly closed."

Clutching old clothes to their chests, they gazed at each other. Unspoken was their wonder, sometimes felt as disbelief, that Muriel was their mother at all. There had been for a long time very little they could discuss with her.

The long lonely caw of a crow flying across blue vastness penetrated the cold stuffy bedroom.

Leigh hung at the door of the room. He wanted to watch the teevee, but he would not enter. He wandered back and forth in the sun that fell on the faded lino.

The women loomed in the filtered light, limbs rising and falling, heads turning and stopping, sometimes to talk, sometimes to hold out a garment to watch its full-length ride across their arms before they folded it carefully. When he stopped to look at them with something like amazement and embarrassment at the attitudes of loving care his mother and his aunt shared, he felt excluded. He was shut out, he believed, by Graces. He stood outside their feminine ritual that required of them deft sensuality. At this time in his life, at his grandmother's demise, he believed he was condemned to observe from outside its cosy ambience, too young to know he would be as an adult its privileged observer.

"Leigh?" That was his mother talking to him. "Make us a cup of tea, will you, darling?"

He hesitated. He wanted to join them.

With the tea on a tray beside a jug of milk and two mugs, he wanted to ask if he could join them in the pink room. He wanted to sink into the soft old eiderdown made strangely beautiful with Muriel's lacy patches. He wanted to watch teevee. But when he smelled the cold absence of his gran'ma, he instantly ran outside to warm up in the sun. He choked off his tears. He didn't understand the hard lump he had to swallow.

Photographs spilled with stories.

Muriel kept her collection stored idiosyncratically in an old suitcase and the wooden box lined with velvet that her wedding cutlery came in. Gillian reached up and Fi stood beside her to catch the unbalanced edge toppling towards her head. They gently levered the suitcase and the box onto the floor.

With their comforting cups of tea beside them, the sisters set to work, leafing through the old photos. Early generations of Dark children in stiff lace collars squinted out of cardboard frames. They sat crosslegged. Perhaps they had been ordered to stare at rabbit ears or a bright ball propped up beside the man whose head had disappeared under black cloth. They looked as if they waited. They promised big smiles when they heard the happy sound of the shutter. One of Muriel, barefooted, leaning against a chair, sash and lacy dress elaborate, showed a smiling girl.

"Where's Lydia?" Fi wanted to know, picking up a large school photo.

But ...

"Have you ever seen such sullen faces?"

Fi looked at it closely. In it, rows of school children dressed in the pinafores of the 1920s, glared forever at the camera's lens. To prove he was in control, the red faced and mustachioed headmaster stood with his cane beside the boys, his heavy head looking straight at the camera.

Fi lowered the photo. "I don't know who to look for," she said. "Lydia, I mean. No idea what she might have looked like when she was a child." She lifted the photo again. "She was too young to be in this, I think." She wrinkled her nose. "Did Mum ever talk about this teacher?"

Gillian said no. "But when I was doing some local research, I came across a report written in the earlier part of the century about some families sending a deputation to Sydney complaining about a sadistic headmaster at that school she went to. It would have been sent before World War I — 1900s — in the time of Gran'pop Hindmarsh. The families were told to leave teaching to the schools' inspectorate, to those who knew best. Some of the families took their kids out of the school. Better to be unable to read and spell than be beaten to a pulp, I guess was their reasoning."

Fi looked at the photo of the sullen children, asking by making the comment "No one took Mum out of the school, away from that ... To be perfectly honest, Gillian, he looks like a thug."

Gillian again said no. "Mum's in that photo." Fi couldn't find Muriel anywhere, and Gillian pointed to a sad-faced girl in the second row. Her hair was black and straight. She wore no ribbons.

Troubled, Fi put the photo down quickly.

Gillian shoved another at her, a photo taken several decades after Muriel's school one of a grinning ten year old — it was Fi — rising up out of spraying sea. "Gawky, eh," she said, admiring her sinewy legs and the wet hair that stuck flat against her freckled cheeks.

Gillian turned up one of a lone boy — "Barry Priddle?" "No!, No! That's Elliot! Bastard!" — who dangled a long dead snake, his kill recorded by camera, his face blitzed by an overbright sun. She picked up one of a row of school children carrying a plaque stating 1956, NEWRYBAR PUBLIC SCHOOL. By contrast to Muriel's school photo, all the children grinned widely at the camera, some near to laughter that might split their sides. Their schoolteacher wore the faded look of a man with a heart disenchanted by the over-exposing sun.

"That was Mr Piggons, wasn't it," said Gillian.

"Oh God yes."

Of school, they recalled nothing special, just days of sports and singing and routines of 'rithmetic/writing/reading.

Then Gillian, waving the 20s and the 50s school photos at Fi like the tutor she was, demanded to know, "What do you see when you look at these photos?"

Fi glanced at the rows of glum faced and barefooted children under the curling cane and the rows of broad smiling children sparkling with ruddy good health. "Affluence," she asserted. "By the 50s, affluence," spinning in mid-sentence to exclaim "that's when we stopped the big Christmases, wasn't it, when Uncle Sid was in Penang and ..."

The mysteries of adult life flowed above the leggy world of childhood.

Gillian sternly waved the photos again. "This photo taken in the 20s was taken only 30 years after our families moved here to farm the land. What you have here, in the 50s, is amnesia. Seventy years after settlement, the violent attitude towards children as well as the aboriginal presence is erased."

Fi perched on the bed like a good student, listening to Gillian's instruction that, absent from the photos, were aborigines.

"Of course not," she snorted. "There weren't any."

Softening her voice, Gillian explained, "Some Arakwaal families stayed along the coast, but the Wiyabul vanished. They were highly regarded as spiritually sensitive, but they didn't stay as guardians of the spirits of their land. One account — a white man's — describes them as melting inland. To live on the reserves, I suppose, and on the river islands."

Cuddling her knees, she explained that she had worked on an oral history project at Southern Cross University. "But I gave it away. There are just so many old hardfaced bastards I could listen to telling me 'My Dad uzta say, never trust a blackfella least of all not one behind ye.'" She rocked slightly, avoiding the truth that she had given the project away because harsh stories came too close to family farms. There was one, one deciding one, about a very young farmer. After a hard day preparing a paddock for the plough, he walked home and as he drew closer he saw his teenaged wife sitting on the shadey side of the shack. She was feeding their first baby. Breast feeding. Did his heart warm at the sight of her, dark hair falling over her pale face, her skin glistening white, her dress a faded rose? The police file simply stated that he saw a black boy of about 11 years of age peering at her through the bushes. The farmer, perhaps reacting from an angry fear that something sacred had been violated, shot the boy dead. No charges were laid.

That's when Gillian understood the expression 'I hate to think'. Even though she herself was an historian, she forced history to mark time, stamp its feet and stand stockstill to attention for more acceptable interpretations.

The baby was their Gran'pop's eldest brother who later died in France.

With Fi, she turned to the more palatable, the large numbers of photos of girls dressed in cotton frocks, lace mittens and curvettes. Fi could not recollect looking the way she did in them, her wrists weighed down by thick bracelets of Woolworths pearls, her neck strangled with plastic beads called poppets. She had told Laine about hunting snakes, rabbits and frogs with Barry Priddle. The very same Barry Priddle whom she did not recognise, the one who made the stubble on her neck stand up and prickle. Would she have said to Priddle *snakes have eyes as cold as frost in hell?* Unlikely. Playmates made rare confidantes.

She picked up another and smiled, recognising herself as *Fi*, hand on a fence post as narrow as she was thin, crisp in her highschool uniform, gazing with perplexity at the camera with all the other pink-faced girls in her class. In the private moments of those days, moments unshared with anyone, she learned to understand that not only were boys like Barry Priddle no longer her snake hunting mates, they were prowling creatures impaired by the constant ache in their crotches. She hated their smell, they excluded her and they turned away from her as if she smelt wrong.

It was about then she began to notice how much she liked the aroma of girls.

Silently, she placed photo after photo, one on top of the other, on the floor of Muriel's bedroom.

Most of those on the bottom of the suitcase were backed by thick cardboard. They celebrated the family's arrival and their successful settlement prior to World War I. Photos of men, generations of men. They were the uncles Muriel spoke about, uncles her daughters only knew as the ones they had a laugh at on wet days when there was nothing to do but rummage through Muriel's old suitcase. They giggled at bushy moustaches, roared, their laughter rude, at the men's self-important straight-eyed and unseeing gaze.

The better ones were framed. One had made it to the hallway wall. Neither Gillian nor Fi could name that great man wearing gloves and a watch chain looped over his white waistcoat. The little girls held their laughing sides and waggled sticky fingers at him. Muriel wacked their laughing legs, reminding them "That's your Uncle Bertie."

On the floor, the adult sisters passed these old photos between them, recalling their disrespectful behaviour.

"Is this Hugh?" — a burly man with large hands on his knees, a moustache waxed wide across his cheeks.

Neither could put a name to that face.

Had they asked Muriel who he was back then?

Lined up in family photographs were proud young men who stared over the shoulders of serious brides clutching big bouquets over the three months fecund stomach. The men wore adult responsibility on their broad chests and big mouths. Later photos showed a ducal look when, as proud fathers of bald babes wrapped up in baptismal lace, they stood behind a blunt young mother. "The Wife," said Fi. Gillian held the photo of one slender young thing, the baby, fussily robed for baptism, falling off her knees. After her careful appraisal, she announced "This one ..." She put the photo down. "I don't think this is a person easily described as 'a little woman'."

Recalling Muriel and her flyaway temper, Fi concurred. "Family failing?" she asked. "Do you think that's a family failing, the lack of ... fainting femininity?"

Apart from jogging memories, what did they do, these photos? Which institutional library, who among scholars, wanted Dark stories and Hindmarsh yarns? Unedited, nor airbrushed for cosmetic purposes, the photos emphasised the complicitous family. No one shrugged off self-deprecation mixed with self-righteousness. They faced the camera without dissembling doubt, but for the children who, seated at adult feet and round adult elbows, wriggled, their twisty heads flinging away from the camera at the moment the shutter fell.

The photographs were still-lives suggesting the whole story.

Gillian told Fi she believed they witnessed in the old photos the temperate pride of new settlers. "They wanted confirmation of who they were, acclamation for what they'd done."

"It also may be," opined Fi thoughtfully, "that they were worried some people thought they were nobodies."

The light behind the faded curtains flickered, the shadows from the trees stroking the closed windowpane.

One set of fingers lifted the war uncles, those known as Returned Soldiers.

A weariness strained the smiles hovering on their still young faces. It was the look of a generation who dragged feet through lives that were marked by nightmares. In the 1950s, with their children grinning around their legs, they tried, these men, but the indescribable had struck outside the frame and shattered them. First, the Depression of the 1930s. Then the cold mud of Europe and the suppurating swamps of Papuan jungles in the 1940s. For the rest of their lives, they were tired.

One thin haired bloke, knee bent, grasped a black ball. Gillian identified him."That's Uncle Phil, the champion at bowls." Fi looked at the mouth that smiled up one cheek. She said quietly, "A champion with women, too, according to Aunty Daphne. Did you ever hear the gossip? She separated from him after finding him in the laundry with the bit who ironed for her."

Gillian passed her one of Uncle Jack, his gaze transfixed on something out of the camera's range. Another — of Uncle Harry and Aunty Marjory fatly beaming beside a new car. Elliot stood under his mother's elbow. A later one of them showed Marjory holding one of their grandchildren as if the baby was made of porcelain. There was one of the younger Uncle Bertie, anxiety oiling his clean-shaven skin, hand upheld, asking the camera to go away, his ravaged face bent over a walking frame. He seemed to have strands of ginger hair flattened against his skull.

"Lorna's husband," Gillian said as she put the photo down.

Aunty Lorna Scott.

Where there were uncles, there were aunties. But of them, there were few if any photos.

One prized family photograph lying at the bottom of Muriel's battered collection recorded a Christmas event. The aunties were young and lovely in it.

If everything depended on aesthetics alone, if there were virtue in perfection alone, then this family photo was a group composition that existed only as a decorative accent. Displayed in a country museum or an antique shop, the Dark photo — for it was a photo of a Dark family Christmas — was the picture of someone else's relatives, thus antique kitsch. It was a study to turn into framed prints that would match other people's furnishings. It could also be a gauzy image 'to bring the whole world home', a ring of eyes and smiley mouths scanned for the pages of a newspaper to fold and later slide under a dog's dinner bowl.

The Darks, the aggrandised past.

Men gathered on Nanna Dark's verandah and down its steps. The aunties — the Dark women — were 'just married', beautiful and round limbed in floral dresses fitted to the waist, skirts full and wide, the necklines scooped and not collared. The aunties stood close to the elderly couple who were seated in the garden below the verandah. In Poppa Dark's eye there was irony, round Nanna Dark's mouth a smile. Azaleas, perhaps a swish of broom, added an insignia to the foreground.

The family ringed with resonances reaching beyond the quiet looping through and leaning over verandah railings.

Uncle Jack, a kindly one, perhaps effeminate, was the small boned man looking straight and without guile. His lips were slightly open, hesitating between apprehension and a willingness to smile. Smudges round his eyes showed a man resigned to the things that haunted him.

To the far right, Uncle Harry somehow stood to one side. Or by looking away from the shutters, Uncle Harry broke the frame. Whatever he did, his gaze was not towards the lens but to one side of it, unsettling the general impression the Darks gave of unimpeachable stolidity.

Outside the border, excluded from the shuttering eye, a blurty girl delivered a cruel "YUK"! and a well-aimed "NYEAH!" That was Fi.

When her daughters swung in trees, a small smile ameliorated the cross perplexing Muriel's gaze. She loved to hear the lightness of her girls' pleasured sounds. True to say, she wanted princesses. She ordered Jim to make the girls a doll's house, just like the royal one she had seen pictured in a women's magazine. Jim complied. He didn't mind Muriel pining for lovely girls, yearning for compliant curly-haired darlings, but he liked it better when he saw she relished the wild surprise of their daughters' growing up.

Gillian and Fiona were agile. They straddled the broad and accommodating branches of camphor laurel balancing a basket filled with treats. They were laughing girls stuffing themselves sick on the sugary cakes Muriel made for them.

The wind, blowing from the northeast, lifted their hair. Turning their heads to catch a sniff of seasalt, they looked down the farmed slopes to the Pacific Ocean. That vast glittering and restless blue expanse may have been scudding up the beaches of Broken Head between Byron Bay and Lennox Heads for all they knew. For them, it was a beauty that so stung their eyes it made them squint. And the prose they used to describe it was decidedly purple. Gillian once breathily said it as like heaven. *More like heaven, you know, Fi,* she'd said. *We're on top of the world in a sort of a way. Like being in heaven, you know.*

Fi was no angel. She looked into the words, suspicious of what it was her sister was trying to say.

Fi sat up on Muriel's bed with one of the family album's on her knees, Gillian beside her, fingers tracing the image of a fit young groom, sun zapping his face to leave a blank with full lips fading into his bride's tulle headdress. That was Jim, their Dad. Dreaming distances. On the lookout for an horizon. For rain clouds. Was that what he was doing at his wedding when he lost his face to the sun? His bride looked straight at the camera grinning from ear to ear, her eyes dazzling happiness.

Staring at the page, Fi remarked, "We hardly knew him." Her voice thickened, her head bowed over the young barefooted farmer, this time standing straight in front of the camera, the brim of a battered hat skating across his nose. Gillian giggled at the edge of the photo in an anxious attitude — shoulders hunched and hands clasped at about chest high — but she looked at the camera, not under the hat to see her face shining in his shaded eyes. The camera didn't find his eyes, either.

They hardly knew him.

Jim was a faceless wonder.

They sat on Muriel's bed awhile. The album lay open, the pages unturned. Gillian looked past Fi's bowed head to Muriel's bedside table where Jim faced the television set. It was the youthful Jim standing to attention in uniform, his light eyelashes fringing pale eyes, his thick lipped smile not convincing. His angled head was framed by an unadorned silver square. Jim. The young Jim. On finely embroidered linen, the border crocheted fastidiously to resemble lacework. This photo stood on the right side of the dressing-table.

Gillian had an overwhelming urge to reach across Fi and

snatch the album from her. She didn't want to pore over photos, she wanted to sort through clothes and all the other possessions, as ragged and worn as they were. Trying to be patient, she said, "Muriel liked to do this."

Fi's body twitched, her neck jerked, and her voice was muffled with tears when she asked, "Wha'?"

"She liked to lie on the bed in the afternoon, remember? On hot days. To tell us how great dancing was. How handsome men in uniforms looked."

Fi raised her head to look at Gillian with amusement.

"I remember."

She remembered: When they were small, they curled together on top of the eiderdown soft with ducks' down and obediently listened to the story of 'During The War'. Their mother was a Dark who sometimes danced at servicemen's balls, at engagement parties, and dances to celebrate twenty-first birthdays. At one of these occasions, she met the man who was the boy she met years before at picnics on the banks of Emigrant Creek. Jim. He wore an army uniform, and he was from a family known to her, the Hindmarsh family. They lived over the neighbouring hills. "Decent people," Muriel said. She guessed he would be too. Then with an uncharacteristic sparkle, she exclaimed, "And such a good dancer he was." Her little daughters giggled, enchanted by the daring Muriel who married Jim even though she knew good dancers in uniforms made men wickedly attractive.

But when they started to get wise, her daughters laughed at her. They threw back their heads and rolled from side to side in unison, clutching their stomachs and sides, laughing laughing laughing at their mother. At the stupid things she said.

Their laughter struck her dumb. Muriel retreated, expelling them from cosy afternoons thumbing through the photos in her bedroom. She ached to weep. She refused to cook. She sat for hours staring at her fists in her lap, her wordlessness keeping her daughters at bay. She sat on the edge of her neatly made bed, not making a dent in the eiderdown, not making a sound for her girls to laugh at. If their derision numbed her, her silence drilled holes through floorboards. It flattened Fi's ears to the sides of her head and made her heart stand up hard in her chest.

She was the one who smashed the silence.

Smash! Smash!

She played ugly games.

Gillian joined her.

Gillian and Fi pretended they didn't know they had caused their mother so much pain. They wound their arms round each other's necks, stuck their foreheads together and pushed hard, rubbing red marks on their skin as they made noises like trucks grinding up steep hills.

Tears held in check, Muriel screwed her fist.

Jim held the doorknob and stared, his lips moist and pink. He faced his wife's anguish with the round frightened eyes of idiot caution.

Unlanguaged, Jim's shadow hovered.

"Gillian?"

Fi closed her eyes as if in prayer, closed the album with one finger inside to keep her place among the pages of images that jogged memories. Gillian put her hand over the album, her fingers touching Fi's.

"We were a pair of headaches, that's what we were."

Both, with broad smiles, put the album down and let it shut. They headed off to the kitchen for a refreshing pot of tea.

Back then, Fi lined up her dolls across the threshold of Muriel's bedroom and systematically beheaded them. "Off with their heads! Off with their heads! Said the Queen of Hearts to all those tarts."

Gillian bent from the waist, her hands behind her back, and she inspected the row of decapitated dolls. She said to her little sister, "My, my. Fine job, Hindmarsh. Fine job."

"Good work, Hindmarsh!"

A single blunt scene of prattling girls at play one sun-drenched morning, little girls who dropped into a queenly fantasy. They had no time to be princesses. They wanted to be regal and use the guillotine. They wanted to swing a sword. They crooked their imperial fingers and sentenced wicked ones to headless deaths.

"Off with it!"
"Off with this head!"
"Off with this head of hair!"
"One!"
"Two!"
"Three!"
"Heads!"

Dolls' heads rolled across the hallway lino.

Little girls, busily at play, bossily ordered one and other. "Line them up! Line them up, Gilgil! Across Mummy's bedroom door."

"That's right!"
"Good one, Hindmarsh!"

They arranged dolls' heads neatly. They fluffed out dolly hair and opened dolly blue eyes. The bodiless dolls emitted no plaintive wails for Mummy at the bedroom door.

"Pretty! Aren't they?"

"Look, Mummy! Look! Doll heads 'cross your bedroom door!"

Mummy's throat ripped with curdled pain. "Oah! Nao! Naoooo!" It was a bovine bellow drawn up from the bowels.

The sisters took up the headless dolls' bodies.

"Drop the bodies, drop the bodies."
"Down the stairs!"

Headless bodies rolled down the stairs. A rat scurried under the house, its tail looping above the dirt.

"There goes one!"
"Now goes two!"

The rat leaped. A snake hissed and struck.

Where dreamtime is exposed to bake under the sun, snaky coils, opalesque and beautiful, slither to lie in wait for a lucky strike. The reptilian eye holds a hellish chill to hypnotise, perhaps to seduce, perhaps, too, to annihilate hope and good luck under the verandah boards where the rats leap. But never underestimate the rat. It will scuttle from its dubious place on a snaky menu down down down a rabbity burrow.

In the brains of some where dreams spread their rosy glow, a white bunny crashed through a mirror to tumble down a labyrinthine burrow. It bounded downunder, through the mirror disguising a silent life on a farm as some kind of bucolic romance. Bunny burst with violence into the glaring light. Where Ratty leaped and Bunny bounded, Snaky opened wide-hinged jaws and sank fangs into hope. Mummy's dreamy belief that her daughters should be princesses bore fang marks.

Muriel snatched at the headless dolls. She bundled up the bodiless heads. She screamed blue murder and throttled Fiona, her imperially dreadful daughter. Muriel's fist gripped Fi's hair. She wrenched and tugged it into a big floppy hank and dragged the girl, pulling her by her hair into the bathroom. With one painful thrust, she threw Fi against the wall and slammed the door shut and locked it. No matter how loud Fi wailed "MumMY! MumMY! MUM … My! I HATE YOU!" Muriel's face remained stony.

Gillian disappeared, She clutched her favourite dolly. It still had its head. She shuddered and her fingers fluttered over the doll's dress as she recited in a whispery voice a story about the wicked witch who locked Hansel and Gretel in cages. "Dare you! Dare you!" she said, acting Gretel when she tried to rescue Hansel. "You grizzle-faced cranky old witch! You're wicked! Wicked! May the Devil get you!" When she said that, she felt calm. Smoothing the doll's dress, she took on the role of the witch, tucking her chin in as if she had none. "Selfish wicked little girl! Girls-like-you are horrible! Horrible!"

Did it happen that way? Or did it happen the other way round? Did the bruised brain come first, followed by the decapitated dolls? Was the decapitation of dolls Fi's angry protest against having to be a girlie girl? She wanted to be horrible. She thought she wanted to be horrible. Consigning dollies' heads across the threshold of the master bedroom may have been Fi's first poisonous act of defiance.

Violence grabbed her heart and shoved it sideways.

Down under the floorboards where the rabbit leaped with the rat to avoid the snake's quick strike, Fi ached for ways out. She looked for exit signs but none glowed red in the dark. She longed to crash through the daily world to find at the end of a hollow log a dreamy garden filled with talkative roses, mad hatters and grumpy queens.

Not one white rabbit came to her rescue, not even in her dreams. No white bunny hopped up to her bedroom door or answered her prayers to show her the hollow log. The long burrow, the labyrinthine way out, was her mystery tour. Nothing cute and furry came her way to give her directions.

In any case, bunnies were bounced sideways to make way for the diseased curse, rabbits with bloated livers, blurred vision and roughened fur. Myxomatosis took the cuteness out of bunnies. Fi knew rabbits moulted in earthy burrows where red-bellied black snakes coiled round each other in reptilian sleep.

Fi's world was horribly real.

She had a hard-nosed disbelief in fantasies, bunnies and a future walled in with illusions that she always but always tested, and never trusted because they shattered.

Frogs, ringing the guttering, croaked. Down in the valley where the creeks meandered, frogs puffed pale throats and spread webbed paws. A snake slithered under debris white and orange with fungus. A marsupial, something small like a rat, pricked up its snout. It sniffed the air. The snake yawned open its jaws, its fangs long, its lunge deadly. What moved no longer moved. But for the frogs. They croaked.

With a soft fall from leaf to water, the males puffed up glistening bodies and the females oozed eggily into cloudy sperm.

Nanna Dark said it was God's Earth.

And it had been going on for centuries, long habits of mating happening right beside a snake's dinner. Where she grew up, mating like snapping up dinner was perfunctory. Violence was part of God's Earth.

Fi's world was horribly real.

And yet ...

...

(A girl-like-you! will say *Play it again, Sam! Turn up the music and turn down the lights and play it again! Here's lookin' at you, kid!* A beautiful girl will lift a glass. She will press her lipsticked lips to the rim of a long stemmed flute where she will leave a lipstick slick, and Fi will gaze across a dimly lit room at loveliness. At the adorable Laine Macready.)

B<!---->each days happened. There were summer beach days and winter beach days. When they were girls.

A beach to the north, Pottsville, was a place Muriel liked to take them to. The beach open to the ocean, dangerously unprotected from the strong ocean currents. There were no lifesavers at Pottsville as there were at Byron Bay and Ballina, so they went there during the winter to run on fine sand.

If Jim had grisly work to do, Muriel liked to go to this small beach where light crackled from sky to sea to white sand. When he had killing to do — when he had to strangle unwanted kittens and put them in a sack with rocks to lower into a stream, or that fraught day when he had to shoot a favourite and very sick old horse and dispose of its carcass — Muriel packed the girls in the car and they headed north. The roads were narrow and winding. They drove through rainforest growing over steep hills, took a sharp bend in the road to cross a sandy heath, and they came out where sunrays refracted like steel blades off pale rough ground. The thorny leaves of the heath speared the brightness that blinded the girls. They giggled and covered their faces, and they made up stories about the spirits of murdered black children dancing like dervishes across the heath. Until Muriel told them to shut up. "Stop it! Stop it this instant! I can't drive when you make all that NOISE!"

They slumped into cranky corners, but not for long. They resumed play, twining their fingers through each others to make cats cradles, their first giggles subdued. Just as they were beginning to let their giggling get out of hand, the car stopped. Fi then Gillian whacked open the doors and bolted over the low dune to the beach.

Dressed in a striped red playsuit, Fi ran with scudding wavelets, toed the foam and waded in until sea broiled round her knees. If a large wave loomed and sped towards her, threatening to knock her flat, she squealed and ran to safety through water to ankle deep wavelets and up the wet sand to the hard beach where Gillian, matching her sister in her striped blue playsuit, bent over something she had dug out of the sand. Heads together, they sank to squat over driftwood tangled in seaweed.

Sometimes they shared the beach with a group of Southsea Island fishermen hauling nets from their boat. The men, Kanakas whose grandfathers used to work on sugar-cane farms, laughed when, their catch precariously tumbling, the boat tilted, once sliding on its side back out to sea. The crunching sound of wood grinding into sand silenced the girls. The men laughed. Slowly slowly slowly they walked through sea around the capsized boat and, heave ho!, they shouldered together. The boat, put right again, bobbed madly. But the net was tangled. Sprawled on the beach or standing up to struggle with it, the men never stopped laughing and joking.

Apart from those men, no one used the beach, glittering green sea rolling and crashing on a strip of white sand marked at either end by outcrops of black rocks.

Fi happily ran towards the sun-soaked width of a dozy Muriel whose flowered swimming costume was a snug fit. A mishappen straw hat squashed her unruly hair, she sat in the midst of a mound of bright towels, the ceaseless churning and crashing calming the wrath in her.

Fi lay with sun on her face. She shut her eyes tight.

Sole sound, the sea.

She tried to shut in the rhythm of the sea, shut out the sun hot on her face. But she squeezed her eyes so tight pink and gold and blue globules of light reddened under her lids. She held her breath. She tried to lie still, daring her energy to languish under sunshine. The coloured lights sprang purple dots over red, triggering a blackness that stabbed at the back of her eyeballs. She rolled on her stomach, scattering the dots. She grinned at Muriel.

Under her hat, the tired lines criss-crossing Muriel's face softened. She clucked at her lissome daughter, ruffled her hair, smiled, astonished by how much she loved her child.

The daughter stood up, her young body wiry and strong. She stood and flexed her calf muscles. The waves rolled in, currents rushing to the shore, rolling in and across each other to crash with a boom on the hard beach. Fi believed she was a sailor judging the power of the ocean and finding it magnificent. She turned around to ask her mother why the currents crossed before pounding beaches.

Down the beach, the big brown men hauled in the fishing net. It was filled with greenish weeds. They laughed.

The sound of the sea rushed through Muriel with the laughter of men who fell in the sea beside the heaving boat. She clutched her ankles. She no longer looked at Fi, but rocked on her buttocks, her eyes closed, engrossed with her inner life. She was vaguely aware a voice like Fi's circled her head. She smiled slightly.

Spinning on her heel, Fi murdered dreams. She kicked sand, sending the spray straight at her mother's closed-off face. The startled Muriel, whose mind had drifted faraway, perhaps to a dancehall where young men sweated in army uniforms, brushed at sand and squalled "FI!" Her daydream floated away on questions about oceans. Eddies and currents were nothing she understood.

The men stopped their laughter, and looked down the beach at three whites, a mother and her daughters fighting it out. Silently agreeing that mothers and daughters were the same wherever you went, they slowly stood at their places around the boat. All together, they pushed and shoved the wooden vessel up the sand and, once again, they bent back and curved forwards, laughing.

Laughter. Waves breaking on sand, on rocks.
The smells of sea breezes. Grass. Fresh cow pats.
The regular thud of a ball bouncing on hot cement.
None of these invaded photographs.

Over the years, she forgot a lot. Fi forgot the funny scenes. Like this one:

The little girl Fi slid out of sleep, her feet swinging over the mat beside her bed. Across the hallway, Jim snored loudly. Fi listened to him gag and grunt. She waited and waited, then a snort ripped the air. Night flipped up and jumped to a standstill.

Gillian rolled over. She tugged the sheet and blankets up to her neck, and she snuggled further down. Her arm under the covers dipped in at her waist and followed the line of her thigh.

Fi kicked free of her bed and its covers. She stood on the mat. It was hard under her feet. She stepped onto the cold lino, then into the hallway. Her bare feet rolled over the string coils knotting the colours of the long runner.

She slowly pushed open the door of Jim and Muriel's bedroom, her eyes anticipating her fear of waking them.

She wanted to snuggle into the big warm bed. She wanted to curl near the warm smell of her mother.

Jim's snores hit the dressing-table mirror. Fi saw the glass bend. A shadow sprang upwards, its flight swinging high, the mirror emptied and innocent.

At the other end of the house, down where the kitchen was, something dropped. There was a clatter followed by a sharp-clawed scuttle. Fi's ears hissed with fear. The fear sharpened the pain of hearing.

She heard Muriel breathe.

She crept to the side of the bed where Muriel slept.

Fi stood above warm skin softened in sleep. She savoured the delicious perfume of a woman's sleeping body. She put her hand out to touch her mother who lay in the manner of a saint with her hands folded over the peak of her high stomach. Beside her, Jim snored. His body bucked and twitched with a terrible snort, and then stopped dead still.

Muriel ground her teeth.

Fi's eyes bulged. Not blinking, she covered her mouth. She skipped backwards, hunching, fingers twittering. She ran across the hallway, back to her bed, fit to burst with the giggles.

It's this sort of scene that settled so deep in her bones where the marrow yellowed, Fi forgot it.

Some say Death is a depthless dark suffocating life out of Life. Some say Life is Death, a galling waste of time. Others who come back from wandering close to Death talk about a place where bright colours shine, where light shimmers, where landmarks lose distinction. A shadowless place.

Raising her eyebrows and making an ugly loop of her mouth, Gillian said that she dreamed or experienced — she wasn't sure how precisely to describe the sensation — Muriel slide through a velvet dark to stand, wreathed in smiles, on a sandy shore. She did not confide in Fi that, when the odourless shape of her mother wobbled through her head like a church statue sallying forth on its relentless journey to redemption, her heart murmured arythmically. She gasped and quickly dissembled serenity to conceal her pain. The cold flaw in the air fingered her veins. She stumbled and lisped over the words when she said that she believed that in Death as in Life Muriel should discover the calm oasis of gardens.

"I'm sure you're right," Fi said, with a hint of compromise in her voice nudging the truth that she believed Gillian was wrong because she knew that Death was final. Finito. That's it. Ignoring that behind and above her a familiar kitcheny presence pulled her cardigan across her chest and hissed while the night insects whirred, and the wind groaned through the trees.

Laine, alive with love, filled her brain with Fi running around creek banks. When she stared blind at a dull article about the tea-drinking habits of early Australian settlers, she looked straight into a boy's muddy palm cupping a small green frog into Fi's palm. Fi's pink palm was streaked with the colour of dung. Laine wanted to have loved her back, the girl smelling of creek water and muddy weeds.

A girl in green plaid shorts under a plain white top ran across the Old Byron Bay Road, cut across paddocks, lifting the barbed wire strung between fences to make a triangle she could step through as she went. She ran away from the totalitarianism of Muriel's sewing room where she was forced to stand still so that pins could be stuck in side seams to fit a new dress to her skinny body. Fi was on her way to find Barry Priddle who she guessed might be playing in one of the streams flowing into Emigrant Creek. She knew his favourite reedy corner. Where the rocks under water were smooth and brown. Where the reeds at the far bank were thick and lime-green. Where the frogs croaked and once, she believed, she heard from under the pendulous branches of the weeping willow the nasal whine of an old dirge sung to the drone of a didgeridoo.

Priddle was there. The sun baked his neck red. He picked at something in his hands, and said nothing. She talked all the time about everything, Fi babbling with the water that she splashed. She didn't dare walk through the water to the bank where the lime-green weeds grew. Jim had told her blue-bellied black snakes were the slow and sleepy inhabitants of thick weedy patches around the creeks. "Y'keep away, Fi. Their fangs're short, their poison deadly."

Priddle knew that, but he listened to her telling him what her Dad said. She described to him how a snake got among the chooks one night and caused havoc. How her Dad went out with a .22 and shot the snake. "Six foot," she said, her eyes huge. "Dad held it up and it was as long as him ... As he is tall."

Priddle twitched. Although she seemed to think she should correct how she spoke, he liked her. She was a lithe figure dancing between sunshine and shadow as she chattered. She went on and on, non-stop. "Disgusting!" she said, her mouth pulled into a rejecting pout. "Snakes actually swallow whole chooks. Can you imagine!" Priddle looked at her, suspicious of and amazed by her prattle. "A long skinny snake bulging at the middle because a whole chook's in there?"

She was Good At School. He was Slow At School.

But when he opened his hand to show her a curved thing, she was respectful. He said that it was a seedpod, and she listened to him. It was long, brittle and gingery brown. "Blackboy seeds." He delivered speech in telegraphic phrases.

She moved to touch it.

They heard swishing. The grass beside the willow tree shook to reveal Fi's cousin, Elliot Dark. Priddle moved away from her quickly, careful not to be caught looking as if he was sweet on a girl. Any girl. Fi Hindmarsh, brainy swot and strangely boyish, was the worst to be Sweet On.

Fi didn't stay. She looked around for a distraction that might take her away from her cousin who made her feel uneasy, and then she took off, up the hill and through the paddocks she knew well. She went back home.

That was Fi's territory, the hills, the creeks in the valleys and the boys who held dirty things in their bare hands. Gillian's was beside her mother, handing her things when she baked cakes and biscuits. She hemmed skirts and sewed buttons on the playsuits and dresses Muriel made. When Aunty Elsie called on them, she praised Gillian as 'Mother's Little Helper'. So too did Lorna and Daphne. Their eyes skated critically over the other daughter who sauntered through the back door of the small farmhouse, shorts filthy and legs plastered with the muddy traces of creek weeds. She had a bold gaze, that Fi.

They came for morning tea or lunch, less often for afternoon tea. All of them lived on dairy farms. If they didn't help the men with the milking, they liked to be home for the afternoon, a busy time of day when they fed chooks and picked fresh green beans for tea, the evening meal of meat and three vegetables followed by pudding. And cups of tea.

Fi loved them. She loved it when they called. She liked their powdery smells, their fastidious attention to hats, the floral dresses that they made for themselves, and their softly permed hair. She slid beside them, squirming at the table which Muriel set up in the garden. Daphne leaned forwards. "Have you washed your hands, Fi?" Fi blushed and rushed passed Gillian who carried plates of cakes to the table near the mayflower bush. Lorna nodded wisely. She said Fi was a very bright girl, and Daphne agreed. Muriel, dismayed by Fi running from the table, held her plates on which she had arranged dainty foods aloft. "She's a trial," she said. "A mystery to me." Made secure by her criticism of her daughter, she self-righteously proceeded to set down on her embroidered and starched linen cloth her cakes and pastries and white triangular sandwiches.

"I'll get the tea," she said, and went back inside with a businesslike flurry.

Over tea and cake and sandwiches, they talked about the latest in puffed sleeves and the resurgence of gingham as a fashion, about flowers and who should decorate the church for Sunday service. The girls witnessed the same discussion about Lydia every time they met at the table.

"Not the same since the accident."
"Believes she has a sister called Rose."
"She does go off. Goes quite off."
"One look at those children tells it all."
"Poor Jack."

Then, always, Muriel clenched her fist and she said, "That bluddy Lydia!"

The aunties lifted lacy hankies to their lips and shuffled uncomfortably in their seats. None of them understood Muriel's fight with Jack about the cake recipe.

Fi told Laine that in many ways her aunts were nicer than their big sister, their mother.

Laine, sliding under bed covers, said that she didn't have a beautiful memory of women sitting around a table set up in a garden, nibbling cakes and sandwiches and sipping tea. "I remember my Mum racing through the front door. 'Meeting!' she'd yell over her shoulder. 'Your favourite quiche … It's in the oven … Ready to eat in a tick,' forgetting that what was favourite when you were two had a habit of not being your favourite when you were sixteen. Lots of quiches went straight in the bin, nowhere near me and my mouth."

Laine's mother loved life after the microwave became generally affordable.

When they will be together again soaking up each other's warmth, Laine will listen carefully to Fi's description of how the aunts called the day after Muriel's funeral. She will hear how the women sat around the table Gillian and Fi carried into the garden so that a gentle memory of sitting under the cassia could be shared. The delighted aunts wagged their fingers at Fi, reminding her she had been a difficult girl. Such a girl. Always smelling of chaff from climbing in the barn.

Lorna covered her lips with her fluttery fingers. She smiled at Fi, the recalcitrant girl who, Elsie chipped in, "Worried us. We thought you were going to become a bluestocking."

How they giggled!

Passing around a plate of sandwiches leftover from the wake, Fi nodded, her eyes bright with irony. They would ask about the men in her life. She took up a soggy sandwich, frowned at it as she inspected the mush, and put it down with finality. She informed them that she had a girlfriend. "I am in love with Laine Macready. She teaches Cultural Studies. At university."

The aunts, as one, lifted cups of tea and beamed through steam. Daphne said, "How lovely, Fi." Lorna opined, "Oh, one day, Mr Right will come along." Elsie smiled with a little ducking of her head, "You'll see."

Nothing about them seemed to change, not from the days they visited Muriel for tea.

Some things changed a long time ago — during the fifties. There were the clan gatherings at Christmas. Those stopped happening during the fifties. Fi told Laine a long story about the Christmas that might have been the very last gathering of grandchildren, aunties and uncles. "At Nanna and Poppa Dark's place. The Hindmarsh Gran'ma died when I was two," she said. It seemed that the Hindmarsh Gran'pop lived a lonely crank's life in a caravan park. "Gone to pieces. That's what was said. Gone to pieces."

Then Jim. When the price fell out of butter and his pineapples failed.

"Mum said the Hindmarshes had no stomach for any sort of change."

The depth of her lover's sadness when she talked about her father moved Laine to love her more deeply. "After fighting in New Guinea during the War, he had nothing left inside himself to deal with change." That began to happen during the sixties when, each day, another family would turn up at school smelling of pain. The soles of shoes fell away from uppers, the youngest children wore castoff school uniforms and sandwiches were thinly filled. Greyness settled over the classrooms. The teachers stood with discomfort in front of wistful little faces troubled by events they barely understood.

Fi smelt it, that smell of pain, on Jim. Frightened for herself, she steadied her brains, steeled her effort and studied hard. She would get out of this place that promised everything and then caved in. She would accommodate herself to a new way of being. As is often the case when affection is sacrificed to ambition, she blamed herself for not cherishing her Dad's bland good nature.

When she travelled around the world, she dreamed of the farmhouse shielded from sunburn by arboreal shadows, and of the plump Jersey cows chewing grass at the barbed wire fences squaring off paddocks, the salt on the air and the glittering blue of sky vast above the far distant restless membrane of sea. The subtle shift of seasons brightened and bleached the grasses that grew in swathes around the farmhouse. By contrast, the skies blasted greys, blues and blacks — inky black for nightstorms, greenish black for hail, charcoal for cyclones — at the windows. Nothing subtle about the storms, the rolling thunder as if accompanying the rhythmic march of an invading army, the lightning crackling and the walls of rain that raced in from the sea to battle with trees, houses, barns.

One night of howling wind and roaring rain, Jim, in his Dryzabone and wearing no boots ran from the house to the barn. He backed out the tractor. A Jersey cow, Rosie, was in labour in the back paddock, the poor thing distressed, and he had to get to her before she beat herself against the barbed wire and destroyed the calf that hurt her. He needed to get to her before the wind and the rain and her own ache made her mad with confusion. Jim bounced in the tractor, riding on his fear that he might fail to deliver the calf safely, afraid too that he might fail Rosie. His need to protect the pretty Jersey from her pain and the wild weather brought the essence of him near to demonic.

God and the wind roared.

Warm and dry in the kitcen, Muriel insisted that storms were "God's way, girls, of telling us we aren't measuring up." She smiled, despite herself.

Although the air was clammy and brittle with fear, Fi looked for a quiet corner to nurse her fear for Jim. She turned the pages of a book, interrupting her reading often to glance at the back door through which Jim might burst, to peer through the window at the black sky.

Jim found Rosie as he expected to see her, bellowing near the barbed wire fence. Her distress increased when the thunder rolled. He jumped off the tractor. He had to work out a way to get her up on the trailer, secure her and drive her slowly back over the hills to the barn. He began to work, teasing out ropes, coaxing the cow, whispering soothing noises and words into her wet ear. Her wide eyes rolled back. His voice calmed her. But the sky crackled, the storm's ferocity inexplicable.

Jim, too, was at the edge of fright.

Standing in front of himself in that moment when the lightning struck its jagged light through the sky, Jim shivered with fear and aloneness. For crazed seconds, perhaps minutes, he stared aghast at a fire-ball crackling across the sky towards him. Fear watered his guts as it had done in the mud of New Guinea. Tears choked the back of his throat, and he stood, comatose, so that he might fall on the soaked grass.

There was an invading memory of a bayonet. He was in a line-up, he faced a firing squad. He should have been executed by exhausted Japanese army boys. With twenty others, he should have been hit by a bullet and left to rot in the jungle's slime.

How long had he been there — in New Guinea's mud? In his back paddock?

Rosie's bellows brought him back to the storm that raged in from the sea with God at its head. Water washed over his ears and eyes. He lowered his head to put aside the memory of stench and slime, of that day when he crawled on his belly for many hours until he found roots that made a safe cage. His hands gripped his aching leg. He had been hit. Blood coagulated with mud in a hole under his kneecap, and it was beginning to fester. The rest was a blur of hands that steadied him and poured on water. He passed out when thin black fingers picked and cleaned the wound. As he secured Rosie, his deft hands working the ropes on the trailer, he recalled the shining black face of his nurse looking down at him. And the warmth of relief flowing through his veins.

Some twenty years later, Jim's fear ached under his skin.

Slowly, he edged over the paddocks with Rosie to the safety of the pen at the side of the dairy. Head down, he turned towards the warmth of Muriel's kitchen. He wished his hands would stop shaking, that the cold of Death would get out of his bones.

On the strength of the wind's howl, he wrenched open the back door. Its wet hinges screeched, and he blew in, the storm's force behind him. He stood, his face stricken, his eyes stark, as if he had seen the finger of God point at him, the feckless farmer and ex-soldier. In his kitchen, he dragged off his Dryzabone. Admonishing him for being away a long time — "... out there. In that downpour, that torrential storm ..." — Muriel put the jug on to make tea.

He sat in his chair at the kitchen table and, taking the towel Fi offered, rubbed his head roughly. The girls hung around his elbows, demanding to know what happened out there in the shrieking air. What happened to Rosie? What did he do? But, with the towel between his hands, he stared as if transfixed by those moments in his life he shared with no one.

With an effort, he pulled himself into the wakeful day. He glanced at his relentless daughters. "Rosie," he muttered eventually to satisfy them. "Well, she's looks alright. The calf's safe." He gave his head a vigorous rub. From under the towel, he said with the bluntness of a practical farmer, "It's a bull calf."

But nothing would leave him. Not the delicate peace of birthing, not the violence of the storm. And the terror of New Guinea lived in him, a shadow hovering beside his heart, distinct enough to be his enemy.

Jim squeezed the handle of his teacup between his thumb and forefinger. Hesitantly, he lifted it, wanting to savour the hot brew, but his hand shook so much more tea slopped in the saucer than wet his lips.

Outside, the prescient Wiyabul muttered among shadowy trees that looked across the treeless paddocks. The earth no longer soaked up rain, no longer oozed to welcome new growth. The rain ran off the naked pastures and filled the wetlands where birds once called out and squabbled. Flooding waters killed fish and drove the platypus into hiding. The old spirit wished to magic the tree ferns to grow again, the bangalow palms sing through the valleys with the tallow and cedar and the lianna vines.

Pointing his spear at the sleeping Fi to draw her warm blood, she woke in shock and called out, "Dad!"

Pineapples, the tractor, ropes and chains. And the dog Jake.

Jim backed the tractor out of the barn. Attached was the trailer covered with a tangle of ropes and chains. Jake slathered in its midst.

Jim sat with his knees wide apart, both hands on the steering wheel. He drove hard, constantly looking over his shoulder to make sure his driving wasn't going to toss the trailer over. Sometimes with only one hand on the steering wheel, he half stood to get a better look at the ground ahead of the tractor and the security of the trailer behind him. Jake's spittle streamed, a silvery plume tracing the bumpy ride.

Fi turned in her dream to run after the tractor. But it bounced out of her reach. It bounced across the hillside to the paddock surrounded by tall hissing pine trees. And the tractor bounced, Jim's hat bounced, and Jake slathered, his spittle streaming into remembered days, the clarity of the imagined scene bouncing with Fi's yearning for her father to look at her with unambiguous love, ropes and chains and the grinding engine of the tractor her background music. Then all of it would fade. She would find herself lying on a bed in the hotel room of a forgotten city, a sheaf of documents flat across her face, the sensation of the tractor and the trailer tangled all over with ropes and chains, Jake in the middle of it slathering excessively, roaring through her.

The tractor, ropes and chains. The dog Jake. Heading off to the paddock where Jim cultivated pineapples.

So there it was, the rows of pineapples growing on the side of a hill. The pines maintained a dappled shade all day, the sprinkler system kept up a steady flow of water, and the corrugated iron shed, shimmering in the sun outside the cooling branches and humming trunks of the pines, balanced on the edge of a deep red ditch. Fi walked and ran there to escape Muriel's advice on how to be a girl men would like to marry, Muriel's outbursts rejecting the sullen girl-like-you who wanted nothing of Muriel's dressmaking pins and sewing needles, hair curlers and latest-in-shampoos to make a girl's hair her crowning glory. "A girl-like-you must have shining hair, her crowning glory," Muriel simpered, smiling at her hands as she prepared to wash and curl Fi's hair. Escaping these instructions, these oft recited words of wisdom, Fi kicked up the red dirt at her Dad's bare heels. Jake sniffed her, nuzzled her crotch, circled away from her and came back to press his wet nose into the palm of her hand. She ran her hands over his back and belly and rolled in the dirt, laughing with the slathering dog that played with her, panting doggy enthusiasm.

But one hot day when her Dad was unusually preoccupied, she sensed his presence rather than saw him at the rim of her line of vision, breathing hard from lifting and sorting and trimming and packing pineapples in boxes. There were his baggy grey shorts and khaki shirt wet from sweat. His battered hat. His bare feet cracked and ingrained with black dirt. The smooth dent under his kneecap where skin stretched and shone. His slight limp. And the dog slathered too much.

Hot and sticky, she rolled up from the red dirt. She rubbed the heel of her hand against her cheek, utterly disconsolate, and then she started at pouting, kicking at the dirt, whingeing for a drink and something to eat, striking at the nothing in front of her. Something boiled inside her. Something tumescent hardened. And soared. A crescendo of swelling rage burst, demanding and shouting and crying until she caught a sob in her throat, whimpered and turned to walk home. Then she came back, running at the shed, striking at her Dad, screaming that she hated him. She hated Muriel, hated the stupid farm and the pineapples, Muriel's idea of nice dresses, her obsession with the latest in hair, boring school, cranky teachers — and she bellowed through her tears that she was going to go away as soon as she could and never but never come back.

Jim held her wrists, held her away so she couldn't hit him. He stared at the screaming termagant who was the daughter he gripped. She kicked at his shins. Her screaming and yelling made her ears ache. Her throat hurt, her voice grated. When he guessed she was sick of herself, when she seemed to have spent her anger, he loosened his grip. She stopped her noise, hysterically alarmed that she should lose his attention. He looked at her and frowned. Through her shrill sobbing, she watched doubt form and flicker across his face. His lips softened. She hoped for ... His arm to reach around her, hug her? Is that what she hoped for?

He turned around and went back inside his shed.

At last, she walked home, the lump in her chest aching, seeping its poison through her veins where it mixed with her blood.

Gillian sat on the verandah, her hair neatly rolled in rows of curlers that sat up like pineapples in cultivated paddocks. Slumping beside her, stinking of dirt sodden with sweat, Fi breathed in her sister's freshly shampooed smell. She wiped her nose with the back of her hand, and sniffed hard. Muriel lumbered through the door with a tray of cup cakes and cordial, her mouth about to say something she didn't find the words for.

The three sat in the sun.

Nobody said anything.

Standing in the cooled evening kitchen, tea purling from the pot into mugs, remembering "The last time with Dad, Gillian, he stood between us, shrunken, old ... And he put his arms up around our shoulders. *My girls*, he said. He actually said *My girls*. So proud of us." Gillian blinked and the toaster popped. Memories gained clarity over yesterday's sandwiches and vol-au-vents with the pouring of tea, the pot and mugs instead of cups and saucers.

"Mum said the second pour was best."

"Never said a word, Dad. Just sat."

"Dad got the second pour."

"Sat silent, looked ... faded."

"He liked that fine bone china cup with the pale lemon edge."

"Talked to his dog. Jake. The blue cattle dog, Jake."

"There was some grey with the lemon."

"Dad'd grunt, Jake'd pant, 'n' the job got done."

"Flowers. Lemon flowers, grey leaves."

"Mum'd put hot breakfasts in front of him."

"It's handle curled nicely."

"Baked beans on toast. Eggs. Sausages."

"The fine curl got lost between his big rough fingers."

"Not a word said, he just ate it."

"Work roughened, Dad was. Gnarled."

"Jake waiting at the front gate, chasing his tail."

"Was too much, the market garden, plus doing the dairy."

"Never a doggy mate, was Jake. Jake wasn't a pet."

"Trying to make it all ... trying ... Trying not to fail."

"Mum said he was a work dog."

"Dad felt guilty, I think. He couldn't fail the farm Gran'pop'd wrenched from the scrub."

"Gillian?"

"Fi?"

"When I was very little, he used to hoist me up onto his shoulders and we'd walk around the garden and up to the barn, me shrieking, looking at the world from that great height, loving every minute of it."

"What?"

"And I had a book about Molly and the circus. After all the excitement of the merry-go-rounds, the clowns and the fairy floss, Molly's Dad carried her home in his arms."

"Yes, I remember that book."

"I believed ... No, I *knew* I was Molly and that story was about Dad and me."

"He was never like that with me."

"No?"

"No. He was ... Fi. Dad was far too undemonstrative."

"Sure. But ..."

She loved him dearly.

Her hand moved vaguely. Somehow defeated. That's how she felt when she sanely acknowledged that it was Muriel who kept things right. Who saw to the smooth running of chooks, garden and accounts. Who ensured the education of girls. She was the manager. Muriel.

"It was in the seventies, wasn't it, when Mum finally replaced the cups and saucers with mugs."

The whole kitchen seemed to perk up, creating the shape of a wide mouth smiling.

The night pressed against the windowpane. The black vacancy of sea, far down the hills and across the valleys and coastal flats, stretched as if to infinity. The prompted laughter of a teevee comedy rolled at the edges of guilt and grief and the division of property. The sisters sat in the kitchen that had been Muriel's domain. "At this table," said Fi, wrinkling her nose at the bready mess she was dealing with "the sponge batter and the fudge mix and the ..."

"... lemon meringue, anzac biscuits ..."

"Got beat. In the big striped bowl."

"And," said Gillian, "it's where Dad and Mum read the newspapers."

"She did too!"

"And listened to the radio."

"Wireless, wasn't it. When did we stop saying wireless for radio?"

They talked about other days when Jim sold some of the dairy farm to buy some acreages for sugar. How it worked well for a while, but "His health!" "Yeah, sure, you wonder what they were thinking. Having him work so hard." Those days. When adult arms strayed across the table towards the teapot. The gauzy silence, with the girls looking in from the door. At Jim's back. At their mother's profile. Those days. When nothing stirred but the brown warmth of the ABC broadcaster presenting *The Country Hour*.

The room, filled with kitchen cosiness, closed an eggy membrane around Jim and Muriel.

And as Muriel and Jim had done before them, Gillian and Fi talked about what they would do. Should Gillian stay on and live in the house? How much of the farm should be sold? Did she want to keep working at the university as a much exploited research assistant whose PhD had been put on hold, permanently, it seemed. Should they set up a trust? For Leigh? What could they do for him? After all, he went to school in Lismore, which was far from Newrybar, too far, they believed, for him to travel every day of the week. If Gillian moved back into the farmhouse, should he go to the small school perched at the edge of the village of Newrybar where he would have to make new friends? The school they went to when Mr Piggons was the headmaster?

He must have walked in at the moment they started to talk about him. For suddenly, a young boy's voice rang clear. He said that he would like to go to school at Newrybar. It looked *cool*. And, anyway, he'd found out he could make some money on the farm by collecting blackbeans. "For bonsai-ing. A man in Byron Bay buys the beans and, like, sells'em, bonsaied blackbean trees, to Japan and Holland."

Stunned, Fi stared after him as he closed the door behind him. Gillian shrugged. "Typical. He's always got ideas about making money. Makes me feel as if I'm failing him. I'm not what he wants, a great provider."

Good. Fi's steady brain calculated. No need to waste money on sending the boy to a private school in the hope that an expensive education might save him from himself.

"Patrick?"

"Always remembers him. Birthdays, Christmas. But no paid holidays. He's ... He's married, y'know."

Fi sank her teeth into crisp toast and stale slices of tomato.

"Lots of kids. He's Muslim now."

She said this with a grin.

"Lives in Penang."

Fi swung her legs up and propped them on the empty chair on the other side of the table.

"Got a nice little Malay wife." Said with a dry rasping edge.

Fi waved her arms above her head to make pronouncements about the way they should dispose of parts of the farm and invest, establish trusts and perhaps buy some land "... or a house to rent. Along Ocean Shores way. Reckon that should pay off really well eventually." She believed her concerns were so that Gillian should be financially secure for Leigh's sake. But to her own ears her voice belled despite its muffled ring — as if it came from the other side of the fog that swirls between the dream world and the one she sat in.

She held her hand against her forehead, the other rested around the mug of tea. Under one foot where the lino shone, the colours faded — under the sheen answering the deep pain buried inside her. Gillian, sitting opposite her and sighing often, talked about the oppressive work load she endured at the university, how each failure to deliver, each repeated bad cold, every haemorrhaging period, was rewarded with less and less tolerance of her. No one acknowledged she had physically too much to do and mentally too many responsibilities to shoulder. The Union, it seemed, was overwhelmed by similar complaints but ...

But what? Fi suddenly found herself looking at Gillian whose eyes shone bright from a terrible withering of spirit. 'The doctor diagnosed chronic fatigue syndrome," she said. "I think RUBBISH!, although it's nice to put a name to an ailment."

"You think as women, we've gained and lost? Is that what you ...?"

Gillian's hands fluttered in front of her head. "No, I don't think we women've gained and lost so much as ... I think we're from a class of people who always cop it in the neck. We worry too much. We worry about getting everything exactly right. About taking all the responsibility and not delegating. We haven't learned the trick to do the head-kicking. So, no, our or MY problem goes beyond gender politics."

Fi put both feet on the floor. She believed that somewhere under her sister's dejection as a member of the paid labourforce was the shrill disharmony of women's history that sapped the confidence and gnawed strength.

Gillian muttered bitterly, "Maybe you've succeeded where I haven't."

Fi winced, "Speak for y'self!" and believed she sounded defensive when she said, "You're too full of self-doubt, and I'm not. Anyway, you've got to keep your head. Are you safe to leave alone out here, Gilgil?"

Without lifting her head, Gillian backed off from self-pity, snapping, "Don't be stupid. I'm not mad, I'm not an invalid." Then she raised her head to settle the issue once and for all time. "We've said nothing, alright? Nothing. I am safe as houses and as strong too. Just ... Get on with what you're good at." Tiredly, and with a tone of appeasement underwriting hope, she leaned towards the sinewy and competent Fi. "I would be grateful if you organised the money. Truly, Fi. Truly."

All night, Fi lay with her arms under her head, hearing Gillian padding back and forth from the bathroom and the kitchen. She seemed to be making tea, herbal concoctions to help her sleep. Fi tossed and turned, wishing she could wander into her sister's bedroom to wind consoling arms around her, bury her head in her neck, caress her gently, ever so tenderly. And eventually she fell into her own deep sleep, fell indeed into a vivid memory that had washed up and through her sleep as a dream — a dream in which Gillian's silent head bowed at a long table, the ribbons in her hair pink and shining.

From the forgotten past — a Christmas celebrated at the Dark household.

The little girl Fi watched fussing women and red faced men who were her aunties and uncles, young adults who had a way of not looking at small children. They smelt anxious, their lips quivered, their eyes slid out of sight. If she succeeded slipping round the hallways and verandahs and out from under sofas, running fast and swinging up and over fences, they missed seeing her. Either they were blinded by her speed, or they ignored her.

She liked them to ignore her.

When she was six, and Fi thought she was six at that Christmas, she liked to be ignored.

Sitting on the bed lined up under the big window in the sleepout at their Nanna Dark's house, the six year old Fi and her cousin Jacqui watched the moon, a gold ball suspended in a Chinese blue sky. Together, they cried out wishes for Santa Claus to hear. They were sure he heard them. They screwed their eyes up hard, buried their knuckles into the sockets, and wished with pain that he was real.

Jacqui wanted a doll in a poke bonnet, a blue striped dress and a white apron, apple jelly, peppermint sticks and a gingerbread man. Fi opened her eyes to look at her pasty-faced cousin, stupid enough to want the things painted in picture books. Fi shouted over the top of Jacqui's wishing. She shouted "I want a ... a ... a FOOTBALL."

Fi was no dopey girl.

She levelled a knuckle-duster at Jacqui's upper arm. Jacqui gasped, and Fi got a shock when she didn't recoil but retaliated with a mighty whack across Fi's head.

Cheerily, Nanna chimed, "Time for bed! Santa will see you wide awake and he'll forget your wishes."

Abandoning harassment, Fi argued that Santa had flown overhead, straight past the moon, and he had, definitely, seen them. He was a fat man with a red nose. Nanna, pulling the sheet up like a tent, instructed "Girls! Get To Bed."

Fi privately hoped Santa hadn't heard her wish for a football. She wanted him to remember the letter she dropped in the red mailbox in AGR's, the department store in Lismore. It stood near the lift, and it wore a note asking children to drop in their wishes. She wrote that Santa should bring her a book about frogs, a teddy bear and a striped beachball. She hoped he read her letter. She hoped it was too late for him to hear her wish for a football.

Christmas beetles dropped on their beds and smashed into the light fittings. Jacqui brushed them off her pillow. She pulled out a book and sat up in Nanna Dark's sweet-smelling linen to read.

Fi clutched a round matchbox, an old one Poppa Dark had given her. She liked the way the lid slid over the base. She curled under the sheet, wriggled, then sat up to catch a beetle in her fist. She poked it into the matchbox, shoved the lid down and pushed it under her pillow. Fi, in possession of a beetle held captive in her matchbox, liked its scratching noises close to her ear.

From one of the bedrooms leading off the sleepout, the girls heard Kel grinding his teeth, fighting the dreams flooding his sleep.

In the morning, Fi and Jacqui ran to the tree where a teddy bear lay beside a large red and yellow striped beachball. Fi squealed. Jacqui pushed Fi sideways and Fi pulled at Jacqui's nightdress but, catching a sob in her throat and forgetting to cry, Jacqui tore at the paper wrapping the box Santa had left her. With eyes wide, she lifted up her wish — a doll decked out in a blue dress and a white and blue striped apron, a poke bonnet pert on her dolly head. Silently, Jacqui pressed it against her chest.

Poppa walked past the tree to the kitchen for his early morning cup of tea and bread and butter he had before rounding up the cows for milking.

The girls cuddled their Christmas gifts and, putting their arms round each others necks, they followed Poppa into the kitchen. They squirmed and watched as he cut thick slices of white bread which he layered with thicker wedges of butter drizzled all over with honey. Jacqui giggled at how it flowed over his gnarled fingers. He let Fi slick the tip of her tongue over his finger. She got the honey. And she got the roughness of his finger. It felt strange on her tongue. She screwed up her nose. "Nyerk!"

Kel sat beside them on his new bicycle. He watched in silence.

As Fi cupped her hand over her mouth and giggled, Jacqui slicked out the tip of her tongue to catch honey oozing over Poppa's rough finger. She drew back, giggling with Fi, and together they screwed up their noses and jumped off their chairs and ran, squealing and giggling into the bathroom for their morning wash.

Following them, Kel made no sound at all. The girls were vaguely aware that he sat on his new red bike watching them play with the Pears soap that melted in its own jelly cupped in a shell on the edge of the bathtub.

Poppa went to the dairy. Kel took off after him, his blue-black hair curling around his thick white skin.

At breakfast, Nanna breathed hot steam over the rim of her teacup, one arthritic finger triangled above the handle. She sipped tea to the bottom of her cup, swirled it gently and, tilting it, showed the girls the tell-tale signs of the future spreading up its side. She took the girls' cups. She read them one by one.

"You, Fiona." She sat back in her chair and turned the cup round three times, repeating, "You, Fiona. You will travel far ... and ..." She held the cup away from her to examine it with her long-sight, not looking at Fi when she said, "You will live an independent life." Nanna Dark had polite ways of saying, "You are doomed to be a spinster."

Her face changed when she peered into Jacqui's cup. The lines round her mouth sadly drew downward, and she said to Jacqui, "You will have ... A Nice Life."

But it was Christmas Day, and the little girls were heedless.

They walked their clammy fingers up her cheeks, she so still it was as if she was adrift in prayer. When she finally roused herself, she sighed and smiled at them. Then the girls ran into the sunshine to meet Gillian who had not stayed the night at Nanna Dark's. She arrived in the car with Jim and Muriel, and that's when Nanna set to scurrying. She worried about stoking the wood to make sure the heat of the fuel stove was full, it had to be, to roast the birds. And the leg of pork. And the vegetables — the potatoes, pumpkin, onions, and sweet potato. She seemed to run above the sink when she washed and pared vegetables, her four daughters, Muriel, Daphne, Elsie, Lorna, beside her. They ran, opening and shutting doors, drawers, doors, searching for cutlery, crockery, glassware. For the mustard spoon which was not with the mustard pot. For salt cellars and pepper pots. For a special knife Poppa Dark used to carve the meats. For the set of vegetable dishes, the cream ones ringed with purple peonies or pansies. God alone knows what the flowers were supposed to do, but the dishes were ideal for beans. Opening and shutting the fridge door for milk and cream and butter. Opening and shutting the pantry door for pastry shells and home-made ginger beer. Nanna Dark marshalled her daughters to turn on Christmas Dinner.

Uncle Harry and his wife, Aunty Marjory, came late, and Aunty Lydia, Jacqui's mother, wasn't there.

As the morning wore on, Jacqui withdrew into an uncooperative grumpiness, her doll clutched tight. Fi tried her best, throwing her red and yellow striped beachball for Jacqui to play catchies.

Anxious and grey, Jacqui faded under the daisy bushes near the side gate. A thought to play dolls and teddies under the bushes wafted through Fi's brain, but it vaporised rapidly.

Kel cycled in ever diminishing circles close to the side gate.

The other kids, Elliot, Neil, Julie — was Sandra the baby? — all in all nine children aged variously from babe-in-arms to ten years of age, sped through the house, the aunties chastising them for getting in the way of hot baking trays and under hot gravies, the uncles asking "Wa'cheget from Santa, eh?" The backs of barefeet kicked up, answering a call to play hidies in the garden. And the uncles were not persistent with questions.

When the smell of sizzling chookie mingled with the resin from the Christmas tree, there was a call, a bell ringing, a message singing through the peach trees. The kids slid down trees and whipped into the house. The adults, moving slowly, swayed into the living room. Fi and Gillian dived through slow legs and leaped onto cushions. Julie poked out her tongue and sat alone in a perverse sulk. Aunty Elsie snapped sharply "Girls should be better mannered. Sit nicely. Legs together."

The girls, eyes huge, mouths pouted, sat still for a second then wriggled, waiting for Poppa to read out the names of the gift receiver and the gift giver, officially distributing gifts. The smelly, knee scabbed scrum of boys squirmed and picked at the thick skin round their grubby toes. All but Kel. He sat perfectly still, large eyes trained on the golden angel spreading her wings on the top of the tree. Then Fi, disturbing everybody, sprang to her feet and leaped out of the room. Paper crinkled, and adults frowned, their thin lips condemning her sudden dash. More so when she burst back in with Jacqui. She pushed feet aside to make room for her cousin. She made Jacqui giggle with her, shoulders hunched, until Poppa glared at them. He lifted up a parcel and called out a name. Someone stood up and reached over children's heads to lay claim to a gift.

And so it went, with the smoggy eyes of aunties and uncles judging choices, condemning extravagances, cooing over small gifts designated 'just thoughts'. Handkerchiefs, socks, ties, petticoats, panties, towels, cakes of soap and eau de cologne massed at feet and in laps.

Nanna gave Jacqui, Gillian and Fi watercolour paint box sets. The boys all received activities-books.

Then Nanna Dark marshalled the women again and the aunties chorused, "You kids!"

"Collect all the paper."

"And Christmas string!"

"For next year!"

"No use wasting."

Muriel and Elsie set up tables in the garden for the children. Lorna and Daphne bickered about an oval dish, ideal for slices of ham. Uncle Harry and Lorna's husband, Bertie Scott, lifted long stools and swung them through the doorways out to the lawn, their throats burbling with noises that may have been speech. The children, they had been instructed, were to sit under the shade of the pine tree by the side gate.

After that was done, Harry and Bertie rocked on the kitchen verandah and drank a glass of beer with Poppa. Jim Hindmarsh and Daphne's husband, Phil Howie, were leaning against the verandah railings, beers wetting their hands, and they talked about pineapples and peanuts. Sid Johnson, Elsie's new husband, looked nervous.

The air was unsettling. There was so much going on with Muriel and Lorna and Elsie and Daphne running in and out of the dining room and across the kitchen verandah with platters of chookie and roasted vegetables and gravy for the children, their strict instructions "Manners!" "At table!" "Please!" shrill, piercing the children's glee. Sid wanted a whisky but none was offered. Marjory fluttered. She put up her finery, lowered her brassy gold fringe and sweated fatly. She wouldn't be drawn into righteous Dark bustling. She wouldn't offer to help out in the kitchen. She wasn't going to budge.

Poppa watched Jim follow a magpie's flight. Sid paced, his face flushed. Phil eyed the anxiety of daughters who scurried under their mother's orders, their flesh enclosed around a morality he wished dead. All Harry and Bertie could do was grunt.

Nanna Dark darted silently at the centre of the family's energy. She was its servant and its piety, its breathless prayer. In the garden, a light breeze cooled the vegetables and the gravy congealed over the chookie and pork. But no one, not the smallest tot, took up their forks and knives until she sat down and nodded to Poppa. That's when he said grace.

When the ginger beer ran out, it was Fi's job to ask for more. She struggled off her chair and grasped the jug and ran to the door of the dining room. Then she walked in slowly, looking carefully around the table.

Jacqui and Kel were sitting inside under Nanna's elbows. Jacqui was motionless. Kel hunched his shoulders, and rested his fork on his plate. He wasn't touching the potato chopped into gravy. Or the drumstick Nanna had especially reserved for him. Their Dad and Mum, Uncle Jack and Aunty Lydia, weren't there. Lydia was in hospital, that much Fi knew, and that meant her Aunty was sick with something.

With her bare foot hooked over a bare knee, Fi fell into a trance, staring across the table at the masticating mouths of aunties, their bright red lips greased from roasted chook and pork, their lipstick smudged from a judicious pat or two of the corner of a napkin. Their aunties' hair seemed to curl round their cheeks and over their foreheads to conceal all their features but their busy mouths. They drank shandies. Fi's uncles drank beer. Their rubbery mouths and greased lips did not stretch into avuncular smiles. Her aunties and uncles frowned at their plates. Cutlery clinked. They silently chewed. One aunty poked her tongue into shreds of chook softly snagged in a dental groove. Limbs jittered. Chins jerked. They did the best they could at the dining table to ignore the gawping Fi. They glanced at Kel. He sulked above his potato. Jacqui sat perfectly still.

A cloud descended.

The world went murky on a cloudless sunlit day.

Muriel made the plum pudding. From a recipe the Hindmarsh family treasured. Nanna made crème anglais, it was her speciality. For Christmas, she allowed a dash of brandy. Fi loved the careful way Nanna lifted the sauceboat to pour crème anglais over the portions measured out with attention to the size and capacity of each and everyone present. Her daughters left their places at the table and raced the bowls to the ascribed child or adult. Everyone waited until Nanna had sat in front of her setting, and the aunties found their table placements again. Then the adults paused, raised their spoons and, as if reluctantly, scooped morsels. Outside, the children squealed with delight, digging threepences out of the dark fruit and cakey mix.

Kicking noisily round the garden, Fi and Gillian ran and squealed and chased after each other's shouts. They wanted to play dollies and teddies and bounce the yellow and red striped beachball. But Jacqui wasn't to be found anywhere.

Muriel's hand descended from nowhere to grab Fi. She and Aunty Elsie hissed incomprehensible things about not being selfish. The word 'sick' was used. Fi, confused by whisperings and hissings, shrieked. A hard hand stung the back of her legs, punishment for being cheeky.

Gillian stood safely to one side. She sat on the side steps and squinted at the afternoon sun. Her hair ribbons, tied in a bow on top of her head, wobbled. Fi sniffled, more from impotent rage than from crippling anger. She sat with a plop! beside Gillian. Together they would wait to see what was killing Christmas.

It was then the girls heard a stumbling and a crashing from under a bush. Like a chook, Jacqui strutted from under the daisies, her doll hanging from her grip, its poke bonnet tugging loose, the ribbons trailing in the dirt. The side garden gate swung open, its hinges screaming, and Kel cycled through at breakneck speed.

Uncle Jack's car bumped over the grassy slope up to the Dark house. Jacqui and Kel gathered up their excitement and stood back like two small ensigns. They waited for the gears to crunch. Jacqui's body quivered with anxiety, and Kel's eyes were huge with apprehension, but they waited. They were Good Children waiting for the snap and slam of car doors. They waited for the permission to run forwards. Which they never got. So they stood like a pair of tailor's dummies, abject, unable to move.

Fi couldn't sit still to watch the agony of it all. She didn't pay it much attention, just took it on board that Jack was bringing Lydia back from one of her periodic stays in Hospital. To Nanna Dark's.

Running around the house, she played safe by keeping out of Muriel's sight. She climbed a favourite crepe myrtle tree and sat in its branches to sing at the broad blue and green vacancy where the moon had hung the night before. She lapsed into her dreamy world, singing at sky.

As it happened, Harry's big face brought her crashing out of herself. When she saw him under her, his hand seemed to be rising to grab her thigh. Shaking all over from the impact of the drop onto the ground, she shook also from her anger and frustration that Uncle Harry believed he had a right to invade her dreamy world with his big fat hand. But in the same moment something else, a lot of noise coming from one of the bedrooms, distracted her from Harry, his fat hands and her dreamy singing.

Uncle Harry grinned at her. "Bit of fun," he blustered, his face big and shining. He cocked his knee up, believing he was the centre of everything in her world. "Didn't mean to frighten you." The skin around his nose twitched, bubbles of sweat stood round and glittery and his eyes disappeared under fat eyelids, she noticed when he said, "Got caught up there, didja?" He laughed at her, at a girl with private moments.

She scowled.

Then Fi suddenly laughed.

Behind Uncle Harry's head, Nanna and Uncle Jack supported the frail figure of Lydia. But Lydia wanted to drift to the window. She looked like a heroine in a matinee movie, yearning to hang through open curtains, but Uncle Jack and Nanna restrained her.

The scene looked sad and funny and Fi, disturbed by Uncle Harry, heard her cruel hard laugh. She stood outside her skin. That's how she saw the whole moment as one made clear with shock — Uncle Harry trying to finger her when she was up a tree, Lydia straining to reach the window, and her barking laugh. It all twisted up, sound and scene blending indecently.

Uncle Harry hated little girls who laughed at him, and he swiped at her head. She ducked, and the girl in her head looked at the one ducking away from the red-faced uncle and heard her laugh harder.

Framed by the window, both the shocked one and the ducking, laughing girl saw Uncle Jack stiffen, his neck long. Lydia swayed. She swayed in despair. Uncle Jack, Fi could see by the way his face contorted, believed she laughed at Lydia. Gripping her knees, she made herself laugh harder, savagely dragging up bitterness from her belly so that the other one, the one in her head, whimpered with disgust.

Brilliance cut through the branches of the crepe myrtle tree. Uncle Jack's face sharpened. The girl in her head raised her hands. She reeled, flew up and disappeared in the cutting rays of light. That's when the laughing girl fell silent.

When she was whole again, Fi found herself staring at the curtained bedroom window. Perhaps Nanna and Uncle Jack and Lydia were on the other side.

Uncle Harry, too. He'd gone.

That's what they'd been, that's what they were, those Hindmarshes and Darks. Perhaps Gillian the historian will say, "That's what we're made of, those people who tried hard to make sense of themselves with photos, po-faces stiff, glaring at the camera." Fi in meditative moments might ponder the thought that the old people tried to make sense of the things they did. Like rip out the rainforest they called the Great Scrub. They suffered strange moods. They tried to live as if the new land was like the old where the ancestors' bones lay under the hoar frost and the iron grey sky. In the kitchen of the farmhouse they grew up in, Gillian and Fi, with the help of whisky and tea, came to the considered conclusion that both the Hindmarshes and Darks had left their trees behind them. They understood dairies and cornfields.

They had no imagination for rainforests. Nor did they understand the trees that they introduced to make new the old land they took as their own.

Was that the ache in Lydia's damaged head? When the hill farms glowed under the full moon, was Lydia lost in a strange land? On those nights when she hugged herself and bayed the full moon, had she forgotten where her home was?

Many was the time that Fi, swimming to consciousness through restless sleep, groped at the bric-a-brac streaming out of her dreams; and, as these weirdnesses vaporised before she could grasp them, Gillian would materialise under the crepe myrtle, her face stamped with dejection, her pink ribbons shining.

In her dreams that may have been nightmares, the crepe myrtle shivered from shame confused with pride and irascibility.

Did any of them know? Did any of them see?

# PART IV

### under the tankstand

Under the tankstand where maidenhair fern frothed and the black snake with the red belly coiled, there lay, there lay ...

By mid-morning, the snake lengthened its slithery back, stretching outwards and sliding its head under a favoured leaf or frond. There the snake with eyes as cold as hell spent its day, lazily dozing, its back soaking up sun.

A giant cherry guava tree graced the sky.

At the place where Nanna Dark reminded her scruffy granddaughter to Walk-Do-Not-Run, the chooks scuttled and a horse flicked its tail across its backside. Like an ad, it looked good and brightly beautiful, a high gloss real like true life where the snake dozed, where trees strode the sky and children played with canoes made out of blackbean pods.

That's what's said. That's what's pictured.

That's what's framed without its mystery.

That's how a kid saw the Dark farm. A kid like Fi. A kid who liked to scrounge behind the dairy where the blackbean tree dropped its pods. That tomboy Fi played with Barry Priddle, a kid from a neighbouring farm. They split the blackbean pods open, flicked out the seeds and made canoes to sail in the stream twisting across the valley floor.

The Dark farm was invested with beautiful contradictions.

At Nanna Dark's, Fi was a girl dressed in shorts and she ran and ran, ran on bare feet through the kitchen and the voices of women hounded her. WALK DO NOT RUN IN HOUSES!

"Walk, girl!"

"Like-a-young-lady-should!"

Fi remembered loving to go there, to Nanna Dark's.

**Three dishes from Nanna Dark's kitchen**

**1: Scrambled Egg**

The child Fi toyed with black toast soaking up the liquid oozing out of egg Nanna Dark scrambled too long on too high a heat over the fuel stove. Fi tasted burnt wood in her egg. The parsley leaves hadn't had time to soften. She pouted. She elbowed the table and cupped her cheeks in the palms of her hands. Nanna Dark expected "Elbows OFF the table!" Poppa Dark looked at Fi and he said, "Urrgh!" which she knew meant she must comply — that her elbows had to be taken off the table and that she was obliged to eat the hard scrambled egg crisp with uncooked parsley.

**2: Apple Jelly**

Fi plundered the fridge for apple jelly and spread it generously on buttered bread. She tilted back her head and pushed thick white slices spread with the jelly into her mouth between declaring, "I love it!" Nanna Dark, her eyes shy, smiled.

**3: Ginger Beer**

Bottles of ginger beer filled the pantry every Christmas. No other ginger beer ever tasted as good. That was a long time ago. Fi told Laine memory may have added an extra zest to its excellence.

**Three favourite Nanna Dark obsessions**
**1: Crochet**
Everywhere. Doilies.
Crocheted cushions, shopping bags, collars and cuffs, face washers, pocket hankies and petticoat hems. More even than Muriel could tolerate.
**2: Manners**
At all times, her vigilant eye judged the several misdemeanours of elbows, feet and hands.
**3: Gardens**
From first light to dusk, she hoed and mulched and plucked old petals from deep green bushes. She chatted to the birds, conversed with the flowers and coaxed the ferns to grow in the wrong places. When her step thumped the backstep, when she shot her rubber boots into the laundry, when, soaping her hands under running water, she sighed over the wash basin, Fi understood in the way children do that her Nanna was getting herself ready to do something she didn't like doing. She didn't like peeling potatoes, stringing beans, cracking the skin off a chunk of pumpkin, ie cooking tea —
  when cows lowed in the afternoon,
  when light quivered then soared,
  hesitated then with night
  swept dark over the hills.
**Three Nanna Dark characteristics**
She
1: said very little;
2: laughed rarely; and
3: smiled dreamily.
She liked going to church where she was made to feel pure.
Who was she? Where did she come from?
No one knew exactly. She was their grandmother. She was an old woman whose eccentricities were no more than those of an old woman. But one morning when Fi leapt into the kitchen after a breakfast of lumpy scrambled egg sprigged

with crisp parsley, she found her Nanna quietly weeping. Fi's mouth dropped open. Surprise stayed her step for an instant before she rushed forwards, knees and elbows spiking the spaces around her, and she dropped her fresh face under her Nanna's chin. She asked a child's direct question, "Nanna, why are you crying?"

Nanna wiped her eyes and blew her nose. Bowing her head in front of the fuel stove, the old woman's back seemed to curve.

Fi thought she was praying. She sat on the hearth at her feet and looked up to study prayer being said outside church. The inquisitive madness in Fi thought such prayer would have a quality unlike the words in church repeated after the parson's drone. Her grandmother was still, the skin of her fleshy face translucent.

After a moment's hesitation, Fi rolled her body off the hearth. The troubled and uncertain world of adults imposed discretion on her. Something big was moving in Nanna, something too big to understand.

Fi ran into sunshine.

Back home at Newrybar, she told Muriel Nanna had been crying.

Muriel's hands stopped sifting flour. "Crying?"

Not to be distracted by her mother's worried surprise, Fi wriggled around the table where Muriel was preparing a lemon meringue tart. Elbows on the table, Fi managed to slap her barefoot over her knee cap. She hunched over the table like that for a second, then released herself, a yogi raising her arms above her head, pressing her hands together as if the pose was devotional and she said, "Mum, does anyone cuddle Nanna?"

Dropping her wooden spoon and with a soft groan, she hugged Fi hard. She smelled of warm flour and lemons.

Fi sometimes stayed at the Dark farm for a few days during school holidays. To give Muriel a break from her incessant wriggling and cranky questioning and combative behaviour.

Gillian stayed with Muriel, always — she never stayed with their Nanna.

She had nothing much to do at the Dark house but stalk her own shadow.

On those summery days when the sky took on the tired grey of old dishcloths, sagged and drizzled, and the long wet grasses stooped over, Fi lent up on a couch, her chin on her hands, and watched. And listened. If she bent her head sideways, she heard the misty wet condensing under bushes to saturate the ground. The darkened trees drooped, bedraggled and absent of birds and their calls. Close to the house, a sigh fell under the monsteria delorosa, and released a dismayed gasp. Heavy-headed hydrangeas languished.

Weariness soaked into the walls of the wooden house. The boards creaked with their swelling damp. A sashcord stuck, a latch slipped, a hinge stiffened. Feeble light spread along the hall runner. Melancholy lapped around chair legs.

Poppa lay on an old couch where he dozed under the open pages of the local newspaper. Nanna sat by the cold fuel stove. She crocheted a cushion cover. Fi's reading eyes darted off the printed pages to look with amazement at sunrays spinning from the hook, the silk thread crackling over bent, dry fingers.

The child read, Nanna crocheted, Poppa slept under the newspaper.

Sinking without resilience under the old sky, those days were voiceless — nobody bothered to talk. The radio did the job of speech, broadcasting the news, introducing a dull song, droning through an episode of *Blue Hills*.

Poppa had no energy to push words that conveyed little meaning across his vocal chords. Words died on his lips for want of conversation. He telegraphed messages of intent or need.

When Fi looked up from her page to blurt out something, Nanna smiled.

Wood swelled from the damp. Hot sun cracked paint thick on wooden windowsills.

There were other summery days when the air stood hot and still and the men seemed to evaporate from the house, leaving it to women and girls and very little boys. On those days, the burnished pattern of the lino shone under the clean soles of bare feet, mellowing on its polished surface the rush and slouch of housekeeping movements, making of them a graceful and feminine choreography that made Fi's body buzz. Those days were luxurious. If the aunties — Daphne Howie, Elsie Johnson or Lorna Scott — happened to be visiting, Nanna gave them cool drinks and salad lunches then, after washing up the lunch things, they drifted from the kitchen to the sleepout. On those days, with a great deal of chattering — about how awful was straight hair and about the new shampoos to make a girl's hair her crowning glory and how uncomfortably sticky were nylon petticoats, how strangely pointed was the newest bra one of them had bought — the women shed their dresses. Firstly brushing up their permed hair, the aunties stretched lazily in their nylon petticoats and pointed bras on couches under windows opened to catch a chance breeze. There they dozed over the *Women's Weekly* or *Harper's Bazaar* or *The Australian Town & Country Journal*. On rare occasions, Fi saw Elsie or Daphne read a novel. Nanna and Muriel never opened novels. They never touched them.

Gillian always carried one with her. She lay with Fi. When Gillian opened her novel, she lay still and ordered Fi to shut up.

When she was seven, they twisted and ran finger tips down their bare chests and tickled and giggled. That was when Gillian liked *The Famous Five*. When she was nine, she rolled away from Fi's tickling fingers, her top on, and she immersed herself with English schoolgirls in abbeys that were difficult for her to imagine. When she was twelve she was so engrossed by *Wuthering Heights* she refused to share a sofa with Fi.

Fi told Laine she liked *Tom Sawyer*. "It made sense, that book," she said. "I could see it happening."

Gillian, retreating inside the covers of novels to live life vicariously, developed longings, obsessions with colourful misdemeanours, nostalgic yearnings for another time and place in history more exciting than the one she lived in. Unlike her, Fi didn't abstract herself. A realist, her steady brains comprehended her immediate moment, adjusting to it as she analysed a better strategy to make the most out of it. As the clairvoyant said, Fi was masculine, a target spotter. Laine said she was like an army commander, capable only of focussing on one thing at a time. So when Gillian's heart ached for Catherine's reason lost to her love of Heathcliff, Fi read about Tom, measuring herself against him, comparing her adventures down the creeks and across the hills to his boy's adventures.

She liked to elaborate these occasions for the benefit of Laine. She liked to suggest that she discovered she was a woman for the love of women on those hot and dozy afternoons. Propping herself up on bony elbows and cupping her chin, Fi will get around to telling Laine that when she was little, "About eight?" and not too bothered with books, she wriggled and squirmed to peer up and down the sleepout, then she slipped off her sofa and pattered from bed to bed, pushing spaces beside her aunties where she could curl without touching flesh.

They protested. "Too Hot! Ooh! Fi! Sweaty!" Saturating herself with their sweet and soapy smells, with the women's soft restfulness, Fi claimed that at the squirmy age of eight she was amazed by women's sensuality. She thrilled, she will disclaim to Laine, on the golden edge of onanism when, after her aunties had rested, they sat in front of mirrors, paused and arched their backs slightly before pulling brushes through their springing hair, the little girl squirming, entranced by every one of their gestures.

"Back bones swerved, rumps shifted slightly," she will remember, their lizard movements — to look more closely at a pouting mouth, the imperfection of skin round the chin and nostrils, where hairline and ear met — exciting the child Fi as it excited the middle-aged lover of the gorgeous Laine.

She loved it more keenly when Lydia visited Nanna and the day was declared "Too hot!" When Lydia, like a creature gliding across the big screen, dropped her silky dress on the back of a Simla chair, Fi heard a whisper whistle through her heart. Lydia was the one whose raised arms expelled such womanly aromas of vanilla and nutmeg, Fi wanted more. She will try to explain to Laine how eagerly she whipped off her shorts and stripped to her panties and, bare-chested, curled on the ridge of her Aunty Lydia's bed, her hands folded in an attitude of prayer under her cheek. She will play up to Laine's amazement with stories of how she tried to guess if there was a hint of roses in Lydia's perfumes. In actual fact, when she was eight she wasn't sure what else she should do to discover more excitement.

Fi kept some parts of her story to her secret self. Lydia's life was all ache, not a tale to be reduced to a funny cameo scene to aggrandise a precocious Fi discovering her sexuality. On tricky days, when Lydia was in something Muriel called a mood, she wore a dress with a handkerchief pointed hem. Under its arms, the cloth, yellowed with age, was in tatters. Perhaps Lydia wore it to signal her disquiet. For in Lydia's eyes on those days was depthlessness. When Fi tiptoed to the edge of her sofa, to her dismay she watched tears roll out of wide open eyes. They soaked the pillowcase under her head. They left shadows on the sheets. They streamed down Lydia's cheeks to soak the neck of her petticoat. She curled like a foetus. She bit the sheets.

The girl knew the desolate self was a pain like no other.

Muriel sniffily said Lydia had a fantasy — she thought she had been a princess in a previous life. Sometimes Muriel liked to add with venom, "She's off again. Lydia's fantasy's up. Fairyland's taking over!"

Fi carried in her head the story she and Gillian constructed of the things adults said about Lydia, believing she unwound her unloved body to stand tall on lengthening legs and bay the moon. How Lydia bayed the moon! Around the ring of hills, her baying echoed and echoed. They heard her, her nieces, Gillian and Fiona, at Newrybar. The hills flung her baying back, the echoes of her desperate wailing clear sharp notes as if ringing with an orchestra, but her tears, dropping at dawn, were another kind of dew.

The lone woman, shorn of all she had valued in herself, her loveliness and her dignity, unfurled to embrace the full moon.

One day, one hot day when Nanna had retreated to doze in her panties and bra and Fi had run outside, she came across her classmate, Barry Priddle. He stank like a sweating horse. "Bin chasing rabbits." Fi at nine was a girl who ran with boys. She looked him over and classified him as Hot. Having learned what women did when men turned up looking hot and smelling sweaty, she offered him a drink. Barry guzzled it then wiped his mouth with the heel of his hand. His red lipped smile of thanks was sheepish.

Barry and Fi walked out of the kitchen together. Relying on their school camaraderie, they went through the motions of swiping at the heads of roses, and they took up sticks to play at jousting. But it was too hot. Even under the deep and sweet smelling shade of pine trees, it was too hot.

Barry leaned against railings, Fi put her foot on verandah boards. The painted wood was hot. She pulled her foot back. Uncertain that following him was what she wanted to do, she skipped to keep up with him when, with his head down, he crab-walked across the lawn to the back gate that was like a stile. That was where they found themselves when her thirteen-year-old cousin, Elliot, streaked with sweat and dust, called out. He had been grubbing lantana in the back paddocks with his Dad and Poppa Dark.

Elliot ushered them, mustered them, rounded them up like a dog circling at the back to force their walking feet to the tall tankstand that stood between the vegetable garden and the orchard. Fi was reluctant but, wanting to relieve the boredom with play, she let Elliot take charge. She liked being one of the boys.

At this age of nine, Fi wasn't sure why she was programmed to follow. She was wakening to the thought that that was what girls did. When doing boy things, she questioned whether she should watch and follow. She wasn't too sure of the cues, not having the confidence or experience to make her own cues. In any case, on that day Fi registered that she did not want to go under the tankstand with Barry and Elliot. And yet she went with the boys. She didn't initiate going under the tankstand.

A black snake, sluggish from too much hot sun, coiled round a cool rock, its red belly hidden from view, its small fangs neat inside its hinged jaw.

Elliot, a sleekly coltish boy, stood with one hand on the blackened wooden struts of the tankstand, an eye trained on the back garden gate. Fi walked around the space under the tankstand, lush with ferns and lichen. Lime encrusted the corrugations of the old tank where water oozed.

She announced the place was snaky. Elliot slid behind her, he avoided walking in front of her. Barry, preoccupied with fiddling inside his shirt pocket, eventually took out a matchbox from which he carefully lifted a small green frog. He put it in Fi's palm. Quite suddenly. Spontaneously. In the ensuing silence, Fi warmed with pleasure. She smiled, stroking the small bright body quivering at the centre of her palm. She looked at Barry, at his shy eyes that seemed to ache, pale yellow flecks flickering across light grey, the pain of being looked at almost too much for him to bear.

Elliot looked on, excluded from this shy exchange of a tiny frog for a smile. He seemed to slip away from his lookout, not caring for Barry's and Fi's complicity when he smacked the back of Fi's hand with a rough whack. The frog went flying. Fi yelled. She turned on Elliot in a fury. His full lip curled and his small eyes disappeared behind his fat eyelids but before she knew it, he kicked her shins with such ferocity, she fell backwards, and sat hard on her rump. Tears smarting, she struggled to get up, but Elliot trod on her hand and ground it painfully on the rock floor under the tankstand.

Diamond bright points of pain blurred her vision. Through tears of rage and pain, she found herself looking at the back of Barry's head. Head bowed, Barry slowly walked away.

Fi struggled and kicked. But Elliot's deft and strong hands held her down and dragged her shorts down. She bit, he grinned. His grin rose above her face as she struggled under him, his hands digging into her shorts, feeling around her vagina. Her teeth sank into his arm, he punched his pointed knuckle into the soft muscle of her upper arm. He had her pinned, his hand exploring her, his fingers probing and hurting her vagina and curdling everything inside her head.

When she broke free from Elliot's blunt-fingered exploration, her limbs were uneasily liquid. She stood up, adjusting her shorts, dusting at scratches and streaks of lichen darkening her legs, fingering the bruise rising on her upper arm. Resting her hand on the strut of the tankstand to steady herself, she tried to shake the dizziness pressing against her eyeballs, blurring her vision. She tried to rid herself of the sight of Barry's bowed head, the back of his hat walking away from her.

"Girl!" Her big cousin spat in her ear. "Y'r a GIRL!"

The sun smacked Elliot's face without succeeding to annihilate his lurid sneer.

Barry squeezed around the side of the stile. Elliot ran to join him. Perhaps the boys walked together down the track to the road. From where she stood, she lost sight of them. She couldn't see where they went. She didn't want to see them.

Her body stung with resentment. The silky skin where her crotch made a v between her legs burned.

She didn't see the black snake streak across the hot path.

Fi opened the door wide enough for her to slam it hard behind her. Greenly streaked, mouth sullen and hair stringy, the wild child she looked like cocked her head at an angle Nanna loved to look at, at the boldness brightening her eyes. She was in a mood to be a challenge. Nanna wanted to know "What y'bin doing? Under the tankstand?" A shrill voice which didn't sound like Fi's pitched forth with "Nuthin' ... Barry ... Gave me a frog."

She repeated it stoutly, "He gave me a frog, a little green one?"

She sat heavily.

"I let it go."

That's what she said.

Should truth be gratuitously given?

Fi sat at the kitchen table and she poked her grubby fingers into a hole she found in the lace tablecloth. A vase at the centre of the table wobbled. Lupins shuddered. The child pouted at her ferreting fingers. Tugging them out of the lacy holes, she pulled the cloth and the vase toppled over. Water soaked into the lace cloth and spilled onto the floor.

Fi's mouth traced a downturned pout. Nanna let free a sigh like a low moan. She lumbered to the sink where she took up a cloth to sponge the mess, grumbling, as she very often did, that *women's work is never done*. Hearing these words, Fi grew sullen with disgust, angered that in her bones and throughout her dreams the old obligations of her sex were fixed patterns and unavoidable. Hysterically screaming abuse at Nanna, she ran out of the kitchen and around the house, uneasy with the thought that something serious had been broken. The pain that seemed to jelly her limbs was searing.

She first leaned against the crepe myrtle tree, then sat under it on the lawn and looked up at the window where

Lydia and Jack, many years ago, played a tragic pantomime of interdependent movements. Lydia, the agonised aunty, the one filled with pain. Did relationships like marriage engulf her body? Did Lydia and Jack demand agony of each other? She was only nine, and she knew beyond her own full understanding what was expected of her in life was not going to be. She hated her breasts budding slightly, she hated the endless going on about what was expected of girls, Muriel's admonishment about "a girl-like-you", about having to look nice for men. Nothing they said, her mother, her aunties or her Nanna, paid even a token gesture towards a girl being herself.

Pressing her chin on her breastbone and looking at her legs sprawled in front of her, she hunkered down to escape the false self. She wanted the one coddled within to gain strength enough to overpower the nice bright little thing they wanted of her. She strove to take a firm grip on her strength to make sure what was going on would not happen. They were not going to succeed at making her stupid. Fi wanted the prime spot in the cosmic order to be hers. There. Way up high. Where the crepe myrtle branches stroked the sky and above the hill rising behind the house and over the barbed wire strung through blue and a horse cropping grass. She was determined to take off, her ambition being to win complacency, to be secure, on her terms.

She tugged at grass, chewed stalks, wondering what the hell would anyone want to marry someone like Elliot for? Even as a friend, he was a bully. His face was cold, his lips slick, his eyes trickily disappearing behind fat eyelids. Kicking her legs stretched in front of herself, she found the chewed grass tasted satisfyingly good. But she was worried. She drew one leg up to form a triangle, her foot flat against the inside of the other knee, and she touched the skin behind the hem of her shorts. It was sore, badly grazed, skin bleeding. She was in pain. Was hers the kind of pain that came with blood? She whimpered. Stood up. Unsteadily.

Inside Fi's brain, there was a dull ache. Not an agony, not a real bad pain, but a prolonged ache.

Bending over herself, circling like a ball, she looked between her legs. She looked at where she had been scratched and where she had been torn. Her face flushed, she straightened and threw her head back, wanting to wriggle into the plump warmth of Nanna's body, but she concealed her pain, snuffling and dragging the hem of her shorts down as far as it would go.

Nanna found her on her bed fighting back tears and tugging at a handkerchief. Nanna, guessing something had gone wrong, drew her into a warm embrace. Fi didn't let go of the handkerchief, nor did she sob — she gripped that handkerchief and clenched her jaw. Gripped and clenched. She wasn't letting go of the truth of her feelings about Elliot and what he did. Fi wasn't going to spill all over the place like a vase filled with lupins.

"God forgot me."

Her voice, roughened and tense, didn't sound like her own.

Nanna touched the purple bruise rising on Fi's upper arm, "Where'd you get that?" gulped under her pious insistence that Jesus loved little children. "Jesus loves you," she repeated, raising her eyes to the portrait of Christ that hung on the wall above the bed.

Bursting to say 'My eye,' Fi fixed her sights on a far horizon. The centre of the bruise under stroking fingers was hard, like the pointed bone of a knuckle. But her throat swallowed lumps of bile with the hateful name of Elliot. If she divulged details, if she said his name, she would dissolve. She would feel singled out, targeted, brightly lit. That wouldn't do. No.

She looked at her Nanna with angry clear eyes. She said, "I want to go home, Nanna. Please phone Mum."

After a moment when the world seemed to hover, transfixed on its axis and perhaps unwilling to change course, Nanna moved, Poppa's dog barked, cows mooed, chooks clucked, the noises of ordinary farm-life flowing through the window, propelling Fi to take control. If she could not get rid of her pain, at least she must allow herself to come to grips with what had happened, understand Elliot's crude invasion of her body, and stake out what she wanted. She vowed never to see her cousin again.

Fi sat on her bed at Nanna's, her face burning with anger and resentment and courage — with the bright energy of one who faced up to the crux of the problem and gave it a name.

Wiyabul slid from under the rock where the black snake coiled around its red belly. A tremor of malignancy sniggered on buffeting breezes, a boy slammed a girl, doubt stalked questions facing the future. The spirit stood on one long leg, grass between his teeth. One thing to love Mother Earth, but women and girls were knockovers. Wiyabul leered, recalling how hard was the laughter when old cousin Arakwaal threw a spear at his first wife's back. She dropped dead, punishment for nagging her husband who liked to go walkabout for drink. That huge joke had the kookaburras and the magpies and the spirits in the trees cackling so loudly the sky broadened, its blue deep, lifting up the sound of a good belly laugh into its vastness. But Wiyabul, far sighted and prayerful, had forgotten the joke. Existence depended on understanding these pale people who respected nothing but toil. They loathed everything that got in the way. Their hearts small and hard, they loathed the natural hills and valleys of the land, reshaping the glades of tree ferns and grass trees with fire, burning and burning and burning until the air stank of wet ash. The air cracked with the sound of the axe, the crash of mighty trees falling through saplings and bushes to strike the ground. The sap of felled trees sprayed up, fountains raining tears of resin for weeks. But the new people were not diverted by the evidence of mourning among trees. They had work to do. They had to make the rainforest known as the

Great Scrub resemble the place they left. They lifted the rocks out of the creek beds, dragged them up and across the hills to square off patches which they scored with narrow lines, planting seeds into shallow furrows. Bared to the sun, the ground sprang with green, grass that grew at their heels, tall wavering green grasses. Some turned yellow. At an unlanguaged signal, men, women and children bent their heads and shielded their eyes from sunshine and they walked along the lines of tall yellow grass, stripping fat bearded cobs as they went.

These people were tight knots of enterprise.

The far sighted old one looked from the past through the present to the future and into the sour heart of Elliot. No redemption there for an ancient love of creeks, the colour of rocks, the beauty of green so sublime it made old eyes weep. Elliot's music was the clink of coins on coins, his orchestra the chain-saw screeching to the percussion of depth sounders and the plastic rasp of his credit card sliding through the eftpos machine.

Listening for hope and hearing only dull hatred, mourning the lost meaning of Earth and Rock, Wiyabul let a baleful moan hover on the misty air where three streams met. There under the overhanging branches of a dark rivergreen tree the old spirit bent over the land itself, but the bora ring had been broken, the nut tree with two trunks and one taproot had been cut down and the wetlands emptied of birds nesting on reedy islands. Wanting to revitalise, to find again preternatural sensitivities, perhaps the old Wiyabul dared to beseech wisdom more ancient than selfhood — when will men and women, black and white, get on together? When will women be free to love the precious girl within themselves?

When will the disharmonic heart beat for the singing Earth?

Out of the blue, Fi said to Gillian, "Such a funny thing is memory, don't you agree, Gillian?" Even as she said it she recalled how much Muriel loved the colours of Spring and Summer — red and pink, lemon and orange elaborately enhanced in the manner of country elegance with an abundance of cream — so unlike the blue fading in the old kitchen lino, smudging darkly and with a hint of menace, the green giving in and merging where black lines used to outline squares. Perhaps it was a remnant of Hindmarsh preferences she had failed to hack out of her life. "Funny funny thing," Fi quietly repeated, bemused by the fact of the lino, and with such intelligent clarity that she was able to convince herself she could understand everything to do with Muriel's life.

She had an overwhelming desire to slip off her shoe and plop her foot on the kitchen table as a fine example of the funny thing that is memory. "Rather like my grossly pronated feet. That's memory." She looked proudly at her white foot, turning to admire it more, arching it on the table. Gillian cocked her head at an angle. She looked askance at her younger sister's long thin and very flat foot, registering mild surprise that the toes, all five in her sights, were painted to match her lipstick. Coloured Cinnamon Rose, the bony shells shielding the end of toey ligaments, shone politely as Fi described memory as "... like my feet."

Looking away from the nonsense that Fi was perpetrating, Gillian remarked that it would be as well for them to take a stroll around the garden, "Just to see for ourselves, and get it right in both our heads, how much maintenance is involved. If we keep the house, that is. Upkeep, Fi. Upkeep is going to be an issue. For both house and garden." But Fi was absorbed by her foot. Supporting her leggy stretch by embracing her thigh, she straightened her knee and pointed her rosy toes at the ceiling. "A podiatrist told me," she said, releasing her leg, the bare foot landing with a thud on faded green and blue squares, "that the little bones of my feet rattle around as if loose in plastic bags. They don't connect." She looked at Gillian whose head lowered and roamed from right to left, seeking to escape the unbearable. "Don't connect," repeated Fi. She pulled her trouser leg into place and settled in her chair, crossing her legs, dancing her fingertips on the tabletop, recalling the pain of those little bones not connecting in her feet.

By the time she looked at Gillian again, she had related her store of sequences, the story of her difficult time finding a podiatrist; being diagnosed and measured for an orthotic device; having the cast made followed by the fitting of the orthotics; the feeling of relief when those little bones were finally supported; and the searching for shoes that she could wear with the blessed things. "Memory," she urged Gillian to think about and then believe, "is a series of events that don't connect, but are shuttered in together to make one thing whole. Like life, like Muriel's life." She pointed at her foot. "Like my little bones. They roll around inside my skin, they are my feet. Events roll around inside a brain, they are the story. They form a unit, make a story, and that's life."

Gillian pushed herself up. She looked around as she did, as if a troubling memory had returned to her. The curtains, the chairs, the range of mugs and cups and saucers smudged behind glass cupboard doors, the chipped paint behind the handle where fingers hit against the cutlery drawer, and the light flooding the kitchen. She imagined Jim's voice cracking across the bare hills when he called Jake to get behind the cows' heels — "Way back!" — the words, rebounding off hillsides, hollowing out the valleys. Way back. Then Fi as a tiny girl toddling fast to keep up with Jim, Jake and the cows, Muriel flapping after her, the chooks springing aside to keep out of harm's way, Gillian on the verandah amazed by the procession raging across the green slope leading up to the dairy.

"Mum gave you so much attention," she said harshly and bit her lip immediately.

She had said it. Fi said nothing. Gillian's sudden bitterness disappeared in the kitchen, then suddenly reappeared.

Inside her head, Fi's rage reddened and inflated. She looked straight at Gillian and watched her flinch away from her outburst. They both knew Fi hated Muriel's fussing about being a girl mixed up with vague ideas about being respectable. Doing well at school was the same as and equal to being respectable. Being respectable was the same as and equal to conforming. Making her daughters the same as everyone else was Muriel's goal.

The light flooding the room shifted slightly, the late afternoon shadows softening hard edges. Gillian could see Leigh digging under the passionfruit vine with a spade as long as he was tall. He was carefully collecting something, dropping what he found and inspected and approved into an upturned hat. She gulped, a fish under water swimming for life, her boy alert in the natural world he found engrossing. She winced when Fi, her voice grating from the pain of speaking at all, cut through her love of him with "At highschool, you had it all. Boys and boys, Muriel loving every minute of it. But I ... I may as well've shot myself."

Gillian shook her head. But she had no idea what she could say in the face of standout scenes of sullen Fi at school, ignoring boys who shouted that her face was like the back of a broken bus and how she, her sister, laughed with them, more from shocked embarrassment than accord. But what could she have done? At the time she felt grubby, her laugh signifying betrayal. And there it was again, all that was unspoken lingering like the pervasive stench of mould and dust in the air they shared, and she leaned against the table, her body like her mind limp when she tried to ask, "But what about Barry Priddle? You and he were ..."

Fi stamped one foot.

"What's ... Oh, I don't know," Gillian moaned, starting up and gathering mugs to dump in the sink, bustling through the pale lemon light with swift kitchen movements, the magpies orange carolling and the kookaburras laughter bringing her the sensation of warm if false relief.

What could she know?

Fi looked at the tabletop, suddenly filled with the unambiguous rush of anger she felt when she first worked out who Barry Priddle was. How she hated to think that someone like him should ever have taken up space in her life! How equally strange that Priddle associated as he was with disgust and betrayal had sunk into the recesses of memory. By walking away, by leaving her with Elliot, he destroyed their friendship, he had betrayed her. Why couldn't she have done something nasty to him at school? She had burned with fury.

Even if she heard Leigh run up the sidepath, she would not have been able to bring herself back from her disgust that she should have been so betrayed. Priddle abandoned her to the possibility of rape. Was it rape? When a boy of thirteen digitally interferes with his nine-year-old cousin, is that rape? She gritted her teeth, the question appalling her. She should have done something to Elliot. But she could not have done anything, not unless she spoke up and said something to her mother. And father. She clenched her fist around muddled images of Muriel brandishing shampoos to make a girl's hair her crowning glory, Muriel sitting at the sewing machine to make pretty dresses to make a girl look delectable to a man's eye, Muriel haranguing that a girl-like-you would never get a man, Jim heading out the door in the direction of the barn, all of it rather like unpolished green bleeding through the black lines in the lino that smudged blue.

She looked at Gillian. But Gillian had her back to Fi. She was intent on inspecting the property, commerce controlling the wild edges of the grief she might, otherwise, have succumbed to.

They went out into the sunshine and walked around the house and up to the barn and to the ruin of the dairy that collapsed beside a broken barbed wire fence. Even though they were upset with each other, they stayed close together, Gillian walking in the heat of Fi's anger, Fi clinging to Gillian's resilience.

Arakwaal, standing in a Newrybar glade, caught sight of their wandering in the same flashed instant as Wiyabul cosmically elevated within a copse of bangalow palms. With a wicked glint to his gimlet eye, Arakwaal called out, cracking a joke that the future was looking mighty shaky for floating fossils, even wily spirits intent on having a go at understanding unpredictable and exasperating women's business things.

The clairvoyant, that wise woman of Manchester, aware a spirit drawing on a wisdom alien in its strength from the one she knew, lit a cigarette and plucked at the hot pink threads spooling round the knees of her tracksuit pants. Then she suddenly desisted, her fingers stilled by a seismic shift in the spirit world, her mouth an empty 'o' as happened whenever she doubted who will love the feminine in this raw land. Wiyabul grasped breathless whirling and hurled his strange energy through her.

When the sisters found Leigh, he was in the barn, counting blackbean seeds and laying out as if for display Gillian's old collection of rocks, axe heads and fossils. He glanced at them and self-protectively looked away from their pinched and blotched faces, but not before the pain of their grief and guilt and remorse shot cold fright through his heart.

A single tear, perfectly formed, rolled down the clairvoyant's cheek.

Gillian poured both of them whisky. She put ice cubes in hers. Then she gave herself the job of making a last meal out of the leftovers from Muriel's wake.

At the back of the kitchen cupboard, she found bread-&-butter plates rimmed with the worn memories of rust-coloured lattice supporting yellow and orange leaves, and Gillian ran her fingers over the decoration that evoked the kind of autumn that never happened at Newrybar. In the fifties, it had been a popular breakfast set, this one with the autumn leaves. Muriel hinted that she wanted it, she hinted very often, until Jim quietly walked in one day after doing some business in Lismore, and he lowered the box onto the kitchen table with a shy nod, Gillian jumping up and down with such evident excitement she embarrassed Muriel.

Gillian sat down. Ice cubes melted into the whisky she drained too quickly. She grasped the bottle to pour another inch of golden amber into the tumbler, perversely enjoying her status of family drunk, even if it were only temporarily earned. She licked her cold lips.

Fi toyed with toast. She pressed her forefinger onto her plate to collect all the crumbs the toast shed, raised her shoulders and swayed her head, making a gesture to tell Gillian that she should stop drinking whisky on ice. But Gillian didn't understand the vague passage of Fi's hand. She lifted a triangle of toasted tomato sandwich, and took a bite.

"Marvellous," she said. "Bluddy marvellous."

Fi frowned, and she studied her sister for a few seconds. Then she asked, "What's so marvellous?"

Gillian said through the stuff in her mouth, "Hmmm ... I prefer frogs legs."

"What?" Fi leaned forward, a smile forming. "*What-what-what?* Wah'd'y'mean ... Frogs legs." Gillian spluttered through munched toast, and both sisters found themselves alive in their grief, guffawing and playing the idiot, one of them whispering tearfully, "We never ate them, did we?"

Finding her voice as she flicked a piece of tomato out of the toasted bread, Fi flicked at the childhood memory of learning to count by counting frogs. "One to twenty. We just counted them, didn't we? Before dinner. I mean, tea. Dinner's what I used to call tea." She talked aloud to herself about tea and dinner. "Dinner was the hot lunch for the men, and TEA. That was the evening meal. Still is, isn't it? Up here, I mean."

She looked up at Gillian, afraid the real crying was going to start before she could get away and back to Laine. Her bubble car Maisie waited to return her to her newfound love and life and home. In a moment of unambiguous joy, she recognised her impulse to make the relationship with Laine permanent. She dropped the toast, threads of tomato and cheesey tendrils spilling onto her little plate.

Gillian burst out laughing, her tone fruity, shrill, hysterical.

Not expecting to witness grief muddling feelings of recovery with the fractured shards of laughter, Fi slapped another sandwich into the toastmaker, presuming she should work hard to keep Gillian on a happy note. She cleared her mind and chatted on about tea and dinner. She hoped she might distract Gillian with engaging candour by burbling on about … Mashed potato. That would do. "Do you remember the years and years of mashed potato? And pumpkin? Loads and loads of pumpkin?"

Gillian laughed until her face was wet and red. Then suddenly she shouted and clapped her hand over her mouth, yelling "Beans!" She couldn't help herself. So Fi, rather than assume the greater maturity, turned off her quiet wisdom and joined in with the fun, yelling "Beans! Done to death!"

"Death be done! By bean!"

One of them sliced the air with a fork, the other one smacked it down with a knife. Over the cutlery, their two faces shone, sisters, shared memories lurid between them, their mad game elaborating how much they had changed and how much they had stayed the same.

"And the wizened chop?"

Pounding her chest, Fi flung herself back in her chair to feign the groan of despair. "Aaaah!"

Encouraged by their clowning, Gillian threw up more pet hates. "Tripe!"

"White sauce!"

"Squash pies!"

"Chokos!"

"Blancmange!"

Her face flushed, Fi tried to control her giggling by sitting very still, her hands folded in her lap as if she was considering saying something serious. But then she exploded, laughing hard, unable to contain the joke that those old fashioned kitchen favourites were universally hated. However, she managed to straighten her back to announce in a parody of formality, "But I lerved, absolutely lerved, My Mum's Lemon Meringue."

Her face hot and red from laughing, Gillian arched her back in the chair and thrust her hips forward, but she felt tears stinging at the back of her eyes, her mouth about to droop and wail. Her mood, swinging too quickly, put a sudden stop to Fi's litany of bad food memories. Even so, she could not stop giggling, wiping at her nose, dabbing at her eyes, feeling a strain at the back of her throat. She managed to ask "Tea? Shall I make more?" and then she very quickly added "Better than whisky?" leaving room for Fi to interpret that the question about preferred drinks may have been an observation.

Fi confided that she loved red wine, "... the warm feel of it in my stomach."

Gillian rolled her eyes upwards. She had questions to ask, and her voice squeaked "Fi," drying up an old fear in her mouth. She moistened her lips.

"Fi?"

Fi looked at the way her sister rested her elbows on the table making tents with her fingers, just as Jim had done. Stretching over the sudden grief rising to constrict her throat, she said too loudly, "What? What is it?"

Gillian blinked. "What?" She stared at Fi, momentarily puzzled by the echoing loudness of her voice. She continued to tent a thought under her fingers, slowly winkling it into the open, choosing her words carefully. About Harry. Had he ever done anything "... you know. Sexual. To you when you were little."

They both sat quite still, Fi rolling an unseen mote of dust between her thumb and forefinger, Gillian stretching her neck and nose across an abyss where blood coagulated to form an uneasy quiet that spread between them. But not for long was the silence unbroken. Water dripped from the tap over the sink. The twiggy end of a branch tapped the window. Perhaps two or three cars roared along the not-so-distant Old Byron Bay Road.

Fi eventually crossed her legs and spoke up. "No," she said. She was surprised how firm and resolute and wise she sounded. When she turned to look at Gillian, she added, "Not Harry. He looks, he thinks, but I doubt that he's game. No. Uncle Harry's okay." The space between them widened, Gillian sniffling at the vacancy as she looked for clues that might offer explanations for the rumours about him being 'icky' and 'urgh!' and 'not to be trusted with the children'.

Her eyes steadily watching Gillian's exhausted face and wondering if the ghosts of Muriel and Jim would ever be appeased, Fi faced her ghostly childself. Her lips moved, the rim around her eyes whitening, her guts softening, her skin, too. She looked remarkably vulnerable when she said in a clear whisper "Gillian, I don't know why you asked, but it was Elliot. He was the one." Then quickly as if afraid the startled silence would erase her words, she added, "Elliot denied me the pleasure of losing … losing my virginity … Elliot denied me the pleasure of my first love."

Aghast, Gillian started forward, her hands and her mouth wanting to say "Fi, I — Did Mum — Did —," and Fi very nearly burst into tears. She drew in a harsh breath to stop the crying, noisily scraping her shoes over the lino, thudding her elbows on the table and adjusting the chair more comfortably under her. But it was all she could do to whisper "Just kids, we were just kids, doesn't matter when it's a child interfering with … With a little girl."

Fi's whisper scratched air.

She bunched her fist at her nose. Sat like that, as still as the Sphinx, until the back of her neck hurt from the strain.

Gillian, stretching forward across the table, leaned into Fi's stiffness, and she shivered in the scratched and scraped air. But Fi said no more, closing the subject by swerving back to their discussion about food. She almost yelled over the strain darkening her throat, "Have you ever eaten *vatalapam*?" At the same time, she lightly hammered the air in front of her face with her fist.

Gillian took a while to stir. Her eyes on Fi, on the pale rims around her sister's eyes, on her bloodless face, on her shuddering jaw, she murmered, "Not in years, Fi." She wasn't ready for Fi to burn bright and snap, "What di'she do all day?"

Shocked, she pulled back, her head rocking like a horse's. "Fi?"

Fi's jaw took on an obstinate thrust forwards.

Gillian stammered, "What do you mean?" Then her face tilted up with the dawning of what Fi meant by her outburst. "Oh," she said. "On the road a lot. Mum was always at a charity thingamee." Thrown off her balance, she frowned and said inconsequentially, "In Penang, they had an oyster omelette. It's a local speciality."

That seemed to bring Fi out of her distress. Her hands flying dramatically above her head, she launched into her list of much loved foods. "Gillian! I love hot salads with sauces made of roasted, peeled and slivered sweet red peppers. Rocket and citrus and sesame seed oil with shavings of castelsardo. Roasted quails tucked in the leaves. Or spec. Grilled spec."

Freed of her alarm, Gillian visibly relaxed, her shoulders sloping, and she dared to say "Greedy Fi, always greedy Fi." Gillian dared. Fi opened her mouth to spike that dare. But she allowed that there was a funny side of herself and hunched over it at the table with her fastidious love of spec. "Not bacon. But spec." Then, for good measure, she inserted the epicurean preference for the cheese Castelsardo. "Not Gruyere."

All of that made Gillian look at how her hands clawed near Fi's fists. She recalled her favourite breakfast. "Roti çanai. In Penang," she said, smiling wistfully. "I very often had roti çanai. It was a favourite. With the gravy from last night's curried chicken."

Fi was scarcely listening. She was somewhere else on her global travels, tucking into roasted pine nuts and buttery rice. Then, straightening her shoulders, her mouth droll, she said, "In Paris, I longed for chilli. And rice. I was there for months. Purgatory, all that butter, wine sauces swamped all over the huge lumps of muscle they eat."

"*Vatalapam*," Gillian sang, wistful again. "Coconut milk stirred patiently with palm sugar, cardamons and dozens of eggs." She sighed, propping her elbows on the table so that her wrists flopped across each other, the discreet pleasures of a good *vatalapam* enticing her to advise "It's no good at all when they use desiccated coconut."

With laughter sticking at the back of her throat, Fi leaned forwards, and let her wrists fall on Gillian's shoulders. Tea steaming between them, they pressed their foreheads together, smiled and moved as one — slightly. "Assam, is it?" "Noooo. Nuriya Elliya." "Oh dear. Broken Orange Pekoe." Yawning "Not a favourite?" Gillian laced her fingers at the back of Fi's neck, and with a soft moan, Fi shifted to make herself more comfortable, and the two women swayed some more, not noticing how the sharp tick tock of the clock, the urgent brush of a leaf against the windowpane, the sudden gallop of a possum across the ceiling interdicted their blue silence. Even when the kitchen door crashed inward with Leigh proudly showing off the perfect shape of a conglomerate rock, they remained as they were, arms around each other's necks, swaying, their meditation undisturbed.

# Part V

**crushed roses**

In Leura where cats curl, the dreaming Laine toasted the toes of her ug boots on the hearth by a fuel stove. She snacked on Seal Bay triple cream cheese. With water crackers. An open bottle of chambouçin, one from a small vineyard on the southcoast, breathed on a nest of carved tables from Java. A charcoal glazed Japanese bowl shared the mantelpiece with British-Indian brass snuffboxes and silver ashtrays, and Thai amulets featuring Buddha in many redemptive poses.

Light brightened her hair.

She hugged her knees. Pulled Fi's big, loose sweater around her lissom shoulders as if it were a blanket. Content. Fi was on her way.

Fi, hell-bent, drove her yellow Maisie, the bubbled Mazda, hard along the coastal highway. Diverted to Hornsby for takeaway, she wanted laksa. Grabbed a box of chocolates, a bunch of roses at the Glenbrook roadhouse. Her heart listed, her brain heaved with apprehension, her head pounded from the incredulity of love, her reason barely able to comprehend that someone as lovely as Laine could love her at all. Her mind turned itself over and over, losing steady rationality to the uncertain imbalance buried in *Play it again, Sam! Turn up the music and turn down the lights and play it again! Here's lookin' at you, kid!* Humphrey's lines muttered with his famous Bogart twitch in *Casablanca*. Fi, gazing across a dimly lit room at loveliness, fell for the beautiful girl who lifted her glass and pressed her lips to the rim of a long stemmed flute where she left a curved smudge.

With a gasp, Muriel, perched in Fi's head, looked down her nose and sneered at the daughter who was having trouble wrapping her mind around the idea that the adorable Laine Macready was where she located her love. That absolute love annihilated Muriel's clenched fist postures.

Were these turns of mind what Fi expected of her mother?

It was barely possible for her to recognise what the beautiful girl meant to her.

Turning off the mountain highway and down the leafy streets, Maisie glided under the deep sky illumined by suburban houses and streetlights until Fi stopped the car. With a kangaroo hop.

She gathered up the laksa, the roses, the chocolates.

Giddy with anticipation, she rocked down the poorly lit pathway through grevilleas hugging the ground under kunzias, olearia, correa, banksias and silver trunked eucalytpus to her home, her love, her ...

A blaze of light fell out of an opening door. Laine. Silhouetted, she stood, her body welcoming with a certain slink ...

In an effort to catch her breath and keep her brains steady, Fi very nearly dropped the chocolates and the ...

Zinging up and over her thrilling points, she clutched in a tight fist the box of chocolates and the grey plastic bag filled with two take-away boxes of laksa and, and as is expected in moments ablaze with passion, Fi crushed the roses against her heart with Laine.

*Fin*

# Acknowledgements

Thanks are due to Leonie Lane, my sister, for sharing with me her considerable research into the Bundjalung nation and the history of white settlement on their land. The Bundjalung nation extended from near Stanthorpe in south west Queensland to the coast near Tweed Heads and as far south along the coast as Coffs Harbour but not as far west inland as Armidale in New South Wales. The nation was divided into tribes and clans and family groups.

Leonie gave me assistance by providing important documents. These included a map attached to an old NRMA map that was filed under Wiyabul in the Richmond River Historical Society. This map, drawn by Robyn Howell, an ex-schoolteacher and local historian, dated 1992, showed the boundary between the Bundjalung Wiyabul and Arakwaal tribes, the former occupying the hinterland as far inland as Booyong and the latter being coastal dwellers.

Leonie also made available to me studies by Marjorie Oakes, '... who did some extraordinary work documenting Bundjalung language, stories and cultural practices in the 70s.' It was from Oakes that I came across the story about the Wiyabul man from near The Channon who threw a spear at his first wife when she complained about his intention to go to Lismore, presumably to drink until drunk. I also learned from Oakes that the Wiyabul were highly regarded by other Bundjalung for their extra-sensory perception. The documents put together by Marjorie Oakes are held at the Richmond River Historical Society in Lismore.

I referred to the unpublished manuscript *Memoirs 1834-1890* by G H Dawson held at the NSW State Library in the Dixon Collection, especially Chapters 11 and 12, titled *Life on the Richmond River and Blacks Ways and Doings; Pearce's Creek Primary School 1884-1984* by Ian Kirkland; *The Booyong District: The History Of The First One Hundred Years* also by Ian

Kirkland; *Reminiscences: Ballina In The Early Days* by the late Mr Jas Ainsworth 1847-1922. Published works referred to include *Rivers Of Blood: Massacres Of The Northern Rivers Aborigines And Their Resistance To The White Occupation 1838-1870* by Rory Medcalf which was published by the Northern Star in Lismore in 1989; and *Men And A River: A History Of The Richmond River District, 1828-1895* by Louise Tiffany Daley, published by Melbourne University Press in 1966.

I prefer to use the word Bundjalung rather than homogenise all of the indigenous people of Australia as Aboriginal. The Bundjalung are as different from the Darug of the Blue Mountains, for example, as the Irish are from the English.

*From reviews of* fish lips, *the first novel of Carolyn van Langenberg's trilogy*

'At the bottom of the sea a miniature juggernaut waits to perform its final, spectacular effect. Carolyn van Langenberg, writing a secret history of women and others who 'escaped' history, adopts a ghost. ... The first book of a trilogy, fish lips had me hooked.' — Loma Bridge, *Canberra Times*.

'An atmospheric work swimming through place as well as time, it connects apparently disparate lives in small accidents of history that arise from impulse, passion or madness.' — Debra Adelaide, *Sydney Morning Herald*.

'It is an evocation of Penang's colonial past of the 1930s and 1940s that the author's terse and powerful language is at its best, creating a cinematic effect. The cinema's images predominate, and the sensuous story of the young lovers is the one most likely to attract the cineaste's attention. ... fish lips is a post-modernist, feminist novel about liberated women, their dreams, fantasies, brave new lifestyles and their rebellion against the histories of suppressed womanhood as represented by their mothers' generation.' — Cheah Boon Kheng, *The Star*, Malaysia.

'If I were to place bets on literary outcomes, my money would be on Langenberg.' — Lucy Sussex, *Overland*.

'It's a real *tour de force*.' — Maria Simms, *LiNQ*